Peril's Portrait

A Stone Boat Cozy Mystery

Book One

Timothy Peterson

Join the Stone Boat Newsletter at
https://TimothysWriting.com

Copyright © Timothy Peterson 2020
All rights reserved.
Cover Design by Author
Adobe Stock Photo

You My Peeps Inc.
Paperback ISBN
978-1-7329770-5-1

For Lisa
I Miss You
Let's continue our argument at a later date.

I have little doubt this book would not have found its way into your hands, without the efforts, readings, encouragement and corrections of Jona, Beverly, Victoria, Robinette, and Lenaya.
With great appreciation
Thank You

And Annamarie,
for your support, patience,
humor and bravery as I grumbled
through the editing process.

Perils Portrait

1
Portraits in Fur Day

"Eat'm for breakfast!" Violet shouted from her ancient baby blue Volvo. "Get em!" she laughed.

The gable-perched tabby swatted wildly at the tall man, his wind-blown hair making for an excellent target.

Benjamin, Violet's ex, struggled with the dilapidated door of the Stone Boat Art Studio.

"What's the matter with you?" she asked.

"Nothing, the door's stuck. We never lock it anyway."

"Why don't you fix it?"

"What a brilliant idea. I'll add it to the list right away."

"You don't have to start the day with sarcasm." Violet chirped with enough enthusiasm to keep him annoyed.

"Yeah, think I do," He grumbled. "No matter, it'll open eventually." Gus, the majestically perched kitty, had his doubts.

"Seize the day, Ben, Carpe Diem." Watching Gus go at Benjamin amused Violet to no end. Benjamin wasn't aware of the cute predator above swatting at him. That was till Gus's claw caught up in his hair. The tanglement yanked the cat off the gable and onto Ben's shoulder just as he entered the building. Beard first and with fifteen minute's prep time, Benjamin

1

set to work for the mornings 'Portraits in Fur' class.

"Thank you, kitty." She yelled. "I didn't think he'd ever get it."

Violet wrestled her electric piano from her car's back seat. Anytime before noon was too early for working musicians, however, she provided musical accompaniment for the studio's art classes. The promise of caffeine kept her vertical, putting one foot in front of the other. She could hear Gus swatting the bells hanging from the door frame. He then leapt from Ben's shoulder, across the three round painting tables, to the supply shelf, finally landing on the trellis above the office door. His spine curled high with a growl and hiss. It caught Benjamin's attention.

"Don't be such a fusspot, I'll open it as soon as I get the class sorted out."

Gus swatted Benjamin's head as he passed.

"What is with you today?" Ben asked.

Gus answered his request for patience by paw punching the trellis window over and over again.

Peeking out the studio's back window, Violet winced seeing her uncle's car. He owned the studio, therefore interaction with the grumpy old coot was inevitable. She made a beeline for the coffeemaker before anyone else made an intolerably weaker pot.

"Ya know." She said. "That cute little furball has your number."

"That furball has everyone's number. He's the alpha of the stone boat."

"That pretty little thing's the alpha?"

"His name's Gus, and yep, he's in charge. Edmund rescued him from the river a few months back. He's stopped all cat-fighting in the stone boat."

"What? is he that dangerous?" She asked.

"If by dangerous you mean the look of shame, dismissal, disappointment, anger, authority, and 'who do you think you are' all rolled into one? Yeah, he's that dangerous."

She grinned, continuing her descent into demonically strong coffee. The tabby changed his intentions. He stopped smacking the trellis window, and morphed into a golden loaf of bread, to better meditate on the matter at hand. It was just as well. The window, being dark, was a sign Edmund was taking a nap between items on his to-do-list.

Behind the art studio sat the locally famous stone boat. It was, in actuality, a boat made of stone. From the river, the bow peeked out over the shore. To the locals it marked the southern point of the town of Mooikill, which meant 'beautiful stream' to the original Dutch Settlers. For travelers, the boat was another charming curiosity along the Hudson river.

Violet pulled the piano stand from the closet. "Dammit Ben, you've got purple paint on my stand."

"Sorry, it's just acrylic. It'll wash off, I'll get it later, promise. Edmund asked me to store it there."

"Blah blah blah," Violet sneered. "You dripped the paint dummy."

Ben ignored her comments while printing out the pet photos being painted in the day's class.

"Gooood morning teacher." Alice and Hector sang as they entered. They were neighbors, each owning a twin golden retriever, their dogs' size and weight repeatedly flattening the fence separating their homes.

The sister's play dates would not be denied. Though secretly, it was a matchmaking plot for their humans.

"Hello parents of Goldie's," Benjamin replied, switching palettes to set Alice and Hector's up first. While he didn't add the gold glitter to their palette, he left it in plain sight where they could commit the crime he could never do himself.

"So," Hector asked, "who made today's coffee?"

"That'd be me, babe." Violet grinned, "How brave are ya feeling?"

"OK then," Alice gripped her mug. "I'm going in."

"I'll try," Hector said. "However, I'm mixing half with water."

"Awww, where's your sense of adventure?" Alice teased.

"I'm up for adventure, just not jittery fur."

Each mug in the cupboard was a donation from one student's kitchen or another. Each seasoned with cracks, chips, paint-fingerprints, and multicolored stains. Yet if the scruffy pad could clean the edge one drank from, not only did Edmund call it good, but it was good enough!

Next to arrive came Doris, immediately taping the photo of her tuxedo tabby, Winchester, on her easel. Jeremiah, the town's retired police chief, and the town's first officer of color to become chief, planned to paint his big brown lab, Dudley. Eunice jumped ahead, making little paint swatches on the photo reference to match Lavina, her moody cali-co's multicolored coat. Ryan was ready for his first attempt with his Rhodesian Ridge-back Rikky. Molly followed him through the door, ready to paint her Shepard mix, Minny.

Violet played with the melody she'd heard in a dream just as she awoke today. The sounds quietly shifted the mood of the room. Shoulders dropped, faces relaxed, and breathing deepened. The love of each painter's pet became the sole focus.

Benjamin finished the palette for a parakeet, whose owner he'd wished would stay silent.

"Oh my goodness, Betty's coming back?" Violet asked.

"Edmund felt I was too harsh on her, even though she cheated us out of three classes."

Violet grinned, "Should I play calming music for her to be less a pain in the neck, or a calming piece so you're not driven crazy?"

"Can you play a song that puts her in a coma?" He asked.

"Are you calling my music coma inducing? Is that what you're doing, Ben?"

"No, I meant—"

"You meant my music's boring, isn't it?"

"Oh, never mind."

"Start the day with insults, why don't cha." She grinned, wondering if she'd done a suitable job of riling him. Apparently not. He was on to her, and in his zone.

Betty Skurmutza arrived by banging open the door. She grunted, looked around the room, and grunted again. Her hair, an explosion of blond and grey hair, that bounced as if on springs.

Violet grinned like the devil. "Betty Skurmutza," she whispered to no one. "The death metal of annoying." Her piano playing teased of anticipation as Benjamin's nemesis entered the studio.

"Where's the help?" Betty squawked, expecting her tone to be taken as an order. "Oh, there you are," she huffed as Benjamin lay out the palettes by each painting. "I trust you to honor this." She flipped a coupon in the teacher's direction and sat by the canvas with the drawing of her parakeet, Poe.

Benjamin bent at the hips to not give the rude woman the satisfaction of picking it up off the floor.

"Oh, Betty?" he responded happily, "This coupon is for 'Painterly Plus.' That's sixteen miles south on route eighty-seven, you'll not be late if you leave right away."

"I'm happy right where I am, thank you very little, and if you don't honor my coupon, I'm taking it up with Edmund."

"Your haggling will not disturb Edmund. Besides, this expired two years ago. Please do not make a scene about payment, again."

The students had seen the drama before. While all heads looked to their respective paintings, sideway glances looked to the theatrical attraction at hand.

Benjamin approached the bargain seeker. "It will be forty dollars, please."

"Do not accost me with your negativity." She dismissed him with a wave. "I'm about to enter my creative space."

Benjamin was under explicit orders by Edmund, to not yell at Betty anymore. So, when this vexation on his soul looked away to check her phone, Benjamin plucked the parakeet canvas off Betty's easel and walked to the prep station. This episodic drama enthralled the room of rapt painters. Betty felt a birthright to never pay for classes, when she could get away with it. Benjamin, who didn't care so much about the money, was adamant about fairness to the other students.

Violet began playing silent film music, fitting of a Charlie Chaplin chase.

"Who'd of thought we'd get a painting and a show this morning," grinned Jeremiah.

"I would have brought popcorn if I'd known," Alice added, stifling a laugh.

"Give that back, you embarrassment to art," Betty squawked.

Benjamin, generous to a fault with anyone in need, had long since realized Betty was abusing his nature and cheating the studio. A bounced check, lying about paying Edmund, forgetting her purse. It woke an anger in him that, while sincere, was comical in its display.

A small hobby of Benjamin's was memorizing Scottish curses. Most phrases involved the reproduction and elimination details of farm animals. During their last confrontation, he released his crude, though not obscene litany, as Betty opened her basket of accusations.

The heated exchange inspired several painters to press the record button on their smart-phones. It kept the tiny town politely giggling for weeks. With a screwdriver he popped open the gesso can, grabbed a two-inch foam brush and dipped it in fully.

"Goodbye Mr. Poe," the angry teacher growled with all the menace he could muster. Arm raised, he paused, reluctant to snuff out this bird portrait that now would never be. The entire room held its breath in suspense.

Betty crossed her arms. "I will have your job," she sneered, "This is abusive and everyone here is my witness."

His dignity challenged, the painterly sword, slashed the white primer across Poe's left wing.

"NO, STOP!," The cheapskate student screeched. He looked up to see her pulling out a checkbook.

"No checks." He graveled in his best Johnny Cash.

She fussed about her enormous bag and pulled out two twenties.

"Here, you horrible man, and terrible painter," She threw the money on the floor.

"In my hand." He demanded. The room went uncomfortably quiet as Benjamin became lost to his anger.

Violet, familiar with this side of him, knew she needed to act fast. She went to the kitchenette and turned on the cold spigot. The teacher's hand swung left, sending the parakeets perch into oblivion.

Rarely aware of anyone else's emotions, Betty knew she was about to lose her welcome to yet another of the town establishments. She scurried over and put the two twenty-dollar bills in his hand, then grabbed the canvas with its amputated wing.

Unable to help herself, she cried to the room, "Look! The vicious brute defaced my property, and my darling Poe."

"It was not your property yet." He grumbled as a cold glass of water splashed across his face. Violet had approached him like a stealth cat on a mission.

He gasped in shock, took a deep breath, and paused

as he found his way back from his anger. He looked to Violet in surprise and guilt. "Thank you," He said.

"They have the strangest relationship" She heard someone whisper. Other murmurings followed.

Violet laughed at the situation, turned to the students and said, "Show's over, you lazy artists, get back to work," as she sat at her piano, playing a major fifth trumpet blast as though charging into battle. The class's attention returned to each canvas at hand.

Feeling guilty for having enjoyed the confrontation more than she wanted to admit, Violet drew from her superpowers and quickly changed the tone of the room with her favorite Debussy piece, Clair de Lune. Curious, with all this commotion, she thought. How has my scrooge uncle remained asleep? Just as well, I want nothing to do with my family, anyway. Looking up, she noticed Gus looking back at her. Violet felt the judgment, and the shame. Ben was right. He is an intimidating little fellow.

Perils Portrait

2
The Brush Stroke of Death

"If you notice," Benjamin spoke in his teacher's voice. "I've given you all an extra helping of burnt sienna. Please take the rough brush—"

"You mean the cheap crappy one?" Betty chimed in.

"Yes, Betty, and for everyone, sometimes a very cheap brush, is the best for the job."

"And for the teacher's pocket." Betty harped after him.

Benjamin continued. "Take the burnt sienna, and with lots of water, wash it over your canvas. Yes, that's it, like hot coco." He watched the warm color drench the canvases until he came to Betty's.

"Betty?"

"What," said the testy artist.

"Why aren't you using burnt sienna?"

"Oh, you mean that brown you plopped on my plate here."

"It looks more like ultramarine blue to me." Alice suggested.

"Whatever the color, it is not burnt sienna." Ben said.

Hector looked over, "Could that be cerulean blue?"

Ben stiffened. "It should have been burnt—"

"You think so, Hector?" Doris chirped in, "I might have called it cobalt blue."

"Not phthalo blue?" Offered Jeremiah stretching

his neck to add an opinion.

The frustrated teacher pinched the bridge of his nose, closed his eyes, and walked away. He appreciated the eager students enjoying their newly learned knowledge of color, still the mother of parakeets had broken his calm.

Betty felt elated, her revenge on the bossy teacher complete.

As the spat in blue came to a close, Violet looked to Benjamin. How can I make this gloomy boy laugh? An idea came to her as she envisioned the melody. Maybe? Could it be? Back in his rock-and-roll days, what was his first guitar song? What sparked his young musical self? She couldn't help her enormous grin while mapping her remedy for his angst.

To Violet, the song sounded like two garbage trucks playing patty cake. However, for a fledgling rock guitarist, it was mothers' milk for the psyche. She dropped a bassy e-minor in the room and lifted off to a jazz version of 'smoke on the water.'

"Now that your deep warm tone is down," Benjamin spoke smoothly now and with a deeper resonance. "Look and see how the light models your subject. Let's bring those mid-tones up in the snout or nose."

Betty coughed.

"Or beak as that may be." Benjamin added rolling his eyes.

"Build those tones up slowly. It's not a race to the highlights. Take your time with the warm base and rock this baby."

With a smile from ear to ear, Violet felt like the

magician behind the curtain. She played on, seeing where it led.

"Nothing smaller than a number six brush. We don't want to get caught up in tiny details too early in the painting."

"Excellent work." he said to the room. "Always check your reference for lighting. You can even scribble little arrows in pencil if it helps."

Violet emphasized the bold starts and structured stops of the heavy rock anthem. Ben's posture relaxed before her eyes, his movement fluid, and breath deepened. Yeah, declarative statements are such a guy thing.

"How ya feeling, dork?" she murmured as he passed.

Smiling, Benjamin asked, "Who's the dork, dork? All is fine. Ya know ya worry about me at the oddest times. I'm just peachy, really."

"Peachy huh," she looked at him like a prized science project. 'Damn' she thought, 'He is just so freaking easy.'

At one-point Alice and Hector swapped each other's paintings, deciding their Goldie's would never complain or honestly tell the difference.

Jeremiah's palette was a healthy serving of burnt umber, burnt sienna, and other chocolaty variants. He added a bit of ultramarine blue, as some areas, like doggy noses and pupils, would need a black that's blacker than black.

The town of Mooi Kill was low to zero on the crime index. Before retirement, Chief Jeremiah did an admirable job of keeping it that way. If he outwardly reveled in not being interested in the political or legal goings on, secretly, he missed the action. However, Dudley worshiped him, and the feeling was mutual, and the hours of walking together did them both a world of good. According to Benjamin and Edmund, he was also developing impressive skills as a painter.

"Very vibrant Betty," Benjamin said, attempting to make peace.

"Not that you've been any help." she gruffed out.

Jeremiah's eyes lit up as he added a bowler hat and bow tie to Dudley's portrait. He was humming along to Violet's cheerful improv on Beethoven's ninth. As the hours passed, the day's painters found their sunny place. The energy of the room sparkled.

"Please come early on Thursday," Benjamin announced, "As I want to put a glaze over your under-paintings before we begin with color. We'll be exploring high drama in chroma next class."

They met his words with a mixture of understanding, amusement, an action pose and a groan from Betty.

"Benjamin," Alice asked, "I wanted to purchase the next five classes, could you make change for me, please?"

"Ah yes, Ben said, I'll be right with you."

He chanced that Edmund's extended nap might withstand a slight disturbance. Carefully opening the door, he tiptoed across the dark room. His employer softly outlined by the windows glow, behind the heavy closed curtains to aid in Edmund's naps.

Benjamin's fingers searched for the cash box on the shelf behind his elderly boss. He squelched a yelp when his hand came down on a small cactus plant. Why Edmund felt the need to keep cacti in his office was beyond him, still Edmund liked them.

With slow careful fingers, he soon discovered the cold metal shape he was looking for. Validated by the tiny metal handle on top, he quietly brought the cash box to his chest just as the lights of the room flared on. Betty stood in the doorway, hands on hips, proudly squawking.

"Edmund, I have a complaint about your rotten employee."

"Shush!" Benjamin spat back at the woman.

"Oh, shush yourself." She shot back.

Benjamin spun quickly to usher the loud woman from the room. Losing his footing, he turned too fast, hitting Edmund in the back of the head with the cash box.

Edmund's body fell forward. His nose hit the keyboard, resulting in many Y's dancing across the screen. An oversized, long handled paint brush stuck out of his back. A figure drawing under his hand slid off his desk.

Betty's scream pierced Benjamin's head as he tried to make sense of what his eyes were seeing. How could this? Who did? Why did this? Grisly emotions strangled his thoughts.

Benjamin recognized the large brush. Two arrived yesterday morning. He was baffled by how this tool for art could be so horribly degraded. His heart sank as Betty's scream screeched through his confusion.

"Benjamin murdered Edmund. He's a killer." She screamed while running for the door. Betty stopped, then backtracked to grab her bag, her canvas, and two brushes that belonged to the studio. She ran for the door again, yelling back to the room, "I always knew he was a monster."

"Violet, Jeremiah, call the police!" Benjamin hollered over Betty's accusations.

He heard the scrambling of chairs. Jeremiah and Violet squeezed into the door frame together. Jaws dropped in unison.

"Oh Edmund buddy, what a terrible end." Jeremiah said. He raised his hand, motioning Benjamin not to move, pointing to the floor.

"Benjamin!" Violet cried. "What the hell?"

"Oh god no" Benjamin groaned, looking down to realize he was standing on a blood-soaked carpet.

"Ben," Jeremiah said calmly, "You need to step out of your shoes, and out of the room."

"Do as he says" Violet odered him.

"It wasn't me," he growled back.

"I know that," Jeremiah implored, "but you're stepping all over the crime scene. Your sneakers are soaked in blood. Please, you need to step out of the room before you touch anything else."

Benjamin crouched, preparing to leap towards the door.

"Stop! leave your shoes," Jeremiah repeated.

With toes on the heel of his sneaker, Benjamin pulled off one shoe and took a long step outside the blood stain. Not having a toe for his other shoe, he used the base of Edmund's chair to hook the heel of his sneaker and pull the other off. Jeremiah cringed at the contaminated crime scene.

Still hugging the cash box, Benjamin pushed himself sideways to get a distance from the pool of blood. He was overcome with sadness, leaving Edmund behind. Losing his momentum, he began falling back towards Edmund's body. Violet and Jeremiah responded quickly. Each grabbed an arm, yanking him from the room.

"Who would have killed Edmund," Benjamin asked them both, "who would do such a thing?"

"I was hoping you two would have an idea." Jeremiah replied. "Ben, your fingerprints and, well, footprints are everywhere. Prepare to wade through this terrible mess with a lot of patience. And do not by any means take off on us."

Violet looked to her uncle with ghastly mixed emotions. Years of anger and resentment tightened her throat. She felt guilty and did not understand why. "How do I grieve you, Edmund?" she whispered. Pushing her emotions down, she looked to the simple mechanics of the situation.

"How strong would you have to be to plunge a paintbrush handle that thick into someone?" she asked the retired police chief.

Jeremiah acknowledged her question with a nod as his call was being answered.

"Hi Eunice, it's Jeremiah, oh yes thank you, I am taking it easy, or trying too. The thing is, unfortunately, Edmund, you know, from the art studio? Yes, well, he's been murdered. Yes, Eunice, I am sure."

Violet turned around to see a room full of shocked faces. Many hands reached out to her.

"We're so sorry for your loss, Dear," Alice said.

"He will be missed terribly." Hector added.

"I took my very first painting class with Edmund." Doris sniffed, "He was so patient. I'm sure the police will find whoever did this. Nevertheless, if you need anything, anything at all, you know we're here." They all hugged her.

As touched as Violet was by their kindness, a ravenous impatience arose in her. She needed to act, to do something. As angry as she was at her uncle, she had to know the big 'why' of this terrible thing and find the 'who.'

3
The Puzzling Still Life

Everyone's head was down in the group hug. Violet looked up to the old workbench. Her mind created a list of items. The big coffee can with paint brushes sticking out, the small bucket of gesso to prep the canvases, the stretching pliers, a crushed delivery box. Had that box held the murder weapon?

She looked to the shelf under the workbench. A hammer, mallet, chisel, and other tools. All of them are easier weapons. So why the paintbrush? Was it a message, or convenient? They locked the front door. Who else held a key? What about the back door? The windows?

Releasing from the hug, she walked to the bench. The identical oversized brush to the murder weapon hung with Edmund's personal collection. Ben's sorrowful face couldn't look away from his departed friend. She prodded him to get his attention. "What can you tell me about these brushes?"

"Edmund bought two. They arrived yesterday morning, one was crushed during shipping." He pointed to the cardboard box on the workbench. "The crushed one was sharp."

With a small thin paintbrush, Violet pushed aside the invoice in the trash and saw the end of the handle. Bulbous and thick on one end, sharp and jagged on the other. "Such big brushes, why did he need them?"

"They're used to paint large areas like skies and fluffy clouds for murals. Edmund hated using house painting brushes. He said life was too short." Benjamin choked back tears.

"So, what was the big project?" She asked him, looking about the studio. I don't see any big canvas.

"Yes, you do." Benjamin smiled weakly. "The entire studio was to be his canvas."

"How do you mean?" She asked.

"This past winter, the cold dark days made him irritable. His plan is," he paused, and took a deep breath. "His plan was to paint the entire studio a light sky blue with clouds. From the ceiling's center, he planned an array of lights all encased in a frosted glass bowl. It would bounce diffused light all over the studio."

"It sounds lovely."

"It was unusual for him. He was even playful about the idea."

"I'm not ready for Florida," he would say. "though I wouldn't mind bringing a bit of it here."

"I was happy to see him in such positive spirits over a project again." He sighed. "He'd even enlisted me to help, hence the two brushes. I'll continue the project if it's at all possible, for Edmund."

She squeezed his arm. Edmund meant a lot to Benjamin. Years earlier, she accidentally introduced them to each other. A strange twist of fate that always kept creative people circling within her life.

"I'm sorry there are no more fluffy clouds Uncle." She said looking back to him. So many conflicted emotions rattling her heart.

"What do you mean, Crupts is unavailable? Eunice? He's the police chief. How can he be unavailable for a murder scene?"

Jeremiah rolled his eyes and waved at Violet and Benjamin. "The dentist? Yes, a root canal is serious, but Eunice? a murder scene outweighs, I don't want to be disturbed. Yes, thank you. Would you at least let my old team know I called this in?"

"Thank you Eunice, yes, I know you're three months away from retirement, no I'm not taking it personally. I'll see you at your golden handcuffs luncheon. What? No, it was a joke. Please let my old team know. Goodbye Eunice." He hung up the phone and moved to see what Violet and Benjamin were doing at the workbench.

Jeremiah put his hand on the man's shoulder. "Touch nothing"

Benjamin cringed. "I've been handling everything since I came in this morning."

Jeremiah turned to Violet as she poked around the workbench with a small paintbrush.

"Look at this brush, Jeremiah, up here on the rack." She pointed. "It's a duplicate of the murder weapon."

"He was sending the other one back for a replacement." Benjamin added.

The former police chief grimaced. "Yes, Violet, that's very impressive, please tell me you haven't touched anything."

"Nope, just with my little paint brush here, I know on TV they use pencils, than again, look where we are."

"It doesn't matter you two, just get away from the bench." Jeremiah said exasperated.

"I can help." Violet shot back.

"Yes, I know you want to, and thank you. He spoke, barely holding his temper. However, you're both on a one-way train to prime suspects if you don't stop. Now, I need you both to listen to me. We have professionals on their way. I know you're trying to help, but you'll only implicate yourselves into a murder investigation. And Violet, you need to keep your boyfriend from touching anything else."

"He's not my boyfriend," Violet protested.

"How am I implicated in the murder?" Benjamin asked.

"Wait, what? Benjamin's not your boyfriend?"

It riled Ben. He grit his teeth. "I told you, I didn't kill Edmund. He was my friend."

"We haven't dated since forever." She added.

Jeremiah looked puzzled at Violet, ignoring Ben. "If you're not a couple, why are you always so mad at him?"

"Why am I implicated in this?" Benjamin said louder.

"Have you met him?" Violet said, throwing her small paintbrush back on the prepping bench.

Benjamin left the conversation flustered and walked to Edmund's office door again.

"Jeremiah, why is Benjamin implicated in the murder?" Violet whispered, "Does that mean he's a suspect? Cause I know he's no killer."

"I don't think so either," Jeremiah answered. "Still, he's stomped all over the crime scene, and he works for Edmund, and he lives above the studio, that makes him a person of interest."

"But he was just getting the cash box."

"I know Violet, I was there. And I'll do what I can for him, however, it's a process. You're related to Edmund, and you're whatever you are with Benjamin, nevertheless, please don't involve yourself any further."

Violet stopped listening and watched her ex. He stood like a statue, lost in thought over his friend, mentor, and employer.

Jeremiah walked to Benjamin and spoke quietly.

Violet felt for the first time, as dysfunctional as it was, her family had just grown smaller.

"Could you help me move him? Jeremiah called to her."

"Edmund?"

"No, Benjamin. I can't get him to move out of the room, he's transfixed."

"Oh, I know that stare," she said. Violet took a palette knife from a nearby bucket and jabbed it into Benjamin's ribs. He slowly turned to face her, as if returning from a far-off trip. "Come-on big guy, let the cops do their thing."

"Please take him outside for a bit. I've got to get contact info from everyone here. Oh, and I'll need both of yours too."

"We'll be in front Jeremiah, I'll keep your most wanted from skipping town."

"I wish I could find that funny." Benjamin said as they walked out the door.

"I do too." She pulled him in for a hug.

Perils Portrait

4
The Walking Talking Toothache

Away from the murder scene, under a beautiful blue sky. Violet's angst purged in a long yell. When it was over, even the birds went silent. Dropping herself to the waiting bench in front of the studio, she pulled her scruffy friend to sit by her. Benjamin remembered those yells. During stressful times they were common. More than one might have been attributed to him.

"Look," she said. "I know you didn't kill my horrible uncle."

Benjamin looked at her, bewildered. "Violet, of course, I didn't kill Edmund. He's been like a father to me."

Astonished, she needed to ask, "How in the world can you say that? He was the grumpiest man who's ever lived."

"Grumpy is just grumpy, it's not mean, it's not cruel, it's not—"

"He stole the house from under my parents, Ben, do not tell me he wasn't cruel."

A police cruiser skid to a stop before the studio. It distracted their disagreement. Though, as always, they would pencil the argument in for a later time. The new police chief, James Crupts, wrestled himself from the patrol car while holding an ice bag to his head. With a pained and sour face, he made his way to the door. At first glance, Benjamin thought the man was foaming at the mouth. He then noticed it was cotton balls.

Crupts had heard stories about Benjamin and Violet as the town oddities. While they didn't blatantly engage in anything illegal, even the hearsay of their strange history gave Crupts a reason to treat them as suspects.

"Donmt Mooov." Blurted the cotton-mouthed chief entering the studio. His attempt to represent authority failed, rather than the comedy to which he ace'd.

"Well, that can't be pleasant." Violet said, not quite hiding a grin. "He sounds like a sick cow, or maybe a sick dog? No, definitely a sick cow."

Chief Crupts was not a year into his post with the MooiKill police department. It was a town as quiet and easygoing as the river flowing beside it. Crupts was considered, by most, an awkward fit for the nature of the community. The accepted rumor was that his uncle, a political figure with the state, had paper shuffled his nephew into the position.

"Willow!" Benjamin cried.

"Right." She said. "Where is Edmunds' dog?" She looked inside the window for Jeremiah.

"Willows' been locked inside Edmund's house all night."

"Hold that thought," Violet said, "I need to ask Jeremiah something. The killer might have keys to the studio, however, they didn't know Edmund never locked the front door. Unless the killer stole Edmund's keys. If Edmund still has his keys, the murderer has to be someone he knew!"

She glanced at Benjamin's face and could see his concern for Willow had taken his attention elsewhere. "Oh, never mind, I'm going inside for a minute, just don't go anywhere." She opened the door, intent on asking Jeremiah, but reconsidered her timing due to the argument in play.

Jeremiah yelled at the Chief. "What do you mean the forensic team isn't coming? It's a crime scene and my crew are the experts. They've decades of training for this. Have you even been on a homicide case or been at a murder scene?"

She closed the door on the two men, an idea forming in her mind. Willow might not be here. Still the stone boat housed a dozen cats.

She ran to the back of the building. Again, the door was locked. Looking to the stone boat, the door was partially open with cats everywhere pacing and calling out for breakfast. Said breakfast was hours overdue. The volume of their meows underscored the lateness.

The previous night's dinner bowls lay on the floor of the stone boat. Each flipped upside down for the crunchy treats Edmund hid underneath for dessert.

Benjamin walked up behind her. "Violet, here's the key to the back door, I have to—"

"What time does Edmund feed the cats at night?" She interrupted while taking the key.

"Between five and six, maybe closer to five. They get pretty yelly the later it gets."

"Do you know if he brings the bowls in right after? I mean, everyone knows cleaning dried bowls is a pain."

"Violet, listen, I have to—"

"He never had the chance to clean up the dinner bowls." She said.

"I have to see to Willo—"

"Ben," she peered inside the stone boat. "Edmund would not have locked the back door in the middle of the feeding regiment. He was killed after he fed the cats, still before he brought the bowls in. Five thirty? Six-ish? What do you think?"

Benjamin was gone.

"If you needed to go, you should have said something." She spoke to the empty spot he'd been standing.

Unlocking the back door of the studio, she carried the bowls in. It was the portrait room, reserved for Edmund's private commissions. It also held the refrigerator and a large steel sink for kitty cleanup. She laid the bowls in to soak and opened the fridge to discover a large bucket of homemade cat food, made up of chicken, sweet potato, and broccoli. She felt the irony that his cats probably ate better than she did. An aroma of linseed oil caught her attention.

A painting was in the works. The large wooden palette rested on the stand. She observed what colors he was working with. The hues were neutral, cold, almost resembling dried wood and pale metal. The paints were still wet. Everything was here and ready, except the painting itself.

Dammit Ben, if you hadn't left you could tell me more about this. She made a mental note to ask him later, and about recent commissions. And how did he record his commissions? A date book?, a ledger? Internet calendar? She quickly cleaned and refilled the kitty bowls and brought them to the boat. She needed to talk to Jeremiah, but not while he was fighting with Crupts.

James Crupts leaned over the murder scene from the edge of the blood-soaked carpet while taking pictures with his phone.

"The crew uses real cameras with proper lighting to pick up the details of the crime." Jeremiah laid into him.

"Thiisss id fime" Crupts shot back as a cotton ball fell from his mouth to the bloody carpet.

"The crew also never contaminates a crime scene with their own DNA." Jeremiah added.

"Y coulll havv yoo arrrests for imeeeding an vestigation." He slurred with the confidence of one who'd never paid for his mistakes.

Violet watched the heated exchange and obvious contrast in professionalism. Being surrounded by the morning's students, neither man chose to take the disagreement further.

Jeremiah's veins throbbed in his neck. "Nuts to you, you've already impeded the investigation and contaminated it." He walked outside and called Margot and Abram, his former forensic specialists. While listening to the ringing he looked over to see the empty bench.

Benjamin had left. Jeremiah knew if Willow wasn't with Edmund, she was home. Or Missing. Or worse, with the killer. Knowing both men's love of animals, he took a leap of faith and assumed Benjamin was on his way to Edmund's house to tend to Willow.

He switched tactics and called Margot and Abram's

office directly.

"Yo Jeremiah, you're on speaker," Margot said.

"Hey old man, is that really you?" called Abram from the background. "We thought you'd be golfing it up on such a morning."

"Painting, actually," replied Jeremiah. "Unfortunately, we've got bigger problems. Your new boss is at the Stone Boat Art Studio, and he's screwing up a homicide investigation. Yeah, Edmund's been murdered and—"

"Why weren't we notified?" Abram asked.

"It seems your new chief—."

"On our way." Was all Jeremiah heard, as the line went dead.

Why hadn't he notified the team, Jeremiah wondered. This was against all protocol. Walking back to Edmund's office, he now found Crupts poking around the dead man's papers with a pen. Jeremiah coughed loud enough to startle the chief who dropped his pen onto the bloody carpet.

"Em-poy-ee," said Crupts, "waar's da em-poy-ee?"

With his best poker face Jeremiah related, "Your lead suspect has taken off."

"Uuu leit hem get-waaay?" Crupts made sounds as close to a holler as he could. Another cotton ball spit out. "What derect-shun."

"Someone saw him sneaking into the back of Betty Skurmutza's car." Jeremiah stated as a fact.

"Fetty Shurmza?" Crupts slurred.

"Yeah, yeah, she's the one." Jeremiah turned to see a glaring Violet demanding an explanation for his slander of Benjamin. He gave her his best 'please work with me' look, and she nodded, though not entirely losing the angry glare.

"Oh, tfaa Betty isss a andfull." Crupts mumbled as he texted instructions to have a squad car meet him at Betty's house.

Crupts turned to Jeremiah mumbling, "Lok-issh plash dowm."

The retired police chief feigned stoic acceptance of his orders to 'lock the place down.' Crupts sped off in his cruiser. Jeremiah turned to the room. "OK folks, I'm sorry you've experienced this terrible sight and even sadder that we've lost our Edmund. If you would all, please sign this canvas here, and add your phone number. Someone from the station will call if we need your help."

The students nodded their heads and murmured to each other as they signed the canvas and moved to the door. Jeremiah walked back to Violet and sighed.

"Why are you telling that foaming idiot, Benjamin's his prime suspect?"

"I need Crupts out of the way so we can get Benjamin to safety."

"OK," Violet said, "so what happens after that?"

"The police, my old team, and me, will find Edmund's killer."

She sudden felt outside the ring of activity.

"I am sorry for your loss, Violet."

"Thank you, Jeremiah, it's very sad he went this way, though I lost him thirty years ago."

"About that," Jeremiah said. "There are things—well, we can talk later. Has Benjamin gone to Edmund's house?"

"Yes, that would be my guess. Willow, Edmund's dog, hasn't been let out since sometime yesterday. He sure loved his animals," she said as her eyes went wide, looking past Jeremiah into the office. He turned to see what Violet saw. Gus, the small golden tabby, stood on the desk, head butting Edmund to wake him up.

5
Farewell my Subject

A long and urgent meow came from Gus, as he head-butted Edmund. In his short time at the Stone Boat, Gus revived many cats who'd fallen from trees and off the boat's roof. Head-butting, nuzzling, and face licking was his prescription. He maintained an excellent record of recovery.

"His meows became more and more demanding as the head butting continued. Yet the slow-moving man, his most cherished subject, despite Gus's best efforts, was not waking up.

His slow-moving man was once quick. Just a few months ago, Gus, barely out of kittenhood, was alone and floating along the river in a woven basket. Edmund was raking leaves and heard the calls. Sliding down the slope to the water, he dove in after the basket, grabbing hold before it floated out of reach.

"Gotcha." He said calmly as he could, standing chin deep in the chilly water. When Edmund lifted the basket out, Gus leapt and clung to the old man's neck and shoulders for dear life. By the time they reached the shore, they claimed each other, as their own. Still, Gus wondered why Edmund bled so much.

"Get, shoo, woof, woof," Jeremiah frantically waved at the cat. The bloody carpet kept him from getting any closer. Violet covered her grin despite the grisly situation. A fitting farewell, she thought. In her mind, Edmund's only redeeming quality was his love of stray animals.

Not for lack of trying, Gus came to realize his loving subject had left this slow-moving body. The human who brought him food, whose arms warmed him, and who saved him from the river, was taken from him. The feline climbed on his head and stared at the odd branch sticking out of Edmund. It did not belong. He sniffed it. An angry hiss emanated from himself. The human who was that smell didn't belong either.

Gus stepped back and pressed his muzzle into Edmund's hair several times. Other cats would want to know. The responsibility was on him to share the tragic news. With a hop and a squeeze, he left through the slightly open window.

Jeremiah sighed, "could this scene get any more compromised? I will never hear the end from—"

"Who ordered pizza" Abram bellowed as he entered the studio carrying his forensic kit.

"Funny how that never gets old to you," said Margot. Setting up her camera lenses and flash, she deftly adjusted her equipment while evaluating the scene.

"Hi ya Chi— um Jeremiah, good to see you. Hello, umm," Abram said. "Oh, you're Violet. I'm sorry for your loss."

"Hello Abram, and thank you so much for coming,"

"We'll do our very best," Margot said, "is Edmund in there?" She motioned to the office.

"Yeah," Jeremiah answered, "plus Benjamin's shoes having walked over everything. Also add your commander and chief's pen on the rug and pen markings on the desk, and a cotton ball from his mouth after a dentist visit."

"What was Crupts looking for?" Abram asked.

"Who knows, still, I've never seen such disregard."

"Oh," Violet added, "and our most recent crime scene guest was an orange tabby in case that helps."

"Who doesn't like a little marmalade?" Margot replied, focusing her camera.

Jeremiah joined Violet in front of the studio. "Can you drive, my cruiser should stay low profile."

Jeremiah bought his own patrol car when he retired. Though slotted for replacement a year earlier, it fit him too well to give it up.

Violet threw a bunch of papers, empty coffee cups, a broken music stand and a laptop into the back seat to make room for him. "Don't judge." was all she said, gunning the gas pedal toward Edmund's house.

"Violet," Jeremiah said. "We have less than an hour to get Benjamin before a judge."

Jumping on her brakes, the car skid to a halt.

"What do you mean a judge?"

"Please just go, I'll explain." Jeremiah pleaded.

She motored on slower as Jeremiah spoke.

"OK," he said, "here it is. Benjamin, 'your whatever,' is a person of interest, like it or not. He works with Edmund every day, Edmund is his landlord, he lives in the apartment right above where the murder took place. I know, though I don't officially know, Edmund worked with Ben's finances, as Ben ran the day-to-day operations for the studio."

"Why are they so entangled in each other's business?" She asked.

"An excellent question, Violet. So today, when Ben stomped all over the crime scene, accidental as it might have been, was the icing on the cake as a suspect."

"Come on!" She cried. "Do you honestly think Benjamin would? No, I can't even say it."

"Do I think Benjamin killed Edmund? I want to say no, however, there's a heck of a lot I need to unravel before we can clear him."

"And the judge?" Violet asked.

"Oh that, I have to arrest Ben."

Violet slammed on the brakes again.

"Why do you keep dropping these bombs on me? And aren't you retired?"

"Violet, we have little time. I need to arrest Ben and get him in front of a judge so we can charge him with interfering with a murder scene. It'll be thrown out because he didn't know it was a murder scene."

"Than why arrest him at all?" She asked.

"If Crupt's gets him first, he'll see it as a slam dunk and charge him with the murder itself. I need Benjamin available to me to understand Edmund's world, the art studio, and who would have murdered him. Retired or not, I can still make an arrest."

Violet floored the car with a new understanding. Coughs, pings and rattles sang from the engine till they reached Edmund's house. Benjamin, was in the yard with Willow as she ate her overdue breakfast. Jeremiah got on his phone to the courthouse as Violet ran to Benjamin and Willow.

She punched Benjamin and bit her lip and punched him again. She hugged Willow, who looked up to Ben with a 'why?' expression on her face.

Ignoring Violet's punches, he looked to Willow. "Good girl," Ben said soothingly.

Willow settled into the hug as best she could from this person who shared some scents with her man. She craned her neck, looking for Edmund. Her everything man whom she loved best in the world. He took her in after others left her in the street. She was not yet six months old when Edmund heard her yelping from inside a dumpster. From day one, they'd been inseparable.

Violet gasped, shocked to see Benjamin's bloody, bare feet. With his sneakers at the crime scene, the gravel road left him no choice.

Jeremiah ended his phone call. "Hey, we're running out of time, once Crupts realizes Ben's not with Betty, it'll not be long before they head back."

Violet ran to the back door of Edmund's house. Childhood memories pointed her to the gardening clogs always left on the steps. She grabbed the leash hanging from the doorknob and filled the watering can before joining the others at the car.

"Stop bleeding in my car" She yelled at Benjamin.

He stuck his feet outside the door.

"Here," She said, pouring the cool water over his wounds while handing him the garden shoes.

Jumping in the driver's seat she tore off down the road asking her car for one more push, which was the thousandth 'one more push' she'd asked of it.

"Benjamin, Jeremiah, did you two talk?" She asked.

"Oh yeah," Ben said. "I'm under arrest now. It was on my bucket list, anyway."

Jeremiah shook his head as Violet smirked, fully versed in his behavior.

The emotions of being at the family house again were catching up to her. Quietly she fought back confused tears.

"Jeremiah, I have to find out what happened to my Uncle. There was a lot of bad nasty anger in my family. If this is connected, or I can discover why—" she trailed off, unsure which 'why,' to focus on.

Jeremiah saw the distress in her face. "I will do my very best Violet."

6
A Well-Directed Apple

James Crupts felt very important in the moment. He blew past two red lights as the cruiser's siren blared through town. Oscar and Regina followed, both officers were utterly embarrassed by the chief's overzealous insistence for sirens and lights. Regina was on the phone, giving step by step paperwork instructions to Justin, the station rookie, as requested by her old chief, Jeremiah.

Regina, who was African American, began her career as a police officer in MooiKill. When only her partner, Oscar, was around, she did a fantastic barney fife impression when answering the station phone as Maybury.

Betty was just getting home from the Foodie Fest. Having splurged to help recovery from her earlier trauma, she hugged her bags close.

Engrossed in her thought's she failed to notice the two squad cars pull up. Especially the one driven across her lawn by Crupts, and now blocking her walkway. Unable to see over the day-old baguettes sticking high out from her bags, she collided with the chief's car, banging her knee. She screamed out as the groceries fell, splaying across the hood.

"What the hell are you doing? You ran into me?" Betty screamed.

"Where bis hee?" Crupts bellowed while losing another cotton ball. "Aibing a fugative bis a crime Skurmuza."

"This is police brutality. Get the hell off my lawn, you fascist."

The yolk of two broken eggs traveled down the crevice of Crupts hood.

"Don't gib me dat crap, Bebby, I know you're hiding—"

"Fine, I did it, but they deserved it."

"Waa, you're admibbing it?"

"Damn straight I am, the pink lady apples were supposed to be on sale. They listed them on sale, but when I got to the checkout, they charged me full price, like I was some kind of idiot." Her fist slammed down on his hood. "They said it was an error. Error my keister, it was fraud, down and dirty fraud. So yeah, I took'em."

Crupts snarl turned sideways as the woman spoke of checkouts and apples. It may as well have been another language as Betty's story continued of fraudulent fruit prices and corporate corruption. Her words of lawsuits brought him back to his senses.

"I can already feel my knee swelling, fascist, you'd better have a good lawyer. This is an abuse of power, and you both saw it." She pointed to Regina and Oscar.

"We're heere to bake an arrest, Bebby, I wunt no more trouble brum you."

Betty slapped her hands on the hood again. "Fine, take them back, take them all back."

Enraged, she reached into her oversized handbag and started throwing apples at the chief. "Here, here." The first two missed him completely, the third hit him squarely between the eyes.

Regina and Oscar's jaw dropped as Crupts grabbed her wrist, holding another plump red projectile. He eventually wrangled Betty into handcuffs.

Oscar looked to his partner Regina and whispered. "Ya body cam on?"

"Yeah baby," she spoke in a state of wonder. "I'm getting all of this."

"Brutality, police brutality." Betty hollered out to the neighborhood.

"Where's Benbamin" the chief bellowed.

"How the hell should I know, pig! Stop groping me, I'm being molested."

"Because he's hibing in your back seeat, and I'm not grobing you, you're bust squirming."

"He's a pervert too!" she shouted, "I should have known."

Crupts approached Betty's car, drawing his gun in one hand while holding Betty in cuffs in the other.

"Get these things off of me, fascist pig." She pulled back and forth, losing her balance, Betty tripped on a tree root and fell into Crupts. The jolt jostled the chief. His weapon fired into the back of Betty's car.

All went silent.

Betty screamed. Her voice pierced through Crupt's head.

Self-preservation kicked in as he looked around for a way out of his screwup. He released Betty, who ran behind Oscar and Regina. Knowing he may have just killed Benjamin, Crupts went sickly pale "Ib was her, she made be fire." He yelled to Regina and Oscar.

Oscar walked past the chief to the bullet hole in the

rear door. He opened it and removed the victim, the canvas of Betty's parakeet Poe. Raising it up, Oscar displayed the grievous wound to the assailant. Poking a finger through the hole where the beak of poor Poe had been shot clean off.

"My dear Poe," Betty wailed out as tears flowed. It was yet another indignity the parrot portrait was to suffer this day.

Without asking, Oscar yanked the keyring from the chief's belt. It was best to release the woman, who, thanks to his commanding officer, now possessed an excellent case for suing the police department.

Regina couldn't resist taking the moment to full advantage. Aware of Betty's low-level pilfering in every town store, she turned to the woman and said.

"We take fruit theft seriously around here ma'am, I do hope you've learned your lesson."

Oscar glared at Regina for going there.

Crupts stared into the back of Betty's car. The bullet hole in her seat looked back at him. Unable to feel shame, his belligerence returned.

"Ib's empty. How dib he getout? Unless Jeremiah lieb too me."

"He must've gotten out at the Foodie Fest Grocer." Regina responded, following with a quieter "you, idiot."

Betty raised her wrists from behind, nudging Oscar to get a move on.

"Book her!" Crupts bellowed, "The susbects on foot so he candbe far from the Foobie Fest. We'll meet ub at da station." He sped off to the Foodie Fest.

"You do that." Regina called back, checking Betty's

wrists for injuries as Oscar took off the handcuffs.

Regina looked to Oscar. "We've got ourselves one dangerous hot-head on our hands."

He nodded. "This could get ugly real fast if we don't nip it in the bud."

Betty broke free and ran to her house in a panic, "I'll never take them again, I swear."

The door slammed shut. The dead bolt thudded.

"Oh goodness," Regina said. "Did she think we were talking about her?"

"Just goes to show ya, some people." He tucked his thumbs in his belt.

"Oh, Dear man, will you never stop quoting Barney Fife? That's my gig. I'm even doing my thesis on it."

He sighed, pleased with himself.

"The very fact you notice makes my heart all warm and fuzzy."

"Oscar," she attempted seriousness. "Nip it in the bud."

Perils Portrait

7
A 'For-Now' Plan

Jeremiah opened the passenger door before the car came to a full stop. Willow pawed at Benjamin with questions in her eyes. Violet's heart sank seeing the two friends trying to communicate.

"We need to hurry," Jeremiah pointed out, "We're almost out of time."

Justin, the rookie cop, held the care package Oscar and Regina had assembled. It needed delivery. He stood at the top of the courthouse steps, frantically awaiting Jeremiah's arrival. New to the district, Justin was not doing well under his volatile chief reign. His phone chirped. It was Crupts.

"Status and wocation." The chief blurted out. The cotton balls were gone, though the Novocain still slurred his speech. With the texting speed of a millenial, he shot a message to Regina, "Capt calling, What do I say?" She instantly relied. You're at lunch, ask the chief if you can bring him anything. Tell him the chicken cordon bleu at Annie's Diner is amazing today."

After the incident with Betty, Regina was in her element to mess with her boss. Oscar turned away, squeezing his eyes and holding his belly. He adored his partner, and supported her real vocation in life, to make trouble with the world at large. Justin proceeded as coerced by his senior fellow officers. His delivery was as awkwardly indecipherable as Crupts pained diction.

"I don't wann any damm chicken." His chief squawked. "I need you at the Foodie Fest, now!"

Jeremiah spotted Justin at the top of the stairs. The boyish man's body jerked back and forth deciding which direction he should run in.

Jeremiah called out, "Hey, Justin, throw it here."

Justin threw the package blindly and bolted out of sight. Willow leapt in the air, catching it before Jeremiah could get close.

"Good girl." All three of them chorused. She gave up the package to Benjamin, who passed it to Jeremiah. She waited for him to throw it again, though it turned out he didn't understand how the game worked.

On tearing open the package, Jeremiah grabbed Benjamin's arm. "Put it here, pal," he said, expertly slipping the cuffs on Ben.

The three plus Willow burst through the courthouse doors in sync-step, and worthy of theme music.

Willow's first activity with Edmund, after her adoption, was to begin her good canine citizen training. She took to it quickly. It helped them both develop a shared language and trust. She then advanced her skills, becoming a certified therapy dog. She wore her certification proudly wherever she went. She looked up and nodded to the man as she entered the courthouse. It meant, *'I'm allowed here.'* he did not argue.

Warren, the guard, was a mountain of a man who smiled as they passed.

"Good morning Warren." Said Jeremiah.

"Good to see you, chief, how's retirement?"

"On hold for the moment, how's Veronica?"

"Due this month, thanks for asking."

"We have to catch up." Jeremiah called back as they entered the elevator.

"Jeremiah?" Violet asked, "we don't have a jail, do we?"

"No, we do not, we have a holding cell. And if our friend here was to be incarnated, he would go a bit north until the trial."

Benjamin, preferring to ignore the conversation, checked Willow's head and neck for ticks. There were none.

Jeremiah flipped through the papers, processing Benjamin's arrest. He did not want to offend the man, yet held little faith Ben could survive even a brief stay in prison unscarred.

"You'll owe a week of free lunches to the station house, ya know."

"I'd happily go a month." Benjamin laughed grimly.

Violet squeezed his arm. "Thank you for this."

"We ain't there yet, ya crazy kids."

The doors opened, and they walked down the corridor to Judge Lynda Barry's chambers.

"Whatever happens, you nod, you agree, you answer every question directly, and you do not lie."

"Got it, will do," Violet and Benjamin said.

"OK," Jeremiah looked upwards, "If you're watching, Edmund, now's the time."

8
Judge, don't Judge

"Welcome." Greeted the judge's assistant, Carol, "Judge Lynda's waiting for you." She ushered them around her desk and into the judge's chambers.

"Afternoon your honor," Jeremiah and Violet said. Benjamin paused and stared at the judge, pressing his memory for where he knew her. The studio? Town? She was so familiar, yet he couldn't place her face. "Oh, good afternoon, your honor." He awkwardly caught up, still trying to remember.

Judge Lynda stood and waved to the half circle of chairs in front of her desk. "Please have a seat everyone." Lynda, an older, slight woman with angular features, earned the respect of the law enforcement community by having an endless supply of dirty jokes. She earned the admiration of the community with fair reasoning and a good sense of humor. They all sat, as did Willow, catching the judge's eye.

"Oh, aren't you the sweetest?"

Looking up bright faced, Willow patted her front paws. Although to properly take stock of the situation, she would rather have the chance to sniff every corner of the room.

Judge Lynda looked to Violet, "I'm so sorry to hear about your uncle. We were good friends years ago, during my painting days. Well, I still think of him as a friend. Life's busyness has a way of drifting people apart. He was quite the looker you know, and certainly chased in his day. Too bad he was not the settling down type. OK, enough reminiscing. Jeremiah, where are we?"

Violet's eyes grew wide. "He was what?" She said to herself, her mind racing through her own history of him. The judge was right, there were no women in his life, except for the nuns he helped with occasional repairs.

Taking the folder from Jeremiah, Judge Lynda examined the papers. "Mhmm, Yes, Mhmm." Seeing everything in order, she closed the folder and smirked at the retired chief.

"Thank you, Jeremiah, it's a nice little present. Now tell me, why are you here?"

"OK, yes, well, you know Regina and Oscar?"

"Yes, I know Regina and Oscar," Lynda shot back. "And you know Regina and I are both in the wine club, so tread carefully."

"As if walking on grapes." Jeremiah grinned. The judge did not.

"Regina and Oscar are tracking down a murder suspect with the chief."

Her eyes rolled at the mention of the chief. "I'm marking off the months till retirement because of that—"

"Understandable," Jeremiah said. "Aside from the murder investigation, Benjamin unknowingly trampled all over Edmund's crime scene. Crupts compromised the scene even further, so even if the murderer is caught, the evidence at the art studio is contaminated and possibly not admissible."

She directed her question to Benjamin

"Did you know it was a crime scene?" She asked him.

"No, the room was dark."

"What time of day was it?"

"It was about noon." Benjamin replied.

"Why was the room dark at noon?"

"The curtains were drawn, I thought Edmund was sleeping."

"Why would Edmund be sleeping at noon?"

"He's been taking a lot of naps lately."

Judge Lynda took a few notes. "Do you help Edmund with any of his business affairs, Benjamin?"

"I've run the day-to-day classes and managed the studio expenses for the last couple of years. Not his investments, but all the art supplies, and studio bills. Oh, and the property taxes."

"Do you have a retirement plan, Benjamin?"

"Well, yes, Edmund set it up a few years ago, why do you ask?"

"Violet," The judge asked. "What caused the rift between your uncle and yourself?"

She jolted at the judge's change of direction.

"I don't want to speak ill of him now."

"It might be uncomfortable, and that's OK, we need to hear it."

"Well, he swindled my parent's house right from under them."

"He did? So you were homeless?"

Violet fidget, her shoulders shrugged.

"No, still, he owned it. My parents were forced to pay him rent. Then he attached his greedy fingers to

my father's paycheck. He always got his money before anything else. It humiliated our family."

"When did this all happen?"

"I was eleven."

"Violet, I'm sorry you experienced that at such a
young age. Perhaps, and I don't mean to intrude on
your personal affairs, however, could there be more
to that mystery?"

The question stumped her. What she'd just told the
Judge, she knew to be true. Her parents repeated it
hundreds of times over the years, yet Jerimiah com-
mented something similar, and equally vague.

The Judge gently probed, "What do you do for a
living now?"

Still disturbed, she gathered her thoughts. "I play
for the seniors in the Morning Dove Nursing Home,
also two nights a week at the Tap & Stance Pub. And
of course, I play music for the painting workshops
with Benjamin."

"Didn't you draw my blood once?"

"Oh yes, I remember. My short career as a phlebotomist. I had to resign. My tattoo scared the patients."

"That's unfortunate, I found your dancing skeleton
an amusing distraction from the needle."

Violet found it unnerving that while the judge's
questions were directed at her, Lynda's inquisitive
eyes never wavered from Jeremiah.

"If your relationship with your uncle was that
strained, why did you play for the painting classes?
Couldn't they just turn on a radio?"

"I don't honestly know, guilt in his old age? I can't
turn away work right now. Even if my parents would

be angry, they've long since left for Florida."

Judge Lynda looked to Willow, who looked to Benjamin. He was her temporary point of security, till she was with her man again. As Willow saw things, Benjamin was part dog, part man. He was good, yet he wasn't 'Her' man.

"Who will take care of Willow and the cats?" Lynda asked.

"I will." Ben said. "I do now about half the time. I live in the apartment over the studio."

"Jeremiah." the judge looked straight ahead. "It looks to me, if I'm seeing this clearly, you have yourself a few rolls of film that haven't been processed yet."

Jeremiah nodded and sighed, running a hand over his hair.

They spoke in a code developed over decades. At times working with, and at times against each other, respectfully. Each having embarrassments and victories, shared and not shared. She lifted the folder of paperwork.

"So, the only legal reason Regina could have signed for the chief, is if he's indisposed. Is he indisposed, Jeremiah?"

"He's currently on a manhunt." Jeremiah replied.

"That was not my question, and knowing you, the manhunt is for Benjamin."

The room went silent.

The judge's nose crinkled up as she put her fist to her temple. "Oh god Jeremiah, what are you doing to me?"

Jeremiah leaned forward and spoke softy, trying to pull the situation back from a hopeless state. "Your honor, chief Crupts experienced major dental work this morning, he's on quite a lot of painkillers."

"So, you're telling me the police chief is on pain-killers, and carrying a sidearm, while on a manhunt?"

Jeremiah nodded in affirmation.

Lynda sighed, "Why couldn't you just retire and paint happy clowns?"

"You're not far off," he said. "I was painting my Dudley when this all blew up."

Benjamin brightened up, "He added a very impressive bow tie and hat this morning."

"Did he now." The judge said, giving Jeremiah her, 'you had better make this work,' look.

She closed her eyes and shook her head. "Just so you know, I'm laughing on the inside, and I'd be rooting for you. Though, this scheme, it's rather minute to minute, isn't it?"

"We're working with what we have." Jeremiah said. "And we've got to try for Edmund's sake. He could be a curmudgeon, but he was our curmudgeon."

"He was at that." the judge smiled. "OK, the chiefs medically disposed, still, why should I not hold Benjamin?"

Jeremiah took a deep breath. "I know I'm retired, and possibly shouldn't be taking part in the case."

"Possibly huh?" Lynda grinned.

"Jeremiah? you said that about me." Violet added.

"No Violet, I'm sorry, but you were interfering."

The judge smirked, "um, Jeremiah?"

"Forty years of police experience says that when I do it, it's not interfering."

The judge acquiesced. "Continue."

"I need Benjamin, he's the closest person to Edmund, and knows his day-to-day behavior."

"Why is this important?" the judge asked. "Simple interviews, you've done it a thousand times."

"Edmund was a closed and private man. Without context, I could waste a lot of time in the wrong directions. Benjamin knew his world. He'll be invaluable to me in catching the killer."

"I can fully help." Violet added. "There was no robbery that we can tell. No obvious enemy. And no witnesses. So far as I know, it was a crime of passion."

Jeremiah took off his glasses and rubbed his eyes. "Violet please."

"I'm sorry, Jeremiah, but to be stabbed in the back with a huge paintbrush? In this town and to that man?"

Lynda smiled, "It looks to me, like you two are starting an investigation agency."

"No." Jeremiah said. "This is just too dangerous."

Lynda looked at him with worry. "Do you have an idea, Jeremiah? Even if you can't yet say?"

"I honestly do not, that's why I need him."

Turning to Benjamin, Lynda spoke. "You do everything he says no matter what, is that clear young man?"

The forty year old man with gray in his beard nodded. "Yes, your honor."

Benjamin's eyes widened, remembering why she looked so familiar. Edmund had painted her. A beautiful figure painting. A painting that was decided, should never be publicly displayed.

"I want clear and naked transparency." She said. "No secrets, it's important that nothing is hidden, and I mean nothing. Can I trust you, Benjamin?" He nodded in agreement as her word choices made his head dizzy.

"I am releasing Benjamin into Jeremiah Woodman's custody. I will set bail at $50.00. Oh, and Benjamin, you'll be wearing an ankle bracelet. You know the drill, Jeremiah."

The judge finished signing the papers, stood and went to Willow. "Aren't you the prettiest girl ever?" Continuing in a baby-doggy voice, she added, "Don't you think these bozos' should get the hell out of my office so I can take a nap now? Yes, you do, yes you do." Willow leapt to lick the judge's face and trotted out with her new found detective team.

9
Fur-Ship

The drive back to the studio was pensive yet hopeful. Violet told Jeremiah about the doors being locked and the cat's cleanup that didn't happen, and asked if Edmund still possessed his keys, or were they stolen. Like a broken record, he thanked her, and told her to stay out of it.

Willow bustled about in the back seat, still looking for her slow-moving man. Her nervous concern brought the emotions of her human friends to the surface.

While usually reserved for gangsters and criminals, Benjamin's ankle bracelet was arguably the most fashionable accessory he owned. Even if only on loan from the MooiKill police department. He eyed it with curiosity, a bit of shame, and uncertainty, unsure how his friend's death could have led to this.

Messaging his former team back and forth, Jeremiah remained under the radar of his successor. The gang on the scene sent Jeremiah a text. Edmund's body had been removed, his crew finished collecting evidence. Due to the nature of the contaminates, Abram and Margot also took Edmund's desk, chair, computer, and rug for a more detailed examination. Jeremiah switched on the GPS tracker and registered it to Benjamin's ankle bracelet. He'd many resources for sure, Violet thought, still, sitting around waiting was just unthinkable.

Violet knew Benjamin better than anyone, and how uniquely creative and frustrating his mind worked. Ben logic, she'd always called it. She was certain Jeremiah would be lost without her help. Pulling up to her usual spot at the studio, the morning class felt an eternity ago. The building, eerily empty.

"I'm sorry to take off like this," Jeremiah said, "but I've got to talk to my crew. Please stay in touch should anything happen." With hugs, he left in his old cruiser already on another call.

Violet opened the studio door as Willow pushed past them, racing for Edmund's office. She sniffed along the floor, circled around and re-sniffed everything. She went to her bed, which had been pushed to the corner, and pawed it back into place.

Standing in the spot of Edmund's chair, she barked at Ben and Violet. Ben got on his knees to hold her, yet she pulled away agitated, once more circling the studio. Vocalizing a whimper, she pressed herself into Ben till he fell sideways. Only then, allowing the dogman to hold her. Violet was in tears.

After finding safety in Edmund, Willow's true self emerged. She was always on the job, even when she didn't know what that job was. And when he fed the cats who lived in the funny-shaped house. She guarded and surveyed the scene from a distance. That was one of her jobs too, twice a day.

Yesterday, they repaired the gate posts between the church and cemetery. Like any old thing, it needed a unique fix every season. And with every repair, Willow heard the same jokes. 'We don't want those saints getting in,' when on the church side, and 'I've plenty of time to meet those neighbors later,' if on the cemetery side. She did not understand what he was saying yet agreed with every word.

Lost in turmoil, her man was missing, and the world was broken. The blood she smelled in the room was him. The dog-man kept utter despair away, barely.

The sound of small paws scampered across the flower box outside the window. Willow wrestled herself from Benjamin's hug and bolted to the door. Her paws slammed it open as the dead bolt shook loose. The flurry of fur charged to the backyard leading to the stone boat. Violet and Benjamin held back. What took place between Willow and Gus needed to be uniquely theirs.

A dozen cats scattered in as many directions. To the felines Willow looked like a woolly mammoth stampeding towards them. Every cat except Gus. He sat center and upright as the distressed beast charged him.

The felines always retreated to the boat when the woolly mammoth was present. She'd never been aggressive towards them. Still, the world was a wild place and it was prudent not to test the canine's nature. Gus, however, had been awaiting their meeting since the bad-thing happened. Testing nature or not, Gus needed the woolly mammoth. A crime against life, love and family had been committed.

Willow forgot she was running and needed to skid to a stop to not run Gus over. He remained motionless. They touched noses and found a centering place within each other's space. With great discipline the golden tabby fought the instinct, hundreds of thousands of years validated, not to scratch the beast's snout and dash out of sight. The sun glowed off both their coats, unified in light and needed communication.

Gus pressed his right cheek to Willow's nose. Her beloved man sprang back to her in scent and nuance, unimaginable to humans. She remembered the moment his house changed from an overnight sanctuary, to her real and forever home. The scent-memory floated in her mind like a tangible thing.

A thousand chores they did together. She, trotting by his side, making sure all was well. The jobs always ended with that long word he made: CouldntHave-DoneItWithoutChaGirl. He looked right at her when making that sound, and his face was smiling. It must have meant I love you, cause that's what her face said back to him. And all was well. He taught her what 'We' meant. And sleeping on the nice thick rug next to his bed was a bliss she couldn't have imagined. She remembered the sounds his body made as he moved slower than usual lately. And that it was OK, cause she would wait for him no matter what. They were a 'we'. Now her joy was gone. She never expected these awful feelings would be back.

Gus turned his snout and pushed his left side across her nose. Everything had changed. This world was darker, crueler, filled with the thing that some humans have, the bad ones, and junkyard dogs too. The broken animals who hurt her when she was small. That was the smell. Though this was a human, who wanted to hurt. Who liked it. This foul smell took my subject, Gus related. This awful smell took your Man.

The cat prince pressed his head to the large beast's upper snout, looking into her clear golden eyes. An intelligent communication by sight, scent and osmosis. A plan was in order. I need your help to avenge my subject. Your Man. Willow was lost in her grief, that such a dreadful thing took him. Unaware the growling she heard far off was her own. Gus felt this growl. Shivers ran up his spine. A dangerous sound to be near. Yet when the beast looked back into Gus's eyes, the growling stopped and Willow's eyes softened. The danger has passed.

Gus allowed himself to be scented with the intent and emotions of the woolly mammoth, her nature, and exceptional ability to be trusted. Gus would share this with the other cats. Some would understand, and some would not. Like Eve, who for all Gus understood, existed only to blink prettily, and dance in the moonlight. Or Donny, who kept scores of mice as pets, hidden in a hollow tomb in the cemetery. They and others puzzled Gus. Still, the man found everyone worthy of kindness, so the cat prince respected his charity.

The large dog and cat walked to the bow of the stone boat. With Gus's assurance, the cats appeared, understanding they were not on the woolly mammoth's menu today. A cool breeze blew off the river. It helped clear Willow's senses from that horrible smell and person. Even if the memory was permanent. And if she understood Gus's intentions, she would need it soon.

61

Perils Portrait

10
Stabbing 101

The next morning, Violet drove to the studio. Wishing the previous day, nothing but a bad dream. She clung to the familiarity of the beautiful stone building with its white framing. Once more her trusty car delivered her and her electric piano, where she needed to be. "Popfff!" A large puff of smoke burped out the exhaust pipe. The car backfired and stalled. She rolled the rest of the way to her usual spot.

"Good morning." Benjamin called from behind the studio. He knew the quirks of her ancient vehicle as well as she did. Walking around back, she saw he was outside feeding the four-footed folks. "Darn," she huffed, "I'd rather have woken him with the backfire." Of the few consistencies of their relationship, annoying Ben was her true emotional safe place.

Willow stood back, waiting. Her usual liveliness was missing as her body sagged. Scanning the grounds for her man and hoping what she knew to be true wasn't. After hugging Willow and kissing her on the head, Violet went inside, leaving Ben and the animals to their morning ritual.

"Here ya go, girl." Ben said, placing Willow's bowl in front of her. He sat close by, inspecting the fence and stone boat for any needed repairs. This, his own way of searching for Edmund and avoiding what he knew.

When the furry people finished breakfast, he took the bowls inside to the sink.

"I'm making a memorial portrait." He said, pointing to the canvas still wet with a warm tone primer. Letting the surface dry, he looked to the photo wall.

"That's nice." Violet murmured, wandering the studio space, not fully listening.

"I don't suppose you have other photos of him."

"Not that I know of." Her focus was elsewhere.

He stared at the wall of photos, picking his favorites, searching for the best picture to honor his mentor and friend.

"Didn't you say Edmund and Willow were inseparable?" She asked.

"They were. He even avoided stores that didn't allow her in."

So why wasn't Willow with him the night he was murdered?

He put the photos on the easel and looked at the big sink. "You're right. The cat's bowls were left in the stone boat, Willow's bowl was untouched. Still, why? Who's so important that he'd leave Willow home for? And is that someone the murderer?"

"I don't know," She said. "Yet."

The photo of Edmund, smiling with his friend Olga, caught Ben's attention.

"What do you think of this one?" He asked.

"It's fine," she mumbled, barely looking. "So he didn't expect to be home late."

"Please, would you actually look at it?" Ben huffed.

"OK, fine, it's a wonderful photo of him. Who's that woman? She looks familiar."

"Of course she does, that's Olga, it's from Edmund's seventy-fifth birthday party. Olga threw it in his honor. She's a nun from the church next door, and the only person who could chastise Edmund out of his grumpiness."

"Olga?" She felt memories of another life, her younger self. Remembered holding Olga's hand and taking in that enormous smile, and watching her wild hair blow in the wind. A solitary clue to a lost childhood.

Violet picked up the other large brush, identical to the murder weapon. Holding it in a way to stab someone, she went through the motions, changing her grip and hand positions several times. Still, stabbing it into the air wasn't enough.

A large slab of clay on the shelf gave Violet an idea. Wrestling it into her arms, she plopped it on the table. From a bucket of modeling tools, she settled on a wooden spatula and began modeling a crude head and torso.

"Should I turn so you can get my good side?" Ben asked.

She didn't answer.

"Reenacting the crime scene?"

She didn't answer again.

He felt a bittersweet warmth. Missing the days when they both worked side by side, happily ignoring each other while creating whatever they were creating. They were some of the best times of his life.

*****

A decade earlier, Benjamin met Violet's uncle Edmund. By chance, the two painters were part of a group showing at the MooiKill art gallery. Violet accompanied Benjamin out of obligation. It was a period when the couple was a couple and trying to make it work.

Benjamin admired her uncle's casual looseness of brush stroke. They were abstract when viewed close up, yet a natural realism from a distance. Landscapes of light, texture and depth existed within a skin tone, a dress, an expression. From years of experience, the man possessed nuanced control in what he wished his painting to say. Ben was hoping to meet Edmund, even though Violet warned him about her untrustworthy relative.

In their small apartment, Violet watched Benjamin produce his 'one' painting for the show. Hence, she didn't see the point of spending the entire night in the gallery. Though her therapist du jour stressed mutual support in each other's passion. In her words, "Ben attends your music events, So, go to your boyfriend's art show, and be nice about it."

"Can we leave yet?" She asked him.

"Is it that awful?"

"Oh, I don't know." She snorted. "Spending the entire evening hobnobbing with people who look down on me. All the while, I try to avoid my uncle, who's a freaking rock star to his fossilized fan club."

Benjamin sighed, "Fine, I'll get my coat and go alone next time." He turned and at once bumped into Edmund, spilling his cheap art gallery wine on the man's jacket. She attempted to squelch a laugh but failed.

After wiping his jacket with seltzer and a napkin, Edmund introduced himself to Benjamin. Violet was sour that the wine didn't leave a stain. Ben apologized again, though Edmund waved it away.

"I don't own a single piece of clothing that doesn't have paint on it." The older artist said. "I don't think a little wine will make a difference."

"You know, I don't think I do either." Benjamin relaxed over his stumble.

"It's good to see you, Violet. Are your parents enjoying Florida?" Edmund asked.

"They are fine." She responded with suspicion. 'Would he try to take their duplex?' she said to herself.

Picking up on her hostility, he looked back to Benjamin. "I see you're doing some experimenting, yes?"

"Um yes." Ben said. He was surprised Edmund could so easily read that aspect of his work, let alone look at it.

"May I ask, If you're leaping into abstractions, why make your foundations so traditional? Is there a narrative you're relating?"

"I'll browse the paintings again." Violet huffed, knowing he'd just been hooked into a heady art conversation. She'd give him fifteen minutes and revisit getting the hell out of there.

Her parents said it thrilled them that she found someone like Benjamin. So happy that they reached out to Ben, secretly 'borrowing' ten thousand dollars from him as an invention investment. The invention was a senior friendly jar opener. They convinced him the success was imminent and the massive wealth would be a surprise to Violet.

The money was half the down payment for work/living space in an old factory, now an artist building a few towns north of MooiKill. After many arguments over where 'his' half went. He finally told her. They did not get the space, and the issue led to yet another breakup.

However, Benjamin's friendship with Edmund led to employment at the studio. Over time, his role grew to managing day-to-day operations.

Olga, Edmund's friend from the church next door, once confided to Ben; She appreciated the younger painter's presence in the studio. He possessed a naturally thick skin to weather the older painter's grumpy and, at times, caustic behavior. A friend who could tolerate his world-weary self.

On the business side of things, Edmund pointed out every mis-sorting of materials, management inefficiency, error in the ledger books, oversight in presentation and advertising, and misstep in client handling.

Undoubtedly Edmund could be a terrible nag. Yet he shaped Ben's professional behavior into a dependable and sought-after portrait artist, and a savvy small business manager to boot. 'Focus young man,' being his most common mantra to the younger artist.

*****

"Focus young man." Benjamin said out loud.

"What was that?" Violet asked as she finished modeling details on her clay victim.

"Just what Edmund always said to me."

She grinned, "So I guess he did know you. He didn't have much to say to me. Probably guilt, still, who knows if he even could feel that?"

Ben frowned. "We don't know the load another person carries. Nevertheless, he could feel as much as anybody."

She tapped the hammer on the chisel, making her cuts on the oversized paintbrush.

"Ben, you didn't know him as I did."

He watched her handiwork. "I know he cared a lot about you."

Checking her cuts, she aimed with more intensity on the second swing.

"Cared enough to keep my family on the edge of poverty for years?"

"Violet." He paused, "There was wine one night, and he talked about all that. There were reasons he did what he did. It tore him up too."

"He got rich off my parents. He was horrible back then." She swung the hammer harder.

"I'm not sure you know the complete picture."

"Yeah, nobody does. Ya know?" The next swing cut the handle in two, just like the murder weapon.

"On the occasions he drank a bit, he'd ask about you, However, he couldn't bring himself to talk to you. He wrote it all in a letter. Did he ever send it?"

Making several minor cuts to taper the new weapon, it satisfied her.

"Nope, I never opened his letters. I know he's dead, but I need you to stop defending him over that." She stopped and looked at him, grinning. "Besides, I think I've got it."

"Got what?" He asked.

Holding up her accomplishment, proud of her duplicate murder weapon, she changed the subject. "What I need, big guy, is for you to stab me." She dropped her hat on the head of the torso.

"Hmm, No."

He turned back to looking through the photos.

"Aww you know you want to. Remember that time I embarrassed you so bad that—."

He huffed, avoiding her persistence.

"I have no desire to stab you, Violet."

"Aww, sweeter words have never been said. Come on, I need to see how you would do it."

He gave up avoiding her and looked to the clay model of Violet.

"Why didn't you make it Edmund's size?"

"Not enough clay and honestly, way too morbid."

Ben looked closer at her sculpture, examined the face, then looked to Violet.

"Good point, and really well done, still it feels wrong. Besides, it doesn't even look like you."

Her frustration mounted. "Wait, so your saying, if it better resembled me, you'd be willing to stab it?"

"That's not what I meant, and you—"

"Humor me sour puss, stab the clay."

He put the photos down and looked at her painterly weapon.

"Believe me Ben, I'd stab you however you're just too dense." He ignored the insult, yet remembered the time she hurt her hand while punching him. He grimly admired her handiwork. The brush handle was sharp and as threatening as any knife.

She swung the brush fast, stabbing her clay model. "See, I could only get it in an inch. I mean, it would hurt, though it wouldn't have killed him." He took the brush and repeated her motion. The brush again plunged only an inch into the clay torso.

"This isn't right." He said.

"Jeez, you're a squeamish weenie," She snapped.

"No, I mean, it's not workable like that."

"What do you mean?"

"Here, let me try." He gripped the brush with both hands overhead and thrust down with his bodyweight.

The sharpened handle pierced the clay torso sticking out the other side.

"So," She said. "I guess we know you're the killer."

"That's not funny." He walked away.

"I'm sorry, you're right. Please come back. You know how I blurt out stupid things sometimes."

He returned to the experiment.

"So we know it's a man as big as you."

"Not necessarily." He handed Violet the weapon. "Just practiced. A serial killer maybe?"

"No," she pondered. "A serial killer, or any planned murderer would have brought a weapon. They improvised this in the moment."

"Let me try." She positioned herself and took the brush from him.

Using Benjamin's method, Violet's first try was unsuccessful. On her second try, the brush flipped sideways. On her third attempt, she dropped her entire body weight into the downward thrust and impaled her clay twin.

She grunted. "I need to work out more," She said

71

winded, "This forty thing isn't working for me."

"I know what you mean. I spent the summer working on the stone boat, and reinforcing the foundation beams of the studio. I also put in new gate posts on the cemetery side. Edmund didn't feel the need for a motorized post hole digger. He said if the nuns can do the church side by hand, I can manage the cemetery side."

"Oh my god Ben, are you telling me you lost hole digging to the nuns?"

Insulted by her snicker, he shuffled his feet.

"Those nuns' are insanely strong. And they weren't even competing with me, they were competing against each other."

Violet was bemused by the strapping man before her and how he was put to shame by the elderly faithful. Though she did admit, gruesome manual labor looked good on him.

11
Returning Habits

Violet returned the weaponized paint brush to its place on the rack. Glimpsing out the window, she noticed a tall, thin figure raking leaves on the churches' side of the gate. A mane of white hair flew in every direction as the wind blew up from the river.

"Is that?" Violet asked.

"Sister Olga, yes. He groaned, oh god, she doesn't know."

Willow, on hearing the nun's name, ran to the back door. Standing on hind legs, she lifted the door handle and head butted the screen door open. Dashing out to greet her friend, Willow leapt over the fence.

Violet continued to stare. "Oh goodness, that hair. It was black years ago. I was crazy about her Ben, how in the world could I have forgotten. I wanted to be her when I grew up."

"Before your family troubles?"

"Yes," she sighed. "She was my hero."

"Edmund used to grumble that she'd wasted her life trying to save his soul. I said, 'Well, everybody needs a hobby.' He didn't laugh often, though he sure did at that."

Violet smiled with worried eyes, "We'd better."

Willow walked beside Olga at attention. She waited outside the boat as Olga greeted the cats. Willow knew not to woof as to alarm them. After a few minutes, 'an eternity to Willow,' Olga exited the boat.

She would normally lift one paw into Olga's hand, followed by the other. It was the greeting they'd developed just for themselves. Instead, Willow moved in close and pressed herself to the nun. The neediness from the animal confused Olga.

"Oh sweetness, what's happened?" She dipped her hand into the bag to give her friend a treat, still Willow only pressed deeper into her.

Violet and Ben called in unison. She looked up to see them approaching.

"Hello Sister Olga."

It all came together. Benjamin's tone of voice was off, his face worried. She recognized Violet, the girl she so loved long ago. They stood perfectly side by side. She'd heard of their stories from Edmund. The two who couldn't agree if it were morning or night, now united in delivering the unwelcome news.

Olga's hands dropped, spilling the cat food she'd offered Willow as she fell to her knees.

"He promised me he had at least three months." She bellowed, the words an accusation.

"Olga, I'm so sorry." Violet said. "I don't, we don't understand."

The nun hugged Willow close, crying into the thick fur of her friend. Benjamin ran back to the studio for tissues. Violet knelt and took her hand. Olga squeezed it far harder than Violet expected.

"Ever since his diagnosis, he said, we weren't finished making trouble just yet."

Returning with the tissues, Benjamin set himself

to wiping Olga's tears till she moved his hand away with a nod and a thank you. Violet was taken by his compassion,

"Edmund wasn't ready to tell anyone yet." Olga said to them both. "His cancer spread, though he swore the doctor said three to four months."

"Olga." Violet replied. "I'm so sorry. Edmund didn't die of cancer. I hate to tell you this. He was murdered."

"He was what?" She gasped.

"Murdered." Benjamin repeated.

A silent, intense sobriety overcame the grieving woman.

Feeling the emotional shift, Willow squirmed out of Olga's hold.

The nun glared through Violet, "Who killed my Edmund?"

Violet felt nervous seeing the scarier side to the woman. "He was stabbed in the back with a big paintbrush,"

Olga was incredulous, "stabbed with a paintbrush?"

"It was a large and long paintbrush." Benjamin explained. "The ones he bought for us to paint the sky in the studio."

"I remember him telling me." Olga nodded.

"Still, we don't know who did it." Violet said. "It happened in his office sometime the night before last. Jeremiah has come out of retirement to see it through. I've been helping, I need too, yet Jeremiah's resistant to my efforts."

Olga sighed. "I'm glad you are and thank god for Jeremiah. That new chief's an imbecile, and the dangerous kind."

Violet was curious how Olga knew the chief and had such a poor opinion of a man so totally out of her circle.

"Would you have any idea who would do this to Edmund?" Violet asked her directly.

"Edmund kept several wonderful friendships, however, he was not the most favored person in the community. He didn't suffer fools and was rarely silent about it." She looked out to the harbor. "No, I don't know. His gruffness may have injured a long string of ego's. Still, to kill him? While practically on his deathbed? Than again, no one knew that."

A hand bell rang from the church. They all looked to see the Mother Superior, Sister Gretchen. She rang for Olga to come. With irritation Olga turned her back to the noise, shaking her head, and clenched her fist. "That woman's impossible."

Willow barked at the bell. Benjamin took his belt off to loop around Willow's collar, "At the moment, I'm the only suspect." He raised his leg to show Olga the ankle bracelet.

Violet looked away, embarrassed at Ben's behavior. Then she remembered Edmund, Olga and Benjamin saw each other as a family. It was humbling and sad; she felt like an outsider.

"Benjamin!" Olga exclaimed. "How in the world are you enmeshed in this?"

"He's really not," Violet said. "He walked through the crime scene with the lights off trying not to wake Edmund, and now he's part of the crime scene... well, I'm just so sorry Olga."

She nodded in understanding that events involving

Benjamin could become messy.

"Gus is part of the crime scene as well." Benjamin added.

"Gus?" Olga repeated. "Is he OK?"

"He's fine," Violet smiled. "However, he took his own sweet time saying goodbye to Edmund, when Jeremiah was trying to keep the scene untouched."

"I'll do my best to help them adjust." Olga braved a slight smile.

Sister Gretchen's hand bell rang out again, resulting in a snarl from Olga. "You would think she was suffering a religious convulsion."

Willow lunged to run at the bell, though Benjamin's impromptu leash held her. He awkwardly pulled his pants up by the belt loops.

Olga rolled her eyes at the interruption. "I'd better go deal with her. She finds such purpose in annoying all of creation."

Violet hugged the nun, memories of her flooding back.

"I hope you'll both be staying on to run the studio. It would have pleased Edmund immensely."

"Will I be able?" Benjamin asked, fidgeting with Willows leash. "I don't mean to be crude talking about it so soon, although I'm not even sure if Edmund had a will. He behaved like he'd outlive us all."

"He did that, and yes, there is a will." Olga looked to Edmund's niece. "Violet, there is so much you haven't been told. Please see yourself fit to re-enter his life. Your absence weighed on him terribly."

Violet had trouble meeting her gaze. "I need to find out why this happened to him. Still, we were barely on speaking terms. I'm hardly sure his affairs should involve me."

"They do, and we'll speak soon. Either way, please keep the studio running. I know Edmund wished that for you both. It broke our hearts to lose you, Violet."

Olga reached down, hugging Willow again. "My best girl, I think he left you to take care of these two." She stood and gracefully hopped the fence, heading for the church's rectory. When she reached the stairs, the mother superior rang her bell again for the crime of having been kept waiting.

In grief, anger, or both, Sister Olga snatched the bell from Gretchen's hands and with an athlete's arm, flung the bell through the air. Violet and Benjamin watched in amazement of the woman's strength of limb and fortitude. Curious if the airborne bell reached the river, they listened, though couldn't hear for the flurry of, 'how dare you' coming from sister Gretchen. Willow, having a superior sense of all things acoustic, heard the splash.

Benjamin released Willow and put his belt on again. Together the two humans returned to the studio.

Willow, in a need to be closer to the man she lost, walked to the car she shared with Edmund. It was a driver's ed. car which Edmund had bought at a town auction. It ran well, although the body exhibited more dents than car. He'd kept a tarp covering it. She pawed the covering away. Opening the special door knob he'd rigged and climbed into the drivers' seat. The knobby rubber grid Edmund attached to the steering wheel, allowed Willow to steer, while Edmund worked the gas and brake. Willow excelled at the paw over paw turning technique. She and her man took many trips into town in their automobile. They turned a lot of heads.

After running over eight or nine garbage cans on the side of the road, she got the hang of steering around things. It was even more exciting when she memorized the left and right turns needed to reach the General Paw, which was always a treat.

Every officer in town had pulled them over at one point or another. The steering, gas, and brake controls were all mirrored on Edmund's side. It was the only thing keeping them out of trouble.

"Don't tell the others." Each officer said. "I can't wait to hear their reaction when they pull Willow over."

So Edmund made up a license with Willow's photo and name, which she wore proudly on her collar, along with her 'Good Canine Citizen Medallion.' They were often waved at, cheered at, and photographed, though they were never pulled over again.

She curled herself on the front seat and dreamt of her man.

Perils Portrait

12
Wet Paint

The following morning Benjamin began an inventory of Edmund's paintings. A few unsold, a few unfinished, and the select canvases he chose never to part with. One stopped Ben in his tracks. The portrait was of Mother Superior, Sister Gretchen. It was still wet, as confirmed by his 'now' blue-gray thumb. Removing the unfinished painting from the rack, he looked to the back of the canvas. A few reference photos and a ledger page were tucked between the canvas and wooden stretcher bars. Missing were the client's purchase order, who commissioned it, and payment details.

"This commission should have come from Father Frank Hayden." He said out loud. Father Frank was the pastor from the neighboring Church of the Holy Spirit. Curiously, there was no canvas for Father Frank or Olga. They'd all reached the age where the decision to immortalize was the prudent path to take.

The bell over the front door rang as Violet entered with a carafe of coffee, a pot of oatmeal, and a bag of nuts and berries. Different today was that she'd brought some for Benjamin too.

"The fossilized Jesus babe looks serious," Violet said, observing the painting. It was her general term for nuns when she wasn't angry over two millennia of patriarchy. When angry, her vocabulary blossomed.

"It's the Mother Superior, Sister Gretchen," Benjamin said. "And yeah. In person, she's even more serious."

"Oh! That's, the crazy lady with the bell." Violet laughed. "No wonder Olga runs off all over the world."

"What baffles me," Benjamin muttered. "I'd no idea anyone commissioned this portrait."

"Edmund kept it a secret?"

"Not a secret, he just never mentioned it."

"What's the difference?" She asked.

Benjamin pulled out the ledger page tucked into the back of the canvas. "Let me show you." She followed him to the office.

The room was stark and hollow without Edmund's desk and chair.

"Your oatmeal's going to get cold." Violet said, holding her own to warm her hands.

"You brought me oatmeal?"

"Course I did, dweeb, I told you so."

"No you did—, well thank you, that was nice of you."

"Don't get used to it." She said, looking at what he was doing.

Shaking his head, he went on. "Edmund tracked all records of money, in and out."

"Yes, he kept track of money, what's your point?"

To the right of where Edmund's desk should

be, was a painting of Violet. She was young and playing tug of war with Leroy, her childhood husky. It'd been in his office for years. Benjamin pressed the picture frame, and it sprung out on a hinge, revealing a secret nook inside the wall. The hidden cubby contained a collection of papers, folders, keys and maps. He reached in and took the ledger.

"What's the deal with the secret panel?" She asked.

"Your family felt the need to keep their business to themselves, I guess."

"My family? Not just Edmund?"

"Your grandparents installed it during prohibition."

"What! Were they bootleggers?"

"More like distributors. They used the stone boat as an inventory mid-point for deliveries to Albany."

"Why didn't I know this?"

He shrugged, "I don't know. Still, your kindly old grandma and grandpa were rather wild. After prohibition, they reigned in the craziness and started the Stone Boat Tailor Shop."

"I thought they were just sweet old folks who knew everything there was to know about buttons. My parents never said a peep about any of this."

"Anyway," Benjamin continued, "I've taken over most of the day-to-day business of the studio."

"And it hasn't folded yet?" she smirked.

"No, it hasn't folded." He shot back. "Not that

it means anything to you, nevertheless, I'm very proud of what I've accomplished here."

"Fine." Violet gruffed. She thrust the bowl of oatmeal into his belly. "Eat, if it's cold, it's wasted."

Ben begrudgingly took the bowl with a whisper of hope she would stop interrupting him. He hadn't eaten since the previous afternoon and resented that the oatmeal was exactly what his body needed.

"Thank you." He said flatly, cause she was still wrong for interrupting him.

"You were saying, ungrateful doofus?"

He rolled his eyes, "Edmund never missed making an entry, or letting me know it needed one. So yes, he was sick. Yet there's no record of this commission." Violet looked to the ledger, put down her bowl and flipped through it. She found the point with the torn-out page, pulled the sheet from Benjamin's hand, and fit the edges together. It was an exact fit.

She flipped back showing Benjamin the previous page.

"Wow, he charged a lot of money."

"He did, sometimes." Ben replied. "Although, he kept the sliding scale a secret. Like this one here. He did the portrait of a pharmaceutical CEO, Oplyn, I think it was. The guy wanted his personal vision for the corporation reflected in his eyes."

"Umm right, and Edmund made that happen?"

"Always. Edmund could paint the best version of any person walking through the door.

The fellow commissioned three paintings in

the last two years. That's been the most challenging skill for me to learn. Edmund could please even the most self-important jerks like him."

Her brows knit together, "So his clients were all satisfied. Good to know he wasn't murdered for a bad portrait."

Benjamin grimaced, "September's page contained a single letter for the entire month. 'O'. He drew it out as an illuminated manuscript."

"It's beautiful," she said, "and we can bet it means Olga."

"What does the torn page say?" Violet asked.

"COHS," he said. "Church of the Holy Spirit. Yet there's no payment schedule or anything."

"Why was that odd?" She asked, "Are you telling me Edmund never took cash under the table?"

"Nope, his fee for Frank or Olga would have been minimal, because for corporate clients it was astronomical. However, his fee was never nothing. He carved his policy in stone. One quarter deposit, one at the first sitting, one at the second, and one on completion."

"So why would he change now?" Violet pondered examining the back of the Sisters' portrait. "What other secrets does this painting have?"

"It's just a canvas, store bought even. He usually asked me to stretch his canvases. I don't get why he kept this from me."

"There's one logical way to find out," Violet said, walking the canvas back to Edmund's portrait room.

"Oh no," he grimaced, "Your version of logic

always worries me."

"Likewise!" She grinned. "Still, I'm always logical, the world simply hasn't caught up yet." She placed the painting on the easel and showed Ben, Edmund's palette.

"You're the expert, though if you ask me, the colors on the right side of the palette, match the skin tones of the painting."

She hopped into the model's chair. "How come you never painted my portrait?"

"I never imagined you could sit in one place for that long. Plus, the you and Edmund thing."

"Good point. Still a lady likes to be asked."

"I'll do my best to remember that."

"I know he liked you a lot." She said. "I mean, he didn't have much tolerance for, ya know, other human beings." She walked around to see the painting and palette again. "Calling them skin tones is a bit of a stretch, don't cha think? We're looking at grayer than gray here."

Testing the wetness of the palette, Benjamin looked to Violet. "Without question, this is the last painting Edmund worked on. And likely on the day he was killed."

Her previous question answered, she looked at him. "So, you know what the 'ahem' logical thing to do is?"

"I'm afraid you think you do."

"Right you are." She quipped. "We need her back here, to finish the painting, and answer our questions."

"What are our questions?" He asked, watching

her flip through the rest of the ledger. "Hey, what would Jeremiah do?"

"Jeremiah would," she paused. "Invite them to talk. He has a way with people."

"Yeah," Benjamin said, "but we don't."

"Excellent point. So hey, sister Gretchen is a fire and brimstone kinda gal, right?"

"I think that's on her dating profile, yeah."

"Let's play to our strengths, she lives to berate people. Well, you're very beratable."

"Wow, you didn't even try to make that not offensive."

Violet threw him a pleased grin that her barb had hit its mark.

"Come on, aren't you willing to put up with a few ecclesiastic insults for Edmund's sake?"

"I guess they couldn't be any worse than yours."

He opened the door and headed up the lawn to the Church of the Holy Spirit.

"I'll try to get an update from Jeremiah." She called after him. "I've really enjoyed spending time together." She added in a near whisper.

Perils Portrait

13
Bumper Cars

Benjamin knocked on the rectory door and waited. He hoped to see Father Hayden, or even Olga, yet he was calling for The Mother Superior, Sister Gretchen. He waited a minute before he knocked again. On his third knock, the door creaked open enough for the nun's stoic frame to emerge from shadow. Her stone-like poise made Benjamin shiver.

"Good morning, sister. Violet and I discover your unfinished portrait. I'd like to schedule a time when we can complete it."

Her dried lips pursed in admonishment. "It's unfortunate he wasn't able to complete his responsibilities."

"We all miss him, yes." Benjamin had never seen a living being with less color in their complexion. She reminded him of the zombie posters decorating the gaming store in town.

"What makes you think you're capable of completing my portrait?" She asked.

"I was trained by the best, sister. The very best. Would tomorrow be suitable?"

She sighed, the sound both hostile and disapproving, "May as well get it over with. I will be there precisely at high noon." She shut the door as if he were a chill trying to get in.

*****

Digging deep into her bag, Violet found Jeremiah's card. Calling him made her feel they were moving forward with the investigation. As the phone rang, she looked out the window. Benjamin stood at the rectory door. The younger version of herself was madly in love with the younger version of him. They were different people now. "What do you want?" she asked herself aloud. "And do you want it with him?"

"Do I want what with him?" Jeremiah asked on the phone. She quickly switched gears.

"Sorry Jeremiah, different conversation. We've found more information that I think is important."

"Violet, what part of please don't get involved with the investigation is difficult to understand?"

"Why do you think I'm sharing it with you?"

He paused. "Just because I don't have a response doesn't mean—"

She dove right in, telling him about the new secret painting, the ledger page torn from the book, and that no info was found on the payments, and that neither Father Hayden nor Sister Olga were being painted, even though they'd all been with the church forever, and finally, the CEO of a drug company wanted to buy the studio.

Violet was bubbling with excitement to take action.

"Violet," Jeremiah snapped. "Do I need to have you arrested? I meant what I said. Touch nothing, do not talk to anyone, do not explore paths of whatever inquiry you decide is important."

Violet felt the wind leaving her sails on an endless

exhale.

"The murderer is very dangerous, Violet, and I need not remind you, has not been caught."

Violet regretted making the call. It was frustrating yet obvious. She has to do this without him.

"I made it clear Violet, should you both come across actual evidence, it will be discarded because you and Benjamin will be suspect of having tampered with it, even for the very act of finding it!"

Violet pacing the studio. She felt uncomfortable having to endure his controlled scolding.

A loud bang blasted through the phone. "Jeremiah, what was that? Are you driving?"

"A truck just hit me. I gotta go." He yelled.

Another bang sounded. "Violet, Call 911, north side of the old interstate, the daisy diner exit. Old black Tahoe, no plates."

After the third bang, she heard a tremendous crash.

Putting Jeremiah's call on hold, Violet called 911. She relayed the events and coordinates to the operator while running to her car. With assurance help was on the way, she dialed again. "Regina, Jeremiah's been run off the road."

Regina, not someone prone to asking wistful questions, asked the coordinates and raced off towards the highway.

"Jeremiah!" Violet yelled. "Helps on the way." There was no answer from the other end. "Just hang in there, Jeremiah!"

Eternal minutes later Violet slowed her approach, watching the red and yellow lights pulse tragedy into the drizzling rain. She tried her best to not imagine the worst.

An ambulance swung around her car, then lurched off the road, pulling besides Jeremiah's old cruiser. The EMT's were immediately all over his vehicle.

Oscar approached Violet, blocking her from the banged up car.

"Violet, what are you doing here?"

"Is he OK?" She called, looking past his shoulder for a glimpse of Jeremiah.

"We don't know yet, so how is it you're here so soon?"

Oscar's suspicious tone irked her, although she had to admit, she would have had the same question herself.

"I was on the phone with him when he was hit. Has he spoken to you at all, Oscar?"

"He's banged up pretty bad. We have to let the EMT's do their thing. We'll know more once he's in the hospital. What was your call about, if you don't mind me asking?"

"I was trying to catch him up on Edmunds murder. Benjamin and I had discovered a few more points to the case." She felt sick at the sight of his wrecked car. "I heard most of it. Still, I had no idea it was this bad." She hugged herself as anxiety rose.

"We'll definitely need your statement, Violet, and your cooperation to copy the phone call."

"Yes, of course," she said, turning to see the entire landscape of the incident.

"The last crash." Oscar explained, "Sent Jeremiah and his old ford off the bridge at the intersection. He landed there on the highway below."

Violet saw the oil and glass spread across the road where Jeremiah landed.

"Fortunately, his car swerved off the road, missing an oncoming RV by fractions of a second." She watched the RV owners giving their account to Regina.

"Oscar, I'm afraid to ask. Do you think it could be related to Edmunds murder?"

"Too soon to tell. Unfortunately, the best person I've ever known for connecting unrelated events is being put into that ambulance there."

Abram approached Oscar and Violet. "The camera footage is downloading, we'll see it at the station."

Margot continued photographing every inch of the scene.

Leaving the old couple in the RV, Regina approached Jeremiah's old ford."

"Who would have done such a thing?" Violet heard the question coming from her bag.

"Hello," Violet said.

"Hey! who the hell is this?" Violet recognized the voice.

"Regina, it's Violet, I didn't hang up, I was on the phone with Jeremiah during the attack."

"Splendid news, did Oscar invite you back to the station?"

"He did indeed, I just wish there was more I could do."

"A copy of the phone call is plenty girlfriend."

Back in her car, she collected herself.

The ambulance drove off. She was so impressed by how thorough and in sync all the officers and medical technicians were. Alone in her car, she asked herself the tough question. Do you really have any business trying to catch Edmund's killer?

Calling Benjamin for support and an update, she filled him in on the dramatic events of the afternoon.

"Is this what Jeremiah was talking about?" He asked.

"I don't know. Was it a crazy instance of road rage? Or was the attack part of the case?"

"Violet, are you OK?"

"Yes, I'm fine, just worried for Jeremiah."

"How about yourself?" She asked.

"I have a minor case of frostbite from my visit with Gretchen next door. But I'm fine. Just be careful. You need to watch your back. At least till we know if they're related."

"Why do I have this sick feeling they are?"

"Stay safe for now. Oh, and I'm painting sister Gretchen tomorrow at high noon, as she calls it."

"High noon? Sounds like a shootout."

"Well, ya know, I'm quick on the draw."

"That was terrible, Ben."

"Ya know, cause I'm an artist."

"Still terrible. Take care of yourself, doofus, I mean it."

"Thanks for the tip."

14
Nun's in the Day

The next morning, Violet was in research mode. Lost in her web searches she'd forgotten Benjamin was in the room as he prepared his palette to match Edmund's. Having studied the elder's process for years, he made quick work matching his mentor's colors.

"OK," his voice broke the silence, bringing Violet's head up from her screen. "I've got my favorite brushes, Edmund's palette, I'll get through this. It's not really lying, is it?"

"Ben," She groaned. "You're terrible at lying. In fact, I can't remember if you've ever lied to me."

"I assume I must have."

"Now, why would you say that?" she asked, rubbing her tired eyes.

"I'm only as honest as my delusions allow. And everyone's delusions have a bit of wiggle room."

She fumbled her coffee mug to her lips. "Your delusions have wiggle room, huh? Good to know you're still my weirdo."

"You asked."

"I did indeed. Back to the plan. We need any information we can gather from the Mother Superior."

"For the tenth time." He said. "I got it."

She shut down her laptop. "The oddities surrounding the nun's portrait and its timing are all we have to go on."

Benjamin hand wrote the questions they decided on, hoping to stop her from repeating the list. She knew the subterfuge would push Ben off center. He was terrible at being intentionally subversive, though brilliant at it, when unaware.

"Just try to stay relaxed." She suggested.

"Oh, like that's gonna help."

"Look, our motives aren't all that transparent, although possibly neither are hers. Either way, if it makes you feel any better, payments have been made. We should complete the portrait, and by we, I mean you."

There was a knock on the door, Olga entered.

"Good morning." They said together.

"I wanted to see how you two are getting on." Olga said. "Are you planning a memorial?"

"I'm arranging a painting auction where his students will paint the landscapes surrounding the studio and the river. The painting day will be next Saturday, and Sunday will be the auction. I hope you can make it."

"What a creative idea for a service, Benjamin. Will it be for the animal shelter?"

"A Paw in Need. Yes. Many of his students have already signed up."

Olga smiled. "I know he would have loved that. Bravo Benjamin. I'll be there."

"Olga?" Violet asked, "could you look at this?"

Olga followed her to the portrait room.

"Oh, my." Olga said, seeing the unfinished painting of Gretchen. "He mentioned, no, he groaned over this portrait. He took it on as a favor to Father Frank, and I suppose, in some manner, to heal Gretchen's animosity towards the studio. Poor Frank, his dementia seems to only be getting worse."

"Is that why only Gretchen's portrait was commissioned?" Violet asked.

"The commission was a donation. As Frank related, what began as a corporation wanting to buy the church property, ended with the same executives making a donation to have the portrait done. He had a talent for wrangling donations out of every inquiry."

"Did any healing come out of the painting sessions?" Violet asked.

"It was Frank's goal to help Gretchen find peace. I admire that about him, always seeing the good in others and never giving up. Yet she relies on her iron-spined anger to get through each day. There would be an unbearable hole if she ever gave it up. Still, she blames much of that on me."

"How was that your fault?" Benjamin asked.

Olga sat in the model's chair. "Well, I didn't put up with it. To laugh at my own self-importance is one thing. However, I laughed at hers. I made an example showing the other nuns they needn't tolerate her abusive behavior."

"So what happened?" Violet asked.

"Well, they transferred away. Some just left the order. The Mother Superior sets the tone of a parish as much or sometimes more than the pastor. Frank interceded whenever he could. Still, it was her role." Olga sighed and massaged her calloused hands. "Because of my work, my time here is limited. I should have taken that into account. The other sisters' exposure to Gretchen was constant. They all deserved better. So now, she's the mother superior in a parish without nuns."

"What made her so angry?" Violet asked as she sat in the painter's seat.

"Her life. Her family sold her into service fifty years ago. I think she was eighteen. In those years, discipline was a generous word for brutality, and while Gretchen suffered it, she also immersed herself in it's psyche."

"Her family sold her!" Violet asked. "Is this where you make me feel sorry for her?"

Olga laughed, "That's up to you, all I'm saying is that everyone has their story. I learned early on her father was a slumlord in the city. Knowing where to tip the scales in the legal system kept him out of jail. He was religious in the most detestable form of the word. Not a shred of humanity, and filled with superstition. He discovered the urban legend amongst Catholics, that if a child becomes a priest or nun, the family is promised a seat in heaven. He quickly made a donation of Gretchen to the church."

"Why didn't she just run away?" Violet asked.

"It gave her an escape from her family, I guess. By the time I met her, she'd embraced it. I'd entered service after a terrible failed marriage. We are so different in every way."

"Did you have a calling?" Violet asked.

"It was more like winning a travel pass to adventure, and the chance to make a difference in the world. I was the perfect blend of youth, naivete, passion, and complete lack of experience." She laughed.

"I sometimes miss those naive days myself." Benjamin said.

Violet smirked. "Why would you?"

"Very funny," he said.

"When I first met Gretchen. I was telling her about a peaceful protest on television, and how it was raising awareness with positive results. Gretchen was vehemently trying to shut me up and slow me down, before I walked into an old school priest. Apparently, he was known for his mean-spirited severity."

"Why do I think this didn't end well?" Violet asked.

"It ended with the inevitable, I'm afraid. I bumped into him. Suddenly, I felt my arm grabbed, and the priest slapped my face hard. I was even bleeding from his ring. I pulled my arm from the creep and felt my cheek. Once I saw the drop of blood, I saw red. Meanwhile, he's motioning me that my place was behind him."

"This must have been before Frank." Benjamin said.

"That dear man would never have allowed it. In those days, they expected women to accept abuse with humility."

Violet growled and shook her fist in the air.

"I responded by punching him squarely in the nose with all the strength I could muster. I'll never forget his expression. Gob smacked that anyone, let alone a lowly novice, would dare strike him back."

He was flush with rage as he said. "You God Damn—."

"So, I'd grown up in a rough neighborhood. I knew exactly what words were coming out of his mouth next. Yet in my training, what fascinated me most, was the power of compassionate communication. How kindness, woven into a simple phrase or sentence, could inspire good action."

"Umm, how does that fit into the story?" Ben asked.

"Well, I said I was young, passionate, and naive, yes? So, with a profound respect for the uplifting and exacting language of our order, I felt it was up to me to save the priest from speaking words unworthy of his calling. So, I punched him in the nose again. This time, however, I accidentally broke it. There was blood everywhere. Gretchen watched the entire scene in horror."

"How in the world were you not thrown out?" Violet asked as Benjamin nodded.

"I explained it all to my Mother Superior, how I instinctively acted in the most compassionate way possible. She turned away from me. Her body shook as she buried her face in her hands. I was afraid she was crying. It was decades later till I realized, she was silently yet hysterically laughing."

Violet was laughing too. "Cheers to young, passionate, and naive." As she raised her coffee mug.

Olga sighed wearily. "The true injury that day was Gretchen's. During the inquiry, she could have described the event that happened in front of her. She could have related my reasoning as she'd seen and heard the priest's behavior. Out of fear, she told the priest's story. That it was an unprovoked attack."

"So how were you not nun fired?" Ben asked.

"If not for the half dozen nuns coming forth to retell their own tales of the priest's abuse, I would have gotten my walking papers. Instead, I was sent to work with, and learn from, the sisters in the field. It was an act that inadvertently sparked my life's work."

"So the story has a happy ending." Violet said.

"For me, yes, not so much for Gretchen. In siding with the abuser, she lost the confidence and trust of the other nuns. She longed to be one of them, to be part of a family. She was in agony over her lie. Yet her fear wouldn't allow her to stand by the truth."

Violet frowned. "Wasn't that her choice?"

"Yes, it was. Still, fear can twist how we see the world. Considering the life she came from, she probably couldn't see it any other way. So now, five decades of buried emotions, and she's hard as iron. She's also bitter as hell, and ready to spit nails at anyone she feels needs a correction in faith. Or rather, faith as she sees it. Oh, and she still hates me."

Olga hugged them, "I must be going, I wanted to check in with you both."

"Let me walk you out." Violet said, "I should let Ben prepare for his painting session." She grinned back at him. "You're my hero today."

"Yeah, sure I am, he muttered," as he finished arranging the portrait lights.

.

15
Interview in Gray

At one minute after twelve o'clock, the Mother Superior sat before Benjamin. Regal and rigid, she was adorned in a genteel arrogance.

"I have prayed for his soul," Gretchen flitted her fingers dismissively, "be that as it may."

Ben cringed at her comment on Edmund's death. It underscored her immunity to empathy.

Her comment, a generation past version of 'whatever.' was all it took for Benjamin's guilt to fall away. His anger rose at the callous response to his friend's murder.

Sitting in the portrait room, Gretchen adjusted her habit, facing the painter whom she understood was a former 'rock musician.' "A failed hedonist?" She joked to herself, yet did not laugh.

Internally belittling his every move, she watched him fumble about with the paintbrush. She judged him unaware of how he embarrassed himself. It hardly mattered. This lost stooge was close to Edmund's niece, so he might be of use. Edmund, she thought, despite all his grievous sins, was a competent painter. She gave him that, though nothing more.

Benjamin did his best to remember the list of questions, the first question at least. Yet his nerves crumpled his memory. He gave up, dug into his pocket and pulled out the list. As he stuck the sheet of paper to the easel where the nun couldn't see it, he already felt he was failing 'Sleuthing 101'. He tossed out the first question mouthing, "Here goes nothing."

Question One - Why was Father Frank not included in the portrait order?

"So, Sister Gretchen, will we be seeing Father Frank in the portrait chair as well?"

"The good father may allow first names, I do not. He has fallen ill and may not see others for some time. At his request, I manage the needs of our humble church. Should the almighty return to the Father his health and senses, the vanity of a portrait would be his own indulgence."

"I'm certain for all he's done for the Parish," Benjamin said. "His portrait would be a far greater honor than indulgence. Don't you think? Besides, what better way to reinforce our shared history between the studio and the church." Feeling she would jump on this statement, he held his breath.

"I pray your 'she coughed' friend, Violet, understands. The death has dropped an unexpected weight on her shoulders. For her sake, I hope you're not counseling her to be saddled with it."

Question Two - Gretchen has claimed the Stone Boat Property belonged to the church. Does she still? Years ago, Father Hayden squashed her campaign to take legal action.

"This? He waved his hand, referring to the studio. We're a modest business serving the community. How would that be a weight on her? It's part of her family heritage."

Though Gretchen knew to stay in place for the

portrait, her obsessed need to vent her opinion on this matter, forced every vertebrae of her spine to risk cracking. She contorted toward this painter's apprentice, and set him straight.

"I have fought for the rightful stewardship of this plot led astray. I've argued that the sins of this church's founder stole it. And sin, as both the lord and I know, hath no legal standing. Although, perhaps, reasoning with Violet's conscience would be the better path. It's not that your question doesn't matter, still, in truth, it does not."

Benjamin delicately mixed paynes gray with titanium white. The veins in Gretchen's neck had become animated, and he wished to catch their highlights.

"I remember Edmund telling me about that. Your assumption that this property still belongs to the church. It's an interesting argument. The transfer happened over two hundred years ago. Was it honestly won in a three-day drinking binge? I can see how that could be a lasting embarrassment."

Her dark, icy glare directed at Benjamin would have crumbled nearly anyone. Luckily, he was looking directly into her eyes to match the piercing black center of her pupils, to the canvas. She felt shaken that she could not belittle her target, crumble him with shame. Nevertheless, he stared back, nonplussed, as if examining a curiosity. Perhaps, she thought, he was just soft in the head.

"Didn't Father Frank squash your campaign?" He asked.

"If others lacked the fortitude to restore this sacred ground, it does not change the truth that it ought to be. That must seem silly to you. Still, each generation's sin begets another until now. Violet may well support your little hobby of dabbling in paint to attract Jezebels, yet can you imagine a more selfish motivation? I can't myself."

As the artist finished painting her eyes, he saw the daggers he'd missed before. Lifted his brush from the canvas, the insinuations slid under his skin. Her accusations went right for his ingrained sense of guilt. This old biddy was a play'a with a plan, he thought. And while she could shame a porcupine into sticking itself, Benjamin bolstered his resolve for Edmund and Violet's sake. Unless he painted a Salvador Dali mustache on her first.

Question Three - Why was your portrait done in such secrecy, and who made the donation?

"You know sister, I agree, Violet will have important choices to make. I am curious about your portrait, though. Who do we have to thank for the kind donation?"

"Blessings of worldly gain are not evil in themselves. What one does with wealth is a trial for the soul. They made the act in humility. I would not sully the donation, nor the giver, with vulgar publicity. You may not understand having failed at a life on stage, however, some people, chaste of heart and action, give of themselves."

"Some people, yes, it almost sounds like you're describing Edmund himself." Benjamin replied. "The man was generous to a fault."

The old nun coughed yet said nothing.

"Can I get you a glass of water?" Benjamin offered.

"No." She replied frostily. "It's merely a cough."

"I hope Father Frank is better soon. It would be an honor to paint his portrait. And now that I think of it, why not Sister Olga? She's spent almost as many years in service as you, hasn't she?"

"Sister Olga's service?" Gretchen's own quills went up. "Her 'work,' as she pompously calls it, has shamefully brought disgrace to us on more occasions than I can count. She's disgraced the order. Arrested eleven times, protesting political matters that were never our business. She has gone against explicit orders by three bishops and even crossed the sea with pirates." Gretchen huffed in disgust. "Tell me young man, how in heaven's name does she warrant a portrait of honor in the church? She's basically a criminal herself?"

He was attempting every painting trick he knew to introduce some color to the woman. Though her particular complexion defied the use of cheerful anything.

"I have to agree with you, Sister. Perhaps an action movie, or at least an action figure. Still, a portrait might be too, hmm, at rest." He was happy for his choice of words and for seeing the bitter nun riled up. Discovering that Gretchen's trigger was, Sister Olga, gave him a reprieve from the gloomy company. He faked a burp to keep from laughing. "Excuse me, Sister."

"Castor Oil." She responded as instruction and more than a hint of disgust.

Question Four - Why did she hire Edmund to paint her portrait?

"Thank you, Sister, I'll see if the drugstore still carries it. I have to say, I've never seen you visit the art studio before. If your relationship with Edmund was, um, strained with the history and all. Why did you choose Edmund to paint your portrait?"

She looked thoughtful for a moment, even sad.

"It was at the good Father's insistence. I am not a young person anymore, and neither was Edmund. Debts to the lord must be paid. And yes, I stated my case during the first two painting sessions. So in obedience to Father F— Hayden," she corrected herself. "I did my best to make peace with the tensions of the past."

"So how did that go? Did you discover any middle ground to build a neighborly friendship?"

Her look of bewilderment came with a tilt of her head. "Friendship? Young man, the borders between us are stone for a reason."

It stunned the scruffy artist. Did this ecclesiastic crypt-keeper just tell a joke? A grimace resembling dried parchment curling appeared on the corners of her mouth. If this passes for a grin, he told himself. Run with it. Making visual notes, he added it to the painting. She could certainly surprise him.

"Edmund," she continued, "pity his soul, was the last of his lineage of embarrassments and offenses to the church, save Violet."

"Umm, wasn't this building made for drinking? It makes the offense you refer to, originate from the church, no?"

"You would be wrong, obviously." She retorted. "This was the church prayer room. As I've said, the men who lost this sacred earth to debauchery have passed the sin down, generation after generation till Edmund."

"Save Violet," Benjamin added, grinning.

"Like I said earlier, young man, do you truly wish your friend saddled with this burden? I wouldn't have thought you that selfish. Are you?"

"I'll be selfish enough to not sway her decisions. That's the most I can agree on."

Gretchen heard his words yet could not internalize them. Life was a matter of swaying others; in whatever direction her sense of righteousness saw fit.

"I am not surprised," she eventually spat. "You see charity of mind as allowing her to dangle in the wind of confusion and doubt. I'd thought you kinder. At least, more so than your former employer."

"Oh, Edmund was remarkably kind, and without a doubt, a complicated fellow. While everyone thought him an old grump, he delighted in helping almost all creatures, well, non-humans above all. Sister Gretchen, what time of day did your last session end with Edmund?"

"Ah, you're fishing for information now. Do you hope it is I who killed Edmund? Where was I on the night of the murder? Is that your next question?"

"No sister, We are trying to define 'when' he was killed."

"I do believe the police have the means to know that. Though I will indulge you. I suppose it was late afternoon. He grew weary and insisted on feeding those soulless urchins in that ridiculous boat in the yard."

"You mean the cats?"

"Whatever the sort, not worthy of breath."

"Another of his acts of charity." Ben smiled. "Although with the cost of cat food, he was possibly buying an indulgence."

"As well were his acts of depravity." Gretchen added.

"You do not have to like the man to see his murder as horrible."

"Only the Lord can say." She whispered.

"So, you're suggesting the Lord condones murder?" Benjamin tensed. He struggled to keep himself from stabbing the painting.

"Vengeance is mine, saith the Lord." For the first time, she looked to him, defending her position.

"He wasn't smitten by God, sister, a murderer killed him."

Gretchen paused and looked right through him.

"What does it matter, the frivolous pitter patter of an old woman. Whether a murder is this or that, only our Lord can say. In the meantime, I'm sure the police will catch whoever did it."

"If I don't catch them first." Benjamin added.

"Do not seek retribution, young man. When walking in the grace of the Lord, there is no violence, only righteous grace. And you are sorely lacking in grace, on so many levels."

"Oh?" Benjamin paused, "That might explain it."

"Explain what?" she asked.

"I've heard saints were an incredible pain in the behind to live with. Miracles-A-Plenty, still, no one to take the garbage out or do the dishes. Kinda useless with any real-life troubles. Grace and righteousness might wear pretty thin after a while, don't you think?"

Gretchen's face twisted in disgust. "On top of everything else, you are crudely fixated on earthly points of convenience."

"No need to cherry-pick my faults, sister. I can get you a deal on a bushel."

The painting was nearly finished. Benjamin was thankful he could do the rest with the photos Edmund had taken. He could escape this black hole of negativity.

"I am not a critical person." Her voice softened. Rough palms opened. Tilting her chin to reveal her neck, and pained, expressive eyes. "With experience, I humbly shine a light on how willful ignorance feeds your suffering. I do not judge you myself, I am merely our Lord's tool."

"Oh, so you're like my paintbrush?" He raised it up to show her.

"I believe we are done here," She hissed.

Perils Portrait

16
Cemetery Chat

Violet sat at the hospital reading a James Harriot book to an unconscious Jeremiah. His wife, Joanne, had arranged a stack of his favorite novels. Any visiting friend could pick one up and read to him. Violet felt in part responsible. Had Jeremiah not got involved with her family's mess, he wouldn't be in this hospital, or in a coma.

She stepped out to the waiting area to take the call from Benjamin. The sound of crunching leaves and blowing wind could be heard in the background.

"Where are you?"

"I'm around the studio." Ben semi-lied. He was randomly wandering through the cemetery, reading the interesting names on old gravestones as Willow surveyed the grounds. He couldn't tell that to Violet.

When he was particularly moody, it affected his posture. She never passed an opportunity to poke fun of his gloomy walk. "You're practicing to be a zombie." And she referred to any cemetery as his office. "Do you have any morbid meetings today? A creepy conference call?" He didn't want to hear it, cause today, it was probably true. He looked to Willow exploring along the fence.

"So it seems," He said to Violet, "Gretchen had a major beef with Edmund."

"Well, duh, Ben, she has a major beef with humanity."

"True, though in particular, Edmund's entire lineage."

Violet's eyebrows crinkled. "Umm, meaning the lineage that's now, oh I don't know, me?"

"Yep," He said. "Still, there's good news about that. She wants to save you from the damnable curse of eternal hellfire."

Gazing out the window, Violet watched the coming and goings of the hospital parking lot. "Gee Ben, all this time I'd thought myself a shoo-in for eternal hellfire. Should I assume there are conditions to my salvation?"

"Why yes, for once you should assume."

Her frustration bubbled up, and she needed to play.

"For once?" She teased. "Why would you say that? When do I ever assume?"

"It was just a joke." He said, trying to calm her.

"It wasn't funny, you make me out to be a hyper-assuming crackpot or something, I bet you made a deal with Gretchen, didn't you?"

"No, I didn't make any deals with her. Though I'm sure she collects souls in jars under her bed."

"When did she show you her bed?"

"She never showed me her bed."

"Did you sleep with her Ben?"

"Jeez, I needed two showers to get the conversation off me."

"Oh? so you took a shower together?"

"NO! We spoke as I painted her."

"Kinky."

"Painting her portrait, not her!"

"Still doesn't prove you weren't ya know. So," She

asked. "Which one was it? The shower or the bed?"

He pinched the bridge of his nose to center himself. Holding the phone away, he didn't want to continue the conversation, yet he could still hear Violet making inappropriate accusations as revenge for suggesting she was prone to making assumptions.

"I'm sorry, must go, jackass." And he hung up the phone. On another day he would have found her very funny. Today, however, after Gretchen, he was sorely feeling the loss of Edmund.

Although Benjamin was thirty when they met. Edmund still became a father figure to him. He knew Violet was just enjoying having a go at him, but he was frazzled from the creepy vibe he'd gotten from the old nun. It was hard to shake, and worse, the fire and brimstone nun might be right.

What if his wanting the studio to continue was a selfish act? Not to give it away to that grim reaper, though, to sell it. Violet would be set for at least a few decades, maybe even for life if she planned it well. And she would not have to drive around in that clunker car that gave its best a decade ago. He could always find work in those franchise paint and booze studios, the one's legitimizing day drinking for soccer moms.

The phone rang. Still, he was lost in guilt, followed by shame over his guilt. A nasty circle. He faced the gravestone of Sister Matilda Angelvine. She'd been Olga's mentor. Olga told stories about Matilda in her frequent visits to the art studio. Since Edmund's murder, he found himself living in those memories. Brushing off the leaves to her grave, he could still hear Olga telling stories during a visit to the studio.

"It was Sister Matilda, who led me down the path of compassionate bad-ass-ery. Matilda referred to it as 'righteous compassion,' however the word righteous feels so distorted these days. She was a woman who took no guff." Olga would shake her fist, grinning.

"Wait a minute." Edmund would say, "In this moment, exactly how are you being a compassionate bad-ass?"

"By convincing the town's most celebrated artist to make posters for the Christmas food drive."

"Oh, is that so." Edmund said. "As you see it, this artist is not doing it because it's a good cause, yet by way of your bad-ass-ery manipulations?"

"Precisely," Olga grinned. "As Sister Matilda taught me, the secret is to always let the patriarchy think the plans are their own."

"Am I now the patriarchy?" Edmund smirked.

"Oh course not dear man, you, or better put, you both, are my minions."

"Whoa, Ben laughed, how did I get roped into this?"

"Because, Benjamin, I've already told Father Hayden, and Edmund here, that the finest artist in town would create the posters. And, well, to be truthful, do we really know who that is, yet?"

"You, Sister Olga, are evil, pure and simple," Edmund could not help but laugh.

"Than, why is it, Mr. Eklund, that you're the one with reservations to hell?"

"I have reservations 'about it' Sister, not for it."

"There are more than a few religious leaders who'd say it's the same thing."

"You just wait, Woman."

She laughed, he rolled his eyes, and Benjamin beamed, feeling part of a family.

So not entirely through subversion, Olga coaxed the friends into competition. Poster after poster they challenged each other with ridiculously overdone, ornate, and over the top designs. In the end, they pulled their ideas back to usable and appropriate posters.

As a playful dig to Olga, Edmund's masterwork for the food drive was a nativity scene surrounded by canned goods, groceries and a large stack of disposable diapers right behind the manger.

Benjamin took the Santa route with a landscape of rooftops and a dozen Santa's diving into chimneys, all overflowing with grocery bags. He added a line of copy at the bottom, saying. 'This Christmas, Be Santa.' For their efforts, Olga gave Benjamin a hug and kiss on the cheek, and then smacked Edmund around the studio with a rolled-up newspaper for his irreverence to the faith she dedicated her life to.

The younger man's confidence as an artist matured, little by little Edmund asked him to take over his classes, and design new classes, and look to the future direction of the studio.

Pulling himself back to the present was a sad chore. Edmund's challenge for him to realize the future of the studio was now a confounded quest indeed.

He focused on Matilda's gravestone. Intricate yet friendly florals were carved into the stone. With a small stick, he brushed away dirt, impacted in the small stone flowers. "Was this even in Violet's best interest?" He pondered. "With the studio just squeaking by, Edmund didn't even take a salary. It'll be a burden on Violet."

The phone continued to ring. He ignored it.

"And with the world so addicted to instant every-thing, who will be interested in learning to paint any-more? Is closing the studio the best idea?"

Benjamin blinked a few times before he could be-lieve his eyes. On the grass before him, just in front of Sister Matilda's gravestone, was a small easel made entirely of leaves. The delicate natural creation shiv-ered in the breeze.

17
Got Your Back

Violet parked at the studio. She phoned Benjamin again, but couldn't hear the ringing. Walking up the stairs to his apartment, no sounds came through the window. Walking to the stone boat, she redialed. A faint ring sounded out.

Amidst the bird calls, Violet focused on the ring to get a bearing. It went to voice-mail. Hanging up, she called again, followed the sound until spotting the man looking out on the river. It always impressed her, his far-off gaze into the horizon. When she tried to gaze in the mirror, she thought she looked like some-one who'd just missed an appointment.

Violet needed to ask him something personal. It made her feel vulnerable, and she hated that. Maybe that's why you were a bit of a jerk before, she thought.

A lost memory blurted out, "If you're gonna claim the piano, you'd best learn the songs." Who'd said that? She thought. The diner uncle Edmund and Olga brought her to. That was it, was it? It was the diner's owner who dropped a song book in her lap when she commandeered the small upright piano. The woman was ancient, though kind of magical. It was a book of song standards from the sixties and seventies. Violet treasured it like it was priceless. In time, every song in the book was memorized on a cellular level.

"Why that memory now?" She said aloud. "Was Benjamin the piano or the song book?" Now she wanted to sing him a song, and now, for the first time, she missed what they could have been.

"That was so long ago. Besides, we never play for each other anymore. Unless I play *to him. When I need to change his mind. Which is manipulative, nevertheless, he's never seemed to mind. She pushed the feelings away. Her feeling pushed back. No. You lose all your bargaining chips when you start thinking cuddly, so just stop it."*

Willow appeared by her side, having finished surveying the cemetery, making sure no one got in or out without her OK. Her coat took on a golden glow in the late day sun. She ran to Benjamin, then back to Violet and back and forth again between the two humans as if weaving them together. She continued her herding, until they were facing the other. She then lay alert on the leaves, proud of a job well done.

Benjamin pointed at the air sculpted easel, hoping another person could see, yet as Violet looked to where he pointed, another burst of wind brushed the easel into the air.

While honoring Violet's wishes, Ben truly wanted to keep the studio alive and well. All it took was a personal sign from Matilda to remind him.

"What?" she asked.

"Oh, it's gone, the tiniest of visions. Still, I think it's important."

They each sat on a gravestone looking out over the river. Golden sunlight bounced off the surface ripples.

"Ben?"

"Yeah?"

"I know we're neither here nor there."

"I'd say a bit more here at the moment." He smiled, "In case you're asking."

"Yes, I'm asking." Picking his phone off the grass, she leaned over and tucked it in his sweater's pocket.

"Well, it's not like you owe me or anything."

"Mmhmm." He wanted to say no, we owe each other a thousand things. He stayed quiet.

"Would you please stay till this mess of a mess is over with?"

Her question made little sense to him. He couldn't conceive of not staying. She didn't know that, and it felt sad to him. Yet it was the boost he needed to flush away Gretchen's insinuations that he was selfish. Maybe they needed to be selfish together. She'll have choices to make when she decides to make them. He looked to the expanse of the cemetery.

"Hey gang," he said to the gravestones. "I'm going to be out of the office for a while. I'll be next door," motioning to the art studio. "Just think of me as a remote worker." He turned back to Violet and said, "yeah, I'm in."

They ambled down the hill to the studio. She awkwardly hooked her arm into his.

"You stole my 'graveyard is your office' joke." She said as Willow pranced beside them.

"I did not steal it. You may have originated it, still, it's our joke."

"So you admit," She said. "I originated it, making it mine."

"Since it's a joke about me. It could not have existed without me. Henceforth, I claim partial ownership."

She paused a moment.

"Oh, and you're a jackass too."

Ben looked to the excited face of Willow, expecting dinner. "Yes sweetie, I'm hungry too." He looked to Violet, "You?"

18
Adulting

The next morning, Violet and Willow arrived early at the courthouse. The message, from Carol, Judge Lynda's assistant, had left instructions for Violet to come that morning and sign documents accepting her role as executor of Edmund's estate.

This day, walking through the town's courthouse, was a novelty for Violet. She'd no parking tickets to explain away, no housing complaints against landlords and no noise complaints for playing her piano too late at night. The lack of drama gave her the opportunity to admire the old building. She was grateful it escaped the destruction like so many beautiful structures from centuries past.

While most dogs were not allowed, Willow showed off her Canine Good Citizen's medallion, and her canine therapy badge, which she wore proudly around her neck. She gave every passerby a 'melt your heart' turn of the head and wag of her tail. Without hurry, they eventually found the ornate wooden door leading to Judge Lynda's office. She knocked and stepped inside.

"Carol?" asked Violet, unsure if she was interrupting.

"Ah, you must be Violet." She waved her in for a split second then back to the keyboard clattering. "I'll be right with you," She sounded deeply focused, "will be juuuuuuust a second." She saved and closed the transaction, before looking up with a smile.

Carol's desk faced the door and blocked the Judge's chambers behind her. A Battlement with a candy dish, and a clear signal to anyone looking to bypass her boss's calendar. Willow's nose reached for the candy dish.

"No doggy," Carol said, sweeping the dish away with the open paperback she was holding. "You're plenty sweet enough as you are."

In her left hand was a steamy romance novel, in her right, the fate of the town's legal system. Literally, single-handedly, Carol entered the information for court proceedings of the previous day. Brain researchers and productivity experts can debate for eternity if multitasking is real or not. However, no one dared question the bright, impish woman's balancing act of aching hearts and zoning permits.

"I'm sorry to hear about your Uncle, Violet. I took a class from him years ago and still have the painting hanging in my den. It's amazing what an excellent teacher can inspire you to do."

The woman's kind round eyes behind owlish glasses made Violet feel both safe and under scrutiny. Legalese was not Violet's strong suit. Carole picked up on the stranger in a strange land vibe. She pulled back the folder of paperwork and made small X's wherever a signature, check mark, or initials were needed.

Like a magician, Carol's pinky finger slid a bookmark from her sleeve of the very hand she held her book. Tucking the marker in place, she laid it on the old oak desk. The cover displayed a bare-chested man holding a beautiful woman in a gown. The characters gaze adoringly at each other. Carol noticed Violet tilt her head towards the cover.

"It might seem trashy," she said, "But it's really quite good. The major characters are each other's grand adventure." She offered her opinion with the near stranger. "I suppose we can dream, you know. Glen, my husband, is my grand adventure, I guess. Though in the books, you never have to remind the hero to take the garbage out. Than again, in the books, there isn't any garbage."

Violet grinned and nodded her head. She penned her way through the paperwork, feeling more at ease. There was a time she and Benjamin would gaze at each other like the characters on the cover.

"I agree." Violet said. "We should all get a 'Once upon a time' at some point in life."

"Oh, I almost forgot," Carol added. "It's not part of the will itself though it was included with the paperwork. It's from your uncle." Carol handed Violet the envelope, as she scanned the will and estate documents into the town records. Willow raised herself on hind legs, sniffing the envelope.

"Do you by chance teach piano as well as play?" Carol asked.

Violet opened the envelope, only semi-listening. "I, um, hmm, I haven't," She responded. "Although honestly, I don't know why not." Willow tucked her nose in the envelope. Violet noticed Edmund must have written this recently for Willow to be picking up on his scent. Was he setting his affairs in order due to his cancer?

"Well if you decide, please call me. I'd love to see my kids involved with something that's not a computer screen." She finished the scanning, handed the folder back to Violet, and lifted the romance novel, all in one fluid motion. Violet thought her eyes were playing tricks on her as the bookmark effortlessly slid back into Carol's sleeve.

"I'm not exactly sure what I'll be doing, but that's certainly an idea to think about." Seeing the words 'Dear Violet,' on the top of the letter made her unsure about continuing.

"Thank you, Carol," She waved the folder of paperwork, "And thanks so much for making this not painful."

In an hour, she would meet in the courtroom with Judge Lynda as she learned Edmund's will was possibly being contested. Gretchen had claimed yet again, that the stone boat property belonged to the church. Violet held no genuine connection to her family's history. Still, the burden of proof would be on her. And she was lost as to where to start.

19
Dear Violet

At the end of a hallway, Violet spotted a bench in front of a window. Ornate framing swirled about the old glass. Leaves were carved randomly into the bench she sat as if they'd fallen in place. The little nook was a spot out of time, and as good as any to read past the first line.

Dear Violet,

Willow hopped on the bench to join her. Delighted when Violet gave her the envelope which she nuzzled into with closed eyes. Violet began to read again.

Dear Violet

Guilt descended on her, merely reading his words. She was betraying her parents. How ridiculous this was, that anger at uncle Edmund was the strongest bond to her parents. Even though he paid her to play at the studio, she always used Benjamin as the go between. 'Just read it.' She pushed herself.

Dear Violet

She stopped again. "For once, please put aside the family drama and read the darn letter."

You may believe me horrible. For what you have possibly heard, it's difficult to consider your feelings otherwise. I've practiced reading this letter to Willow a dozen times. So, if the editing is not up to snuff, you've her to blame.

She looked to Willow, her nose over the envelope,

paw's slightly shifting.

Yet it's difficult to write all the same, and possibly to read. Most likely, I've passed. And worse, I've failed to make amends with you and your parents. If you're reading this and any other situations have arisen, please talk to Olga, she's usually right, just don't tell her I said so.

Images of Olga sifted into her memory. Forgotten joys.

I've missed having a brother and a friend in your mother, and I've missed you most of all.

"I barely spoke to you." Violet murmured. "And you've barely spoken to me. How could he say this?"

I caused the break in our family, and if it were to happen again, I honestly don't know if I'd have done the same. It broke my heart to lose you, nevertheless at least you were safe.

"At least I was safe? What in the world does that mean?"

Your parents were crazy about each other, I'm sure you knew that. They adored you, aside from their sickness. Please know, I loath to criticize, yet for you to understand, I'm afraid I have too.

"What sickness?" She said to Willow. The dog was deep in scent sleep.

When your grandma and grandpa closed their tailoring business to retire to Florida, they asked your father, and I who wanted the house, and who wanted the Stone Boat Shop. Your parents lived in a small apartment in town and were thrilled to move into the family home. I'd been living in an artist community and decided the time was right to grow up. My dad strongly nudged me to take a few business courses while in school. So, the Stone Boat Tailor Shop be-

came the Stone Boat Art Studio.

Violet found it calming to read the letter to Willow, who occasionally opened her eyes to push the story on.

Your Mom and Dad were a match made in heaven. Inventor geniuses, both of them. And like many geniuses, they were blessed in one area, and sorely lacking in another. Their inventions were brilliant, though sadly, they did not sell or help secure any form of financial backing. The upside and downside to their frustrated genius was traveling through life with feet planted firmly in the clouds.

When you came along, Violet, I felt certain they would address the realities of parenthood. They did not, and my admiration fell to worry.

Your parents invested in get rich quick schemes to fund their inventions. At first, losses were small and seemed harmless. Though instead of agreeing this was not the way to go, your parents decided they hadn't gone big enough. Each past scheme and loss of money was a lesson learned to make the next plot even bigger.

With each escalation, their addiction grew. Forgetting even the reasons for starting the schemes in the first place. Over time, they stopped inventing and their entire focus became centered on these dangerous financial endeavors. When I tried to sway them from the craziness, they accused me of all kinds of jealousies for questioning their fervor.

One day, I made a visit unannounced to drop off some washers for your sink. Your Mom mentioned it was dripping. What I saw was the last straw. Your parents were at another get rich quick seminar. You were having belly aches because you had not eaten anything. In the cupboards was a half a box of macaroni and cheese, and nothing else.

Do you remember that night? It was the last time we saw

each other before it all went bad. You gobbled the macaroni and cheese as I drove us north. We went to my favorite old rail car diner run by Olga's aunt and uncle. A couple of magical old hippies wanting to make the world a better place. You ate like a little bear that night and it broke my heart.

I knew you were feeling yourself again when you claimed ownership of the small piano in the corner. You played a duet with the black cat who swatted the lower keys. You forgave her for scratching you, even though the owners were very cross with her. You said, 'you got to suffer to sing the blues so that must be what they meant.' I agreed, and we drove home with as many meals as I could pack into the back seat. The yelling you heard that night was me. I started the fight, and eventually your parents threw me out.

Your home was on the verge of being lost for back taxes, I purchased it in a foreclosure. Then I did something I shouldn't have done. Our horns were locked, and your parents were already furious with me. I arranged jobs for them at the county office, I told them if they didn't take the jobs, I'd throw you all out of what was now my house.

It was a bluff that worked. They took the jobs, and you would never be homeless. In my business, I was painting the portraits of the townsfolk. I used my connections to keep an eye that your needs were being met. Still, Olga and I missed you terribly.

If you're wondering why I didn't tell you sooner. It wasn't for me to drive a stake between your parents and you. They had an addiction and were lost to it. I forced a cold turkey resolution to the problem, and they never forgave me. It was better you believed in your parents and see me as the villain, rather to know what happened and risk you losing faith in them.

So, I ask your forgiveness for my anger, my mishandled intentions, and any distress I've caused you.

You've owned the family house now for a decade. I sent you a letter with a copy of the deed and title when your parents moved to Florida. Also, I've thought about this long and hard. I'm leaving the Stone Boat Studio to yourself, and Benjamin. I'm sure you can make a success of it, if you don't kill each other first. I've trained him as best I could, so now it's up to you both.

On a lighter note, It's clear to everyone who knows the two of you, that you're meant for each other. You share a beautiful, fascinating, and creative kind of crazy that should only be inflicted on each other. Don't let go.

With much love
Your Uncle Edmund

Violet sat back, the letter dropping, as tears blurred her vision.

"How am I going to find Edmund's killer when I can't even see past my own family mess?" Willow didn't have an answer either. She sat re-reading Edmund's words till it was time to see what Judge Lynda had to say.

Perils Portrait

.

20
Start Your Engines

Judge Lynda felt empowered. Stepping out of her car, she strut across the town square to the courthouse, enjoying the brisk air. To anyone looking in her direction, she showed off her deep red wool jacket with a high collar. Her favorite feature was that it folded closed. There was no zipper, or even buttons, but a leather strap tied around a polished wooden latch, decorated with a Celtic knot.

She'd recently immersed herself in a historical romance. A Celtic couple who could neither keep out of dire trouble, nor within their cloths. So if she couldn't go to the eighteenth century and smack sense into her favorite fictional lovers, she'd bring the eighteenth century back to herself - in a fashion. Also, she felt a need to be ready for battle.

The contesting of Edmund's will struck a chord. Something was off. She ensured the matter landed on her own desk. Lynda never lost a sweet spot for her once heart throb. Was it wrong to still wonder how he'd look in a kilt?

That Jeremiah's accident was no accident, it nagged at her. Her brother in arms was still unconscious. She was now suspect of everyone's intentions, and a predator to all motives.

"Today, I will run my sword through all grandstanding idiots." She said, climbed the court steps two at a time. Not even the fact checker in the back of her mind dared admit. She didn't own a sword.

Her lithe frame sliced open the doors as the determined rhythm of her boot steps claimed the grand hallway.

Willow and Violet awaited outside the courtroom. Olga and Benjamin were late. Not having access to Edmund's office desk, they searched the town's records for the property deed, and any other documents they could find.

Gretchen, Crupts, and her lawyers were already waiting inside. Judge Lynda's jacket came loose. She did a spin in place to get a hold of the strap and re-tighten on the wooden latch. Willow remembered a game she played with Edmund for treats. She stood on her hind legs and spun in a circle, finishing by placing her paws into the judge's hands.

"And good morning to you, Willow," Lynda said.

The judge's anger melted, "You're right, beautiful, we need cooler heads for this." She smiled at the furry face with expectant eyes. "I will never forget your dad either." Lynda leaned close and kissed her head. Willow's collar charms fell into Linda's hand. She viewed her good canine citizen and therapy badges, along with her MooiKill drivers license.

She had an inkling, the meeting of all parties would become heated. With Edmund's murder investigation still in play, she thought it best to let the drama unfold where a video camera kept a memory of it all. Lynda entered the courtroom, followed by Violet and Willow.

Seeing the new police chief sitting at her desk swiveling in circles in her chair while playing with her gavel, triggered a nuanced and targeted sentiment.

"Get the hell out of that chair you incompetent, moronic, brown nosing, inbred, nepotimistic, mean-spirited, self-serving, disrespectful waste of space!"

Lynda hadn't expected that it would be herself getting heated and doing the yelling. She approached her office and position with solemn respect and deep responsibility.

The courtroom fell silent as Crupts fell out of the chair. The scolding shocked him. He stumbled his way back between the three lawyers and Gretchen.

"You have no right to talk to me like that." Crupts huffed. "I'm the police chief."

"What was that?" Lynda shot back. "This is my domain, there is no should or shouldn't unless I say there is."

"It's not respectful," Crupts growled, recovering from his embarrassment, his fists almost clenched.

The judge's boots gave her an added two inches, still the focus of her anger was a head taller. She glared up at the miscreant. "Be respectable." He could no longer make eye contact. His fists fell empty. She continued with her unblinking eyes.

Willow sensed what was happening. She growled quietly and awaited a reason to take the growl further. Violet was unnerved. How would she hold Willow back if events went sideways?

"Why are you here?" Judge Lynda asked Crupts point blank.

"This Will, involves suspects in an ongoing investigation. With all due respect, it is my job to be here."

Still glaring at Crupts, Lynda called out, "Court officer Phillips please relieve the chief of his firearm for this proceeding."

"What the?" Stuttered the chief.

The court officer took the side arm from the reluctant chief.

Olga and Benjamin quietly entered the courtroom and moved to Violet's aisle. Olga looked to Violet, whispering "Three lawyers? What in the world?"

Gretchen's three nearly identical lawyers sat in identical suits. They murmured back and forth. The first tugged his lapels, preparing to speak. The second took notes of the exchange into her laptop. The third text on his phone.

"Good morning." Lynda said to the room. "Today's gathering may be seen as a pre-discovery, it is a courtesy of the MooiKill court. And while this is not a legal proceeding, honorifics and proper behavior will be expected." She spoke glaring at Crupts who was glaring at Benjamin..

"Perhaps your honor," Gretchen said. "If the youthful folly has subsided," nodding to Crupts. "We might move on to the issue at hand."

"Proceed." Lynda replied, "examining her desk for anything askew."

The first lawyer began "Thank you your hon—."

"Our town records," Gretchen interrupted, "started in 1839. Forty years after a legend, based on the inebriation of all active parties, took place."

Her befuddled lawyer sat down dejected.

"Gretchen? Lynda asked. Do you have any documented proof stating otherwise?"

"The land itself, your honor."

"OK, explain yourself please."

"The church property, the cemetery and the triangle plot of land in between, were all obviously once connected."

"And while Erland Petri and Ada Dotter, might make quaint local legends. There are no records for their birth, marriage or death. From a legal standing, as charming as others might think, they were mythic characters. In other words, they played the role of the town's Mr. And Mrs. Santa Claus."

"So." Began Lynda. "As I've always understood it, there are two legends. The first has Erland Petri winning the Stone Boat property in a three-day binge of cards and drinking. The opposing legend is that Erland Petri and Ada Dotter risked their lives treating half the town's population for yellow fever, and were then given the land by the church in thanks for saving the town. Are you telling me Sister, these people never existed?"

The lawyer again attempted to be party to the conversation. He raised his index finger. He was unsuccessful.

"To the disappointment and gullibility of our townsfolk, I am afraid both stories are little more than fanciful fables."

"And the stone wall defining the studio property? And the stone boat for that matter?" The Judge asked.

"Your honor, based on church records and professional examination, the same hands built the church walls. The builders, I emphasize, were workers of the church. While the stone boat is still a curiosity, we can only conclude that they built the walls between each section, to keep the livestock out of the cemetery, not to define separate ownership."

"Olga?" the Judge asked, "Are you in the same opinion with the Mother Superior?"

"No, I am not your honor. I clearly remember Father Frank disallowing this path of action by the Mother Superior in the past. She is using his temporarily weakened health for her own selfish means."

Lynda made a few notes. "And for the question of the stone boat property deed. Olga?"

"Benjamin and I have just come from the town's records." Olga looked to Ben.

"It's not that there are no records," Benjamin said. "It's that they've been removed. The microfilm section has an empty space where that time frame of records should have been."

"The original town records." Olga added. "Have also been taken. We found no records for the stone boat property."

"You're a murder suspect," Crupts sneered, "Who gave you permission to go anywhere near the town records."

"I am no murderer, you incompetent bast—"

"Benjamin!" Lynda cut in, "Did you by chance film what you saw?"

"I did your honor." He walked to the bench showing the Judge the photos records room.

"Why is a murder suspect allowed to submit evidence this way? He staged the photos. He should be behind bars."

"This is not a trial," Lynda began, "And the records are public property. Unless you have additional evidence, remain silent. Benjamin is suspect of tripping through a murder scene, and from what I understand chief Crupts, you are equally guilty."

"All I can say is the case is growing against him." The chief threatened.

"Than, I will say, the court awaits your findings."

Lynda addressed the others. "Violet, Olga, Benjamin, Gretchen, it appears this issue will lead to a discovery, and possibly a court case. I suggest you all dig deeper."

"How do we know these three aren't in on the murder together?" Crupts blurted out.

Gretchen raised her hand to smack him, then stopped.

"You are speaking out-of-order chief Crupts," Lynda said. In addition, how do I know you're not behind this?"

"Did you just accuse me of murder?" Crupts gasped.

"And on whom would that proof be?"

He stared at the Judge, angry and confused, though he gave no response.

"If only I could take your lack of an answer as understanding." Lynda said.

Violet leaned to Benjamin, quietly whispering. "Edmund left us the Stone Boat Studio, as in, to share."

Ben's eyes widened, surprise drew across his features. "Apparently he wanted to torture us."

She elbowed him in the ribs.

21
A Rectangle Question Mark

After leaving the courthouse, Olga hugged them both and kissed Willow. "I'll see how Father Frank is holding up. Where are you crazy kids off to?"

"Benjamin's helping me pack my apartment." Violet said. "I'll be moving into the house tomorrow or the next day."

"Or in about a week, if she's still a hoarder." Benjamin laughed.

"Coming from the man who owns a toothbrush, a phone, and an unused comb, and the clothes on his back, everyone's a hoarder."

"I prefer the term ascetic." He said in mock defense.

"Ascetic huh?" Violet smirked. "Is that what I've been smelling."

"OK" Olga said, "Try not to kill each other before I see you again. And seriously, please be careful." She left in a hurry as they walked the scant distance to Violet's apartment.

"Would you give me a minute?" Violet said. "I need to pick up Edmund's financial records from the bank."

"OK than, coffee and a muffin break for me. You want?"

"Thanks, why not?" She smiled, watching him walk into 'A Rise Above' bakery. Between Ben and Olga, she was not alone during this ordeal. No matter what happened.

Fifteen minutes later, Violet stormed out of the bank spitting nails. Ben was already in her apartment, bundling up pictures and boxes of books.

"Are you ready for this?" Violet growled.

"Umm from your anger I might not be, still, spill it anyway."

"Edmund had investments."

"Yes, I'm aware of that. It's a shame he'll not be able to retire on them."

"Although Olga will."

"What do you mean." He asked.

"The morning Edmund was killed, his investments were liquidated. The following morning, as in the morning we found him, that money was transferred to a nonprofit foundation presided over by Olga."

"How much money." Ben asked.

"One and a half million dollars."

"No," Ben gasped. "Not Olga. Phone her, She has to have a reason behind this. But that much money? She should have let you know." Ben wrote Olga's phone number out and handed it to Violet.

"This happened an hour before they locked his financial activity down."

She dialed Olga. It went to voice mail. She hung up. "I honestly don't even know how to ask her."

A carload of packing later, they drove to the art studio. It would soon be feeding time for the cats, Willow, and themselves. Willow ran to the door to paw it open, but Benjamin had locked it.

Violet had been lost in thought, re-reading Edmund's letter. It gave her back the childhood she'd buried away. Now, she faced a fight for her family heritage, that until recently, she didn't know much about.

"OK girl, we'll get you in for your rounds." Ben said to Willow.

A loud bang and clattering came from inside the studio. He hurried to open the old lock. Willow leapt in first as the back door slammed shut. She did her perimeter check on the studio as Ben ran to the back door. By the time he opened the door, the car had left the yard. Violet heard the car and raced to the front door. She saw Olga's station wagon speeding away.

Benjamin came back to the teaching area. He stood in disbelief. A big rectangle hole was cut into the wall. Willow sniffed along the edges. Olga had carefully placed the cutaway wall on a sheet to minimize the mess. A can of spackle paste, putty knife, and a bit of paint were set to make the repair.

Looking from the front door, Violet called out, "Ben, that was Olga, oh crap." she said, on seeing the large hole as well. "What did she take, Ben?"

That's just it. I haven't any idea. I didn't even know Edmund stored things inside the walls.

"Ben, I love how idealistic you can be, but he wasn't storing anything. When it's inside the walls, it's called hiding. To make things worse, Olga just stole it."

"Though look," he said, pointing to the spackle and paint. "She planned to fix the hole. Oh damn, OK, don't say it. It wasn't to fix the hole, but to hide what she took."

"You got it." She put her hand on his shoulder. "That's the curious part. Hiding the theft might be as important as what she stole. We have no deed, no town records, and an accusation that you interfered with a crime scene, and over one and a half million dollars swooped out of Edmund's investments. Why would Olga do such a thing?"

"Look," Ben said. "Earlier today she was with me, helping to find those documents. She knows we'll lose the studio if we can't prove it's always owned by your family."

Violet called her once more. This time leaving a message.

"Olga." Violet said. "Please call me. It's about Edmund's investments being liquidated, and whatever was in the wall." She hung up.

"I don't like what happened," Ben said. "Still, maybe she has some sort of plan. We don't have answers, yet I know Edmund had complete trust in her."

"Than why wouldn't she let me in on what she's doing? Would an explanation from her be so hard? I'm sorry, it just isn't right. And I can't even call the police because the chief is a nut-job."

"Violet?" Ben asked. "Were those investments listed in the will?"

She paused and took a breath.

"Now that you mention it, no. The only money listed was the working capital for the studio."

"So, until we hear from her, we can only work with what we have."

"When did you become so level-headed?" She poked him.

From the workbench, she took a flashlight. Inside the hole in the wall, was a mess of old newspapers being used as insulation. "Eureka." she said. Benjamin laughed.

"What's so funny?" she asked, pulling out an old rotting newspaper.

"Eureka?" Shall I get you a pipe and magnifying glass?

"It's a clue," she said. "And a clues a clue. Look here."

When he leaned in close, she shook the dusty old newspaper in his face. He gasped and sneezed.

"That's disgusting." He coughed.

"Elementary, my dear Benjamin," she laughed. "We have two discoveries. First, the age of this newspaper, see here?"

"Oh, like I'm gonna fall for that again."

"OK spoil sport, October 15th, 1985. That's forty years ago, Ben."

He was washing his face in the sink.

"Ben, what happened forty years ago?"

"I discovered Punk Rock. I drew black eyeliner on all my sesame street books in solidarity."

"Thanks Ben, you're an enormous help."

"Violet, we were five, had your family troubles started?"

"No, those were the wonderful years."

He returned to the wall, drying his face. "What was so wonderful that needed hiding?" He asked.

"And stealing." She added.

"Hmm, oh, what was your second discovery?"

"Much simpler," she grinned, "You have mice."

"On the contrary, dear Violet, 'WE,' have mice."

"Oh, yeah," she said, "I'd forgotten that for a moment. Say, why did Edmund put up these walls, anyway? The stone's so much nicer, don't cha think?"

"Edmund didn't put up the walls. That was your grandparents during prohibition, to store the booze that wouldn't fit in the stone boat. They were all removable panels. As they rotted out, Edmund replaced each section with sheetrock."

"Ah, that explains the dated newspapers, Violet surmised. He's giving me clues to find the very thing he was hiding, but now Olga's made off with it." She looked to the back door, Olga's getaway.

Ben went to the toolbox for the drill and screws. "I honestly couldn't bear it if she were working against us. I have to believe she's on to something that she can't share yet." He positioned the cut-away section back in place. "It's not a permanent fix, in case we need to open the wall again."

"I want to believe that too Ben, and it would be heartbreaking, but hear me out. She has keys to the studio, and raced off as we arrived. She's been in Edmund's life a long time, and she knew exactly where to go to find what she wanted. And the murderer has keys, acted on impulse, and still left without a trace of identity."

"Still," he added. "She and Edmund adored each other."

"You know what they say Ben, we don't know what we don't know. Nevertheless, I agree, we will give her that, until we learn more."

She watched him screw the wall panel in.

"Why three lawyers?" She asked rhetorically.

"I know, it's not like the church has the money for even a single lawyer. Edmund's been using his mini tractor to cut their grass and snow plow their drive-way when he saw it wasn't being done. Father Frank was grateful, yet Sister Gretchen focused on all the spots he missed."

"Which can only mean the money's coming from someplace else." Her eyes scanned the studio. "Do the art classes make enough to keep this all running."

"The studio," Benjamin explained, "barely squeaks into the black every year, I'm fairly certain I'm the biggest expense."

"Oh, and on so many levels." She laughed.

"Guess I walked into that one. Still, there you have it, we're a top quality studio, though financially, we just make ends meet."

"You know, Ben, that's not the true value of the place. It's waterfront property, and worth a pretty penny." Her mind was churning. She looked out the back door before closing it. "And that's nothing com-pared to the bigger picture."

"How do you mean?" He asked. "What's the bigger picture?"

"Here Mr. Artist, I'll give you a visual." She pulled a big sheet of paper from the storage racks. In the cen-ter of the page, she drew the shape of a pizza slice.

"This is us." She said.

"We're the pizza." He grinned.

"And like you said, a pretty penny. About a quarter acre?"

"Mhmm, yes, something like that."

She then drew the church property followed by the cemetery on the other side. "Here's the big picture," she said. "We could sell this plot for what, four or five hundred thousand? Not much land, however, it's waterfront property on the Hudson river. Still, is that worth three lawyers showing up?"

"OK, I'll bite," he said. "No, what is worth three lawyers showing up?"

"The whole enchilada." She spread her hands across all three plots.

Benjamin grinned. "I was going to have pizza for dinner, though now I want enchiladas."

"So does Gretchen and her three lawyers. If she can get control of the entire property, it's worth a fortune. And don't forget Olga's story. Gretchen's father was a crooked slumlord. Who knows who else is involved in this?"

"Yeah, I see." Ben said. "Three lawyers make sense now, but she doesn't own the property."

"No, she doesn't, however, she has power of attorney for Father Frank during his illness. She can act on his behalf. And as the only functioning officer of the church, she can sell it. If we can learn who the lawyers are truly working for, we'll know the interested buyer. And maybe how it relates to Gretchen."

Benjamin absentmindedly began drawing his favorite monuments on the cemetery plot. "Do you think Gretchen killed Edmund?" he asked.

"No." Violet said. "I know she disliked him. Yet her plan to grab the property was already underway before the murder. As we learned today, that's what she's after. The murder investigation will only delay her contesting of the will, and if a court battle, even longer. They need it all to happen as soon as possible."

"How do you know that?" He asked.

She gave a crooked grin, "A tidbit from this stack of executor and property notes Carol gave me this morning. Edmund recently registered not only the stone boat property as a historical landmark, but the church and cemetery as well. I inquired to learn, that will take about three months to process."

"I'd bet the whole enchilada, he did it at the request of Father Frank before he was sick." Benjamin added.

"Let's hope we have the chance to find out. I'm tired and starving."

"What are you in the mood for?" He asked.

"Mexican ya goof, what else?" She turned to find a very expectant Willow, and Gus staring at them both, with the unmistakable demand of "Where's my dinner."

"OK, furry people, I'm on it," He said laughing.

Violet looked out the window as Ben went through the feeding routine. "Ben, our mice issue seems to be leaving us."

"How do you mean?" He asked.

"That kitty, there, seems to be marching them off someplace else."

Ben stretched his neck to see without moving from the prep area. "Oh, that's Donny. He keeps mice as pets. He must have noticed the disruption when the wall was cut open. He's moving them someplace safer."

"Umm Ben? Is that normal?"

Ben grinned. "Welcome to your new normal. Ya know, you could teach here as well. It might not feel like it yet. Still, it's really yours."

"Ours" She reminded him with a sad smile. And

thought, 'I wouldn't have it any other way,' and then felt a tinge of guilt for not telling him out loud. "I wouldn't have it any other way." The words blurted out before she could stop them. Embarrassed, she couldn't look him in the face. Benjamin stared back, equally awkward, near incapable of accepting compliments.

They left for the Mexican restaurant in an awkward silence, yet comforted.

22
Familiar Ghosts

Early next morning Violet was on a mission. Proof of ownership for the Stone Boat property had to be somewhere. She would start with the family house, and then the studio. Making do with so little for so long made the reality of owning a home intimidating. A good cleaning would help towards the feeling of it being hers. Where did that thought come from? Am I becoming domesticated by home ownership osmosis?

Whatever it is, first things first. She needed to find the deed, or some form of paperwork proving ownership. Taking on the countless stacked boxes in the attic was a daunting task, yet a logical first step.

If you'd only read Edmund's letter back when, she berated herself. You could have avoided a decade of crappy apartments and crappier landlords. When her parents abandoned the house, moving to a retirement community in Florida, Edmund had put the property in Violet's name. He wrote to let her know the home was hers now. He had hoped to talk, to explain his side of the story and why he acted as he did.

Out of loyalty to her parents, she didn't open the letter. A loyalty forced on her by emotional gas lighting. However, when Edmund did not hear from her, he asked Benjamin to make sure she received it. She told Benjamin she didn't want it. She meant his letters, but he thought she meant the house. So, he moved into the house to keep it occupied and Benjamin moved into the apartment above the art studio.

"OK, to it." Pulling on the rubber gloves, she dove in with a vengeance. Her brows knit together while deconstructing her childhood's crime scene. Dragging out the collection of financial scams, inventions, funding proposals, and their own get rich quick schemes, she finally understood how deep her parents' addiction had become.

With the attic windows open, she pushed box after box of her parents' compulsion into the daylight. Keeping a diligent eye for anything that was family or property related, or helpful to save the studio. When she finished, the 'save' pile was sadly lacking, though not a surprise. The 'get rid of pile' now comprised twenty big paper trash bags she'd thrown into the yard.

The last bag was the heaviest, and wouldn't fit out the window. She dragged it down the stairs, pausing in the living room to take a breath. By chance she looked up at the painting above the fireplace. In itself, not unique, yet there was something familiar to its shape. The very dimensions of the rectangle cut out from the studio wall. While dialing Ben, she found a tape measure in the kitchen drawer.

He answered. "Ben, I need you to measure the wall cut out." Putting him on speakerphone, she took the painting down.

"It's thirty-four by fifty inches. Does that mean anything?" He asked.

"It might. Work with me, please. Can you go to the

back racks where Edmund stored his paintings? How many are thirty-two by forty-eight inches?"

"I don't need to, that was his favorite painting format."

"Ben, I believe it's a painting that Olga took from the studio wall. The hole is two inches larger than his favorite painting size."

"That makes sense," He said. "Still, what painting would he need to hide in the wall?"

"What happened in nineteen eighty-five?" She asked, "And don't talk about discovering punk again. Did he ever discuss that time with you?"

The painting she held was a landscape of the Hudson river. Glancing behind the painting, she saw several photos and a preliminary drawing tucked in between the canvas and stretcher bars.

"Nothing out of the ordinary. Though he was never accused of over sharing."

"Ben, I'm winging it here, will you check the other paintings? Especially the ones in the locked cabinet. Do they all have preliminary drawings tucked into the back of them?"

"I'll get back to you on it, and most likely yes. But why especially the ones in the locked cabinet?"

"Just a hunch. Remember the drawing beside Edmund's body? The nude that fell behind the cabinet?"

"Yes, I do, It's an old draw—. Ohh, So, if Olga took the painting, who is she trying to protect?"

"That's just it." Violet said. "We don't know."

"OK, I have the drawing here. Thank goodness it slipped behind the cabinet and didn't go to evidence. The drawing is beautiful."

"Can you make out who it is, Ben?"

"Sorry, that side of the drawing is crinkled. Her face is smudged and in shadow. Her hair is short. I'll check it against the other paintings locked up. You know, I've heard he was a sought-after bachelor in his day."

"Are you calling my uncle a man whore, Ben?"

"No." He rolled his eyes, "I'm simply saying it happens. There are crazier ways to meet someone."

"If Olga acted to protect this person as she did, be assured it was no casual relationship."

"Excellent point. Has Olga returned your phone calls?"

"No, she hasn't. I'm back to the deed search. Let me know what you find."

After dragging the last bag of attic trash to the yard, she went to the bedroom Edmund occupied. She checked the dresser drawers, wall cabinets, and finally emptied every drawer of his roll-top desk. Yet found nothing till at last, a gray folder tucked deep in a vertical side panel caught her eye. Slowly opening the folder, she carefully separated its contents across the bed.

While difficult to read, the text was exciting, and proved her family's history. Written by the church's first Bishop, he spoke of what became of the first inhabitants of the stone boat and townspeople. He wrote of Erland Petri and losing the prayer house in the famous three day drunken card game. He wrote how Erland refused to accept his winnings. The Bishop also wrote of Erland's wife, Ada Dotter. How they were pivotal members of the community and according to the Bishop, Ada Dotters skills in treating the ill, saved the town from certain peril when the yellow fever struck.

What she could not find was the deed. She was missing the last page. Numbered: one of five, two of five, etc. The last page was gone. If it were the deed or a continuation of the story, was anyone's guess.

Searching the house, poking behind every painting, in every cabinet and desk, she eventually found herself in her childhood bedroom. After moving out, her parents converted it to a business office, or a war room, as they chose to call it. But this was not the war room.

It must have been restored by Edmund. Her bedroom was near as she remembered it. He had rescued her dresser, standing closet and bed from the attic or barn. The posters hadn't survived. In their place hung paintings of her childhood pets. Sally, the parakeet, Gary the hamster, and Victoria the cat who ate Gary the day she and Edmund took a trip to the aquarium. She was ten years old. It was an upsetting introduction to a predatory world.

Behind her dresser hung a chalkboard. He saved this childhood treasure. Ticket stubs to concerts and postcards of so many places they went. Often with Olga, the same big beautiful smile as she remembered. Edmund would drop them at the entrances, then find a place to park.

She and Olga would walk hand in hand, waiting for him. She had big wild hair. Violet remembered asking her if it was alive. She told her it could certainly be disobedient. Edmund laughed and then her hair flew in his face. It proved Violet's hypothesis.

Were Olga and Edmund more than friends? A couple? How could this be?

A faded postcard caught her attention. It pictured an old rail car diner painted up in a flower power motif. The sign read 'The Morning Star Diner.' She flipped the postcard, surprised to see a note.

To my new friend Violet. Come back and play for us again. Magic is afoot, Namah.

The piano, the old hippy woman, the very black cat, the jukebox. Her memories were hazy. She closed her eyes, and the image cleared. It was the last time Edmund took her anywhere. She knew he was very upset yet put on his best face that everything was OK. She was eleven and knew better. Things weren't OK.

The old woman at the diner also had crazy hair. Olga's aunt? She remembered Benjamin telling her that she would go up north to tend to her. Was Namah her Aunt?

After safely putting away the old documents, she mapped out the address to the diner. Patting the dashboard, she encouraged her tired car for one last trip again, and chugged out the driveway, her driveway. Checking yet again the postcard in her pocket, she headed north.

A crisp starry night gave her mind a chance to clear. Unconsciously playing Mozart on the steering wheel made the time pass quickly. Unsure why the old diner tingled this hunch in her. If nothing panned out, she could at least have dinner.

Sixty miles later and playing a requiem on the steering wheel, she nearly missed the exit off rt87. If the radical turn didn't jolt her attention, the black cat landing on her shoulder almost made her jump through the roof.

"You scared the life out of me." She said to Eve.

The cat responded with a purr and rubbed herself across Violet's cheek. Checking the back seat, she realized Eve must have slept there all day.

"You got yourself in it now." She said to the sleek feline. Eve stretched herself from the armrest to the dashboard and watched as the exit sign took them to a smaller road, then an even smaller road. It continued a few miles more, till the diner on the postcard became a reality.

Pulling into the parking lot gave her goosebumps. Early memories shifted her sense of time. She was eleven years old again and in the mood for French toast. The building was covered in dust and leaves. A tree branch grew into one window. Still, it did not look decrepit, merely hibernating.

Opening the car windows a few inches for Eve, she closed her door before addressing the freeloading cat. "I'm sorry, however I have to lock you in. There may be hungry critters about who might like a bad kitty who sneaks into cars and goes for rides, almost making me crash." Eve looked at her curiously as she eyed the door locks plunking downward.

"We'll stop on the ride home and get you something to eat."

23
Of Diners and Dreamtime

With an extra tug on the old door, she entered the diner. The sun nearly set, yet its glow illuminated her way in the shadowy space.

Dream-like in its atmosphere, she remembered gobbling food with her uncle. Nothing ever tasted so good. She remembered Olga joining them. Taking the flashlight from her pocket, she looked at the post-card again.

To my new friend Violet, come back and play for us. Magic is afoot, Namah.

The piano was just where It had been all those years ago.

Memories of the old woman came back to her. She kept her laughing while Edmund and Olga spoke to each other in serious tones. Namah's hair! It was exactly like Olga's, only white. Were they mother daughter? Aunt and Niece? Yes, that must be it. Olga recently traveled north for a few days to tend to her Aunt. Namah seemed ancient back then. It's often the case through a child's eyes.

Sitting at the piano, she lifted the lid and positioned her flashlight above the keys. A warm shadow spread out in both directions. To her surprise, Eve had found her way out of the car, into the diner and now completely at home, sitting gracefully on the piano.

Testing the keys lightly to not intrude on the quiet night, she played. It was the very first piano she'd ever touched. Exploring sounds and combinations of notes, and different volumes of phrases and rhymes as if playing drums on the keys.

It was primitive and joyous. This is how she played before she knew songs. Before she learned to finish a song by looking up for approval, and permission to continue. She played to her own personal magic.

"I must be dreaming." she said aloud. Her voice echoed off the walls. "Or possibly, I'm seeing things." To her left, her eleven-year-old self, sat on the bench playing right along with her. The younger was in awe of what her older self learned. Together they played on as sparks bouncing off their dancing finger tips.

In this magical duet, Violet chose to believe she brought this temporary delusion on by the stress of current battles. Eve continued to look back and forth at the two versions of Violet. What should be disconcerting, she enjoyed. The cat, who's normal gaze spoke of knowing everything, now looked astonished.

Her younger self noticed it too. Feeling encouraged, she challenged the elder with wilder, crazy melodies to match and go higher. "This must be in the key of kitty?" she suggested laughing.

"Exactly," said the woman. They played their life in a music uniquely their own.

As the last note rang out, they both took a breath as if they had ran a race. "We have to do this again." They said in unison. They laughed together. It startled Eve, and she leapt away. The girls laughed even more.

Still grinning at her mischievous innocence, she

closed the lid on the piano.

"See ya later, alligator." And the girl was gone. All alone, the quiet was deafening.

Violet's eyes opened as the flashlight flickered. Her head rested on folded arms over the piano lid. As groggy as she was, when Eve hissed into the darkness it got Violet's attention. Another cat? A larger critter? Impossible to tell. Eve leapt onto Violet's shoulder and growled. She knew it was time to go.

Driving home in silence, she wondered if she really met her younger self in the diner. And how this enchanted gift and playfulness had been pushed to the very back of her life. Other memories surfaced. Putting the dots together from Edmund's letter, and saving the house for her, she knew he was only trying to protect her. Still, what was Olga up to? Was she still the warm soul she remembered? Or had the years turned her cold like Gretchen.

A week after the family fight, an electric piano showed up on her porch. It took every bit of strength to lug it upstairs to her room. She hid it in her accordion door closet, practicing only when her parents went to their 'get rich quick meetings.' They sold the TV set in the living room to fund the schemes, and the family stereo system. She knew in order to keep the piano; it had to stay hidden.

A mysterious card arrived for her twelfth birthday. It included prepaid piano lessons for Miss Diane's school of melody. On her eighteenth birthday, before high school graduation, she received a scholarship she didn't remember applying for. It took her to college, where she earned a bachelor's degree in music.

She pulled her car into a highway rest area. It had all been Edmund, doing the things her parents couldn't be bothered to do. Family scabs are painful when pulled off. Eve climbed onto her lap and licked the tears as best she could.

24
Expressionism Takes Flight

"Good morning, no noon, good afternoon." Unless Benjamin was giving painting or drawing instructions, he was not his best when speaking in public. "Thank you all for taking part in the 'Edmund Eklund's Memorial Painters Auction.' It's an honor, I mean, I'm honored that you've all chosen to celebrate him today by painting the view from the studio."

"I know it was brief notice," Violet added. "And I'd like you all to know, you are helping 'A Paw in Need Animal Rescue.' It was Edmund's favorite charity. I also hope this helps heal the tragedy of his loss within our community. The breakfast auction will begin at ten thirty tomorrow morning. And of course, please invite all your family and friends."

The baker's dozen of painters applauded both hosts.

The baker's dozen of cats eyed their hopeful next meal, currently tweeting from the trees.

"So, let's begin." Violet said.

Violet and Benjamin relaxed into their familiar roles. For the special occasion, Violet brought her Cello. Beginning with Hayden, she made mental notes to visit Bach, Vivaldi, Beethoven, and Mozart before the event was over. The birds, chirping up their own concert, would hopefully approve of her selections. Willow surveyed the grounds and helped herself to any treats offered by the painters.

"Whichever medium you paint in today," Benjamin said, "As Edmund taught us, I'm suggesting, to build your colors layer by layer, deepening and brightening as you proceed."

While Benjamin spoke to the artists, Violet looked to the church. Gretchen's three lawyers were leaving the rear entrance.

The white-throated Sparrows sang a response to Violets Vivaldi. The Northern Mockingbirds chirped in as well. The Wood-thrush interrupted, though only out of impatience for Beethoven. Violet indulged her fantasy that the birds were singing with her. The tweeting sounded more than coincidental. Yet to believe it was anything beyond fancy, her confidence wouldn't allow.

Benjamin's voice pulled her out of her inner musing. "You're working with the golden ratio today. For anyone taking Edmund's classes in the past, you'll know it was his favorite method of composition. A natural relationship of patterns found throughout nature. The pencil marks I left on your canvases or watercolor paper are to define your foreground, or water's edge, or distant mountain range. In short, wherever in this composition you wish to bring the viewer's eye."

Gus and the dozen other cats paced back and forth on the roof of the stone boat. Each bumped into one another, excited to have their hopeful dinner singing to them.

Violet watched the predatory nun and her lawyers. Even from a distance, she saw the disapproval etched on her face. With papers in hand, Gretchen and the suits began walking towards the painting event. Willow, who lay beside Violet, stood and growled quietly. Resisting the current feathered temptations, Gus heard the growls and the crouching tabby readied himself.

The class painted away in excited silence.

"Go away," Violet hissed under her breath. The Cello's tones turned darker.

Whatever the papers Gretchen held; Violet knew would be unwelcome news. "Go away." The Cello burned under her fingers as the birds fluttered in agitation.

Willow looked to Gus, acknowledging the impending battle. But instead, Violet's feathered co-performers took her cue and took to the air.

"Go away." The Cellist growled.

The figure in black stopped. A white splotch appeared across her shoulder. A gray splat hit her other arm. The third landed on Gretchen's head veil. Unfettered, more attacks followed, splattering across the lawyers.

"Does someone need water splashed in her face?" Whispered Benjamin.

Violet returned from that angry place, hearing the thrashing ruckus coming from her Cello. She calmed her inner tempo, and the music, and in time, the birds. A few painters looked on in concern.

"Thanks," she said as they watched Gretchen storming back to the church. The lawyers ran to their hired car. The last feathered comments, the birds wrote across the windshield, before returning to the trees by the boat.

"If I didn't know better, I'd say you spun a bit of Mojo there." Benjamin grinned wide eyed.

"Honestly, I've no idea what just happened. All I remember was wanting them to go away." Somewhere deep in her psyche an eleven-year-old girl could not stop laughing.

Benjamin walked amidst the painters as Violet arched her neck to get a look at everyone's progress. The painter closest to her was working in bold brush strokes with exciting, vivid color. Could it be? No. Violet was certain Betty would not dare to come back after accusing Ben of murdering her uncle.

She looked at the woman's hair, obviously a wig. The oversized sunglasses helped make her look anonymous and ridiculous. And the purple tartan poncho would make anyone look like someone else. Her painting, however, was unmistakable.

"Betty?" Violet asked.

There was no answer, yet the woman's body stiffened.

"Betty Skurmutza? Is that you?"

"Please," said Betty, lowering her sunglasses. "Please don't give me away."

"I'm just surprised to see you." Violet said, bemused.

"You know, I loved Edmund as much as anyone else here. And truth be told, I think he was a little sweet on me."

"In that case, we can keep this between ourselves." Violet said.

"Thank you, Violet. Um, also, I overheard that terrible boyfriend of yours say, you did that trick with the birds. I need you to help me with my neighbor. His

166

rotting apples are falling all over my driveway and—"

"Betty, today's not the day to push your luck."

"It wouldn't take—."

"Betty!"

"Yes, um, OK."

Regina, also in earshot, did her very best not to laugh. Though she did sort of sputter instead. Never one to miss Edmund's landscape classes, Regina was here today on official business, to keep tabs on Benjamin and his accomplice, Violet. Personally, she would not have missed it.

Hours later, the paintings neared completion; the afternoon came to a close. Violet waved Benjamin over to her.

"I'm playing at the nursing home in fifteen minutes. Let's catch up later." She bowed to the birds and quietly scooted off.

"I see so many beautiful paintings." Benjamin called out to the group. "If you like, find a stone and move it to where your easel is positioned for tomorrow's auction. And remember to post the wet paint card above if you painted in oils. It'll take a few more days to dry."

Regina's heart sank when the call came in. Displayed across her radio screen, the arrest order was for Benjamin and Violet. It conflicted Regina. "Violet's gone," she grumbled. "And no way I'm arresting him while he's teaching, or while the other artists were present."

She text back, "One suspect spotted, awaiting him to return in his boat to shore. We will not need back-up." She forgave herself the little lie, quickly texting the warrant info to the other key players.

The meditative painting session ended. Several

students stretched themselves from that relaxed and focused state within their landscapes. Regina's fingers searched her utility belt. Sadly, she would need her handcuffs. They were missing. Where? Oh, yeah, She'd been playing with her niece and nephew. She'd arrested them for not brushing their teeth before bed. After compliance, Regina released the adorable felons, and sent them to sleep. The cuffs, she surmised, must have slid behind the couch cushions.

Benjamin walked up beside her. "You've brilliantly understood the muted tones in the background. I believe you're the queen of understated shadows."

"Well, if that's not bragging rights for tonight's wine club, I just don't know what is." She beamed in pride.

"Benjamin," Regina whispered, seeing the last student packing her bag and putting her painting in the drying rack. "Have you got any of those long plastic ties?"

"Um, yeah, I think we do," He went inside to the supply cabinet as Regina packed up. "Here ya go." He called out, returning. "What cha need it for?"

"Benjamin, do you trust me?" She asked.

"Well yeah, I mean as much as anyone can trust the fuzz." He grinned. She wanted to find the joke funny.

"I'm gonna need you to trust me on this big time, you see, I've orders to arrest you."

"Arrest me? For?"

"Well, let's not go to why just yet. With a bit of luck, we'll never even make it to the station house."

"I don't understand. You will arrest me for something unknown, then release me?"

"Umm yeah. That's the plan." She replied.

"And if I say no?" He stiffened.

Regina moved in and hugged him. "I know you're hurting, Ben. But you are not alone in this, not by a long shot. You've got Margot, Abram, and Oscar, all rooting for you. And even judge Lynda's stepping in. Also, we haven't seen a bit of actual evidence that you're any part of it."

After bringing the drying rack of paintings inside, he quickly fed the cats and Willow, then locked the studio. He didn't fight, as she put the plastic tie around his wrists, yet he was not at all happy getting in the back seat of her cruiser.

"You know," Ben said. "If anyone got arrested today, it should have been Betty."

"Sorry Ben, but I'm not the fashion police." She grinned, starting the engine. "However, you should be happy she went through all that trouble to hide from you."

Regina let the car idle its way towards town at about five miles per hour.

25
Evening Visit to the Morning Dove

Abigail used her cane to hold open the activity room door for Violet. "Welcome dear."

Violet's grin was more of a grimace as she lugged her piano into the dayroom.

"Oh my, that's one grisly smile." Abigail exclaimed.

Pausing, sighing, and taking a deep breath, Violet started again.

"I'm sorry Abigail," An honest smirk found its way to her face. "How are you?"

Abigail walked back to her favorite overstuffed chair, not needing her cane, still carrying it all the same.

"I'm fine, dear. Was the painting memorial well attended?"

"It was. Thanks for asking. The painters had a wonderful time." She looked about, unsure of the best place in the room to set up. The other residents in the room were busy in a card game. Abigail pointed to the spot right in front of her.

"Ah, so you're my audience tonight." She put her piano and bag of accessories down.

"Don't take it personal Violet. The Morning Dove Poker Championship begins tomorrow after breakfast. They're practicing."

"You're not taking part?"

"Regina's taking me to the painting auction tomorrow. Oh, and I've got some wonderful news."

"I could do with wonderful news."

"Well," Abigail said. "The cancer is in remission, which has been a daily nuisance, and today, the yoga teacher complimented my warrior one pose."

"That's wonderful." Violet hugged her. "You've certainly been a warrior through all of this."

As Violet opened her tablet to peruse what songs she might play today, Abigail reached into Violet's accessory bag containing the power cord, sustain pedal, lyrics bracket, water bottle, and an assortment of plugs and wires.

"Maybe some Ella Fitzgerald, a little Ray Charles, and Elvis." She said to make conversation. "And as always, I take requests." She threw the suggestion out to Abigail.

"Oh no," She said, "What you play always turns out to be exactly what I need to hear. So, don't you go-a-changing baby."

When Violet looked up from her tablet, Abigail had mounted her keyboard on its stand and plugged it in. The sustain pedal was screwed on, and the sheet music rack hooked on the keyboard. It had taken a couple of visits to recognize that Abigail was far more technically capable than she, or anyone she knew for that matter.

"You are amazing." She said to Abigail.

"My hands are frustratingly bored these days. I miss my sewing machines."

The daughter of an engineer and seamstress, Abigail could disassemble a sewing machine, repair, lubricate and reassemble it in under an hour. She and her husband Ronald converted the sun-room on the side of their house into a sewing machine repair shop.

Ronald was an ace mechanic with his own auto shop in town. He'd passed away a decade ago. Abigail moved into the nursing home when her hips became too argumentative to manage on her own.

"I was so sorry to hear about your uncle, Violet. I know you weren't close, although any family passing is difficult."

"Thanks, Abby. The thing is, with everything I've learned since his death. I feel closer to him than ever."

"Funny and sad how that can happen." Abigail leaned back in her chair and closed her eyes as Violet began finding melodies. "So tell me," she said. "Is your sweetheart, or not sweetheart, helping you through these hurdles?"

Violet swept into an Ella melody. She was certain Abigail could see her glaring grin through closed eyelids. "Yes, Benjamin's been my knight in paint-stained sweatshirt. Nevertheless, we are better off as friends."

"How did you kids meet, by the way?"

"Oh jeez, you really wanna hear that?"

Abigail's eyebrows nodded with authority.

"He was, as few people know today, a wonderful musician. We were rock-and-roll purists, so we tried our best to not get famous together."

"See. I've learned something about you both already." Abigail laughed. "OK, don't tell me, you would not give in to commercialism and succumb to the man?"

"In a word, Yep, exactly."

"But you didn't go the way of drugs, did you?"

"Hey." Violet protested, "who's telling this story, anyway."

Abigail raised her hands, "Oh excuse me miss wall-flower, the stage is yours."

"Well, there were some drugs, and some drinking, though honestly, we'd both known hunger. But every drunken stoner was a billboard sign for what not to do."

Abigail peeked her eyes open. "Smart."

"Anyway, his quest was for the 'real' as he called it." Doing air quotes for Abigail, "or 'real' as a twenty-year-old idiot can interpret reading the existentialists."

"Aww," Abigail said. "Men can be so cute when they discover thinking."

"Oh, he was, and I can still remember his soapbox rant at the 'open mic' events. Let's see, it goes something like this."

"We are all bumbling, fumbling ape descendants, projecting meaning and importance onto artificial hierarchical social systems of behavior. And we do this, to avoid looking into that insurmountable void of inevitable death and the meaningless of self."

"Or, ya know, something like that."

"Um yeah, Violet, that is one mouthful of gibberish."

She laughed, "Oh it was, still, he was so attractive saying it. Well, for that time of life he was. Let me put it this way. To a young woman, Benjamin looked like a soulful man with passion and angst, committed to living a deeply meaningful life. To an older woman, Benjamin was practicing his brooding to attract overly poetic young women."

"And you were that young woman?" Abigail asked.

"I was born to be that young woman." She laughed. "It was adulthood that threw me for a loop."

"Doesn't it though." Abigail huffed. "OK, so when did you know?"

"Well, there was a gathering at a loft in the city. We were circling each other like puppy predators. He played his guitar out of tune to annoy people into listening to his rant. I needed him to know me and that I understood him. I didn't agree with him, yet I didn't care."

"Please tell me you didn't un-tune your piano." Abigail said.

"No," Violet grinned. "I played an experimental anti-musical genre piece in the chromatic scale."

Abigail made a face of confusion.

"Well." Violet said, "To borrow your terminology, I made up complete gibberish."

"Ahh gotcha, and then he kissed you?"

"You would think so wouldn't you, but no. He just stood there, gob-smacked."

"Oh, it's just men, my Ronald was just as clueless."

"I'm glad I'm not alone." Violet smirked, rolling her eyes. "It was January and freezing. Several of us crashed on the couches at the event. There was a lot of couch crashing in those days. Benjamin accidentally slept with his face on my piano. He awoke with the keys of my Wurlitzer pressed into his cheek."

Abigail giggled. "Not what I'd call romantic, so let's see where it goes."

Violet continued. "Billy Preston's 'Nothing From Nothing' came on the radio and I just took the chance.

I knelt on the floor next to him and said, look at the C Major on this guy's face. We can't let this go to waste. So I played along with the song, poking my fingers into his face till he'd had enough. He wrapped his arms around me so I couldn't poke him anymore and kissed me like it was his plan all along."

"Finally." Abigail huffed. "Why in the world do they wait so long."

"Hmm, only the good ones wait. The bad ones were only too happy to be all over me."

"Oh, I'd never had the chance with the bad boys. At the River Tavern, my dad announced regularly he had a fifty-gallon drum and a free trip up the river for any boys looking to get lucky with me. I'd swear, walking down the street, you'd think I was radioactive."

"So." Violet asked, "How did Ronald get past your dad?"

"Simple. She laughed; Ronald never went to the tavern. He had no idea I was a danger to his health, and by the time I'd fallen in love with him, there was nothing my dad could do. How were your folks with you, bringing home a philosopher musician?"

"Oh, I was pretty much on my own by then. With crappy jobs and crappy apartments, we lived happily ever after, until we didn't, and then we did again. Rinse and repeat for the next twenty years. Kind of a dysfunctional mess if you ask me."

"Nonsense, Ronald and I may have been very traditional, though that doesn't mean you have to be. Regina taught me that. Who would think of my granddaughter, the cop, giving me life lessons at this age?"

"I honestly don't know where Benjamin and I

stand right now. I should probably make the break permanent so we can get on with our lives."

Abigail smiled at her with soft eyes.

Violet continued, "Yet we're always pushed back together somehow."

"Is that why you're playing 'Will you still love me tomorrow?'" Abigail asked.

"It's just a song," Violet defended.

"Oh, course it is dear, of course it is."

Perils Portrait

26
The Not So Secret Wine Club

Regina continued to inch her cruiser towards the police precinct. "Please believe me Ben, we are working to find the killer, even if certain parties have made that difficult."

"So Crupts got his way? I'm being charged with Edmund's murder?"

Regina sent a text, cursed and sent it again. Ben wanted to yell about the absurdity of the situation, seeing nothing happening for Edmund. He held his tongue despite the frustration. Regina didn't deserve his anger, but that didn't keep it from growing.

"There's a bright side big guy, I've a good feeling, they'll be an order to release you soon."

He grumbled and watched the trees go by in slow motion.

"This whole being arrested, not arrested, it's really just, I don't know. Don't you have your wine club tonight, anyway?"

"Ben, tell me we're still friends." Benjamin gave her a forlorn look, "Friends" Benjamin said, "get invited to wine club." He gave her half a smile.

"It's women only," She said. "However, I'll see what I can do. Just remember, we never talk about wine club. It's a secret."

"Umm, everyone knows about the wine club?"

"Yes, but you see. We're hiding in plain sight."

Her painting sat on the seat next to Benjamin. He held the landscape in place with his left leg to keep it from falling to the floor.

During the day's painting session, Regina intently listened to Benjamin's chat about the golden ratio in painting and how the old masters relied on this system to plan their use of space when composing their creations. Her painting's horizon line was at the far edge of the river. The stone cliffs rose above it. By flipping and using the ratio on the bottom of the painting and the top, Regina added what Benjamin called a second horizon line.

On this second horizon line, she added the town water tower. Instantly everyone in the yard recognized the exact location with "oohs and ahhs." For fun, on the water tower itself, she painted the Christmas tree that mysteriously appeared every holiday season.

No one knew who carried the Christmas tree that high up the water tower, hung it where there was no catwalk, or provided electricity for the lights that mysteriously lasted the entire season. At the station, they made bets each year on who would catch the local hero, and every year the money went to the charity box.

"Do you think you'll catch the Jolly Daredevil this year, Regina?" Ben was trying his best to not be negative.

Her eyes perked up, looking into the rear-view mirror. "Honestly Ben, I hope we never do. Cause whoever it is, they are awesome!"

As slowly as she attempted to go, the police car eventually inched into the town square. Her phone lit up.

"Yes!" she exclaimed, having a reason to pull over while only four hundred feet from the station house.

"Yes, your honor, we're at the top-secret meeting place now. Wait, I've got a call from the station." She switched to the other call.

"Hello there Chief, what can I do ya for?" Reaching back to Benjamin, she grabbed his hand and shook it in hers. "Yes sir, I have apprehended the prisoner. I'm bringing him now."

Benjamin slumped into the seat. Being arrested for Edmund's murder triggered a sense of hopelessness. He couldn't help but expect the situation to spiral from bad to worse, and worser still. Regina's charm and good humor had met its match in Ben's penchant for gloominess.

"Taking so long? Chief? I'm nearly burning the rubber off the tires. No sir, just the one. Yes, Benjamin." Her phone buzzed. "Chief, could you please hold a moment, I'm getting a call from Judge Lynda." Ignoring his sudden burst of demands, she switched calls, unable to stifle a laugh.

"Yes, your honor, the prisoner has been apprehended." She spoke in a performed seriousness. "What's that? You've signed his release?" She waved and patted Benjamin's knee. "Well, I guess I've no excuse to hold him any longer. Yes, I agree, I'll have the restaurant bill it to your account. What's that, your honor? You want both our dinners billed to your account? My goodness, that's so generous. Oh, the signals getting weak your honor." Regina made a pretty good static noise, hung up the call and switched back to her boss.

"Chief? Chief? Oh well, I guess he's got other urgent things pressing." Shutting off her engine, she hopped out of the car.

"OK, Ben," she said, swinging the car door open. "You're not under arrest anymore."

"Who's the other?" he asked point blank. "Was Violet arrested?"

"Violet? Oh goodness no, Violet's at the nursing home playing oldies for my grandmother."

"Oh, thank god for that." He reached into his pocket awkwardly as his hands were still tied together. Pulling out a small pocket-knife, with a bit of dexterity, he raised the locking notch of the tie and released himself.

"OK, Ben," she laughed. "We don't have to share that part of the story with anyone." She opened the door to the Tap & Stance Pub and Nosh and waved him in. "Come-on slowpoke, dinners on town hall tonight."

"I don't understand." Ben caught up to her as she claimed the biggest table in the back.

"Ya gotta stop saying that Ben, you're starting to sound like a real Bambi."

"OK, who's paying for dinner, cause I really can't afford to eat out right now. Is that clear enough?"

She looked at him, a little stunned. Taking his face in her hands she said, "Pookie, I know you've more than your fair share of stress lately. I hope this makes you feel a little better."

They settled into the party-sized table and waited for the menus. Regina opened her bag and pulled out a double-sized bottle of Merlot. She filled two glasses and slid one to Benjamin.

"This may be the best Merlot fifteen dollars can buy brother. You see, it's been my mission to prove to my snooty friends that cheap wine is not necessarily bad wine. And that expensive wine doesn't mean it's any good. Or at least, any better than this."

Benjamin drank like a man who needed to forget the past hour in a hurry.

"And how is that argument progressing?" Benjamin asked.

"We drink a lot of wine. Oh, the painting, Regina exclaimed." She ran outside and returned with her admirable landscape. She topped off Benjamin's glass just in time to see a serving cart approach their table.

"Hey, we didn't even order yet," she said

"Regards from our honorable Judge Lynda" said the waiter with a lovely accent as he placed the dish in front of Benjamin. On lifting the lid, it surprised him to see salmon and asparagus, with slices of lemon.

The waiter served Regina's dish. On lifting the lid, she discovered a burger with fries.

Regina looked confused. "Hold on there, are you sure you didn't switch the orders by mistake or something? This can't be right."

The waiter looked to her with a face that could not have held less expression.

"The honorable Judge Lynda says bite me."

This time the waiter's accent held a little less Belgium and a lot more New Jersey. Regina laughed loudly as they dove into their meals. She discovered that she did get salmon, however; they disguised it inside lettuce leaves and a burger roll. Benjamin's anxiety visibly loosened as she told him the story of

Betty's arrest.

"Can you tell me what tonight was all about?" He asked her.

"Well, Crupts, by now you know, has it in for you."

"That much I get." He felt the wine doing its job.

"Well, if it stuck or not, Crupts got a judge from the city to sign an arrest warrant for you. It was an idiot's attempt to undermine our local judge. AKA, our Lynda, AKA she who buys you dinner. So first she got hold of the compromised judge and blasted him appropriately. Crupts, at this moment, is probably hiding under a rock from her, or I would have heard his nonsense by now."

"So," Benjamin smiled over the news. "When does the secret wine club arriv—?" At this point, he was interrupted as the door burst open with Della, Maggy, Carole, Bella, and Philina. Their singing was neither good nor in tune, but at least it was loud.

"Cheer, cheer the gang's all here, somthin, somthin, something. Hey Regina, you know the words?"

"Nope." Regina said. Her mouth full of fries. "Ask Maggy, she's the librarian."

"History and bibliography section, mind you." said Maggy.

"I thought I knew it but, but," Philina stood next to Della trying to pluck the words from the air. "I just don't remember. Oh, well."

Maggy stomped her boot, "You'll not lower my standards with these drunken debauchery songs. Now someone imbibe me before I'm overtaken with the vapors."

The Judge walked through the door waving as she

ended a call. Benjamin stood, greeting everyone with an enormous grin at the end of his wineglass. Judge Lynda stopped in her tracks and made a beeline to him. "Benjamin!"

"Oh, hi Judge, I can't thank you enough for what yo—."

"Shut it and get out."

"What?" he asked, stunned.

"You cannot be here," she said, "I intend to do some serious wine comparisons tonight and if you and I were to fraternize, I'd have to recuse myself of any and all manner of this case. That includes keeping you out of jail. So scoot, scoot."

Regina scurried to the scene and escorted him outside. "Well, Ben, I'm glad I could keep my word. Still, the judgy girl is right, you're not out of the woods yet. Let's get you home."

"Oh, but we're having such fun." He paused, letting the reality of the situation pass by the wine. "OK, I understand. Still, go back in, Regina. The studios only a mile away and the walk will clear my head."

"Ya sure Ben?"

"Very sure, Regina. Enjoy showing off your painting."

"Ben?" Regina said, wanting to say more. "You take care of yourself, ya hear?"

He saw his friend smiling, and he smiled back, and wished he knew the right words to say.

"Will do Regina."

He began the walk back to the studio, then heard her call out one more time.

"What was that nice thing you said about my painting?"

"You are the queen of understated shadows." He yelled back.

"Awesome!" she laughed. He heard the slam of the thick wooden door, then silence.

With a wobbly spring in his step, he began his way home.

"Lighten up, dude." He said aloud. "You made a good friend tonight. That's gotta be worth an arrest or two."

27
The Intruder

The sound of water lapping the shore soothed Ben's nerves. His walk to the studio was in near pitch black. Unsure why the streetlights were out, he occasionally pointed his phone outward to check he wasn't walking into a ditch. Feeling his way around the curve on River Road, he thought, halfway home. His phone rang.

"Ben," Violet called out the split second he answered, "please tell me you're sleeping at the studio tonight."

"I am, what's up?"

"I'm still packing the last of my apartment and then I have to clean. Anyway, I'll be sleeping here tonight and just discovered my building doesn't allow dogs! My landlord is such a jerk. I had to drop Willow off at your apartment. Who in the world can look at Willow and not say yes?"

"Sorry to hear that, and yea, I'll be home in twenty minutes."

"Oh, also, I tried to feed her, she hardly ate. She wouldn't touch the burger I gave her."

"Was it by chance a veggie burger?" Her voice went silent.

"You know she's not a vegetarian."

"She ate the bun." Violet defended.

"It's OK, I keep burgers in the freezer, she's covered."

187

"Thanks Ben, hey, I guess if you had any news you would tell me."

Ben paused. His voice was nonchalant. "Well, we're all set for the auction tomorrow. I bought a platter of crackers, veggies and cheese. If you want to bring wine, it'd be nice."

"I've already left the wine in the studio. Come on Ben, first things first."

"Oh, and Regina arrested me tonight," he added. "It was ordered by Crupts, then she released me before we even got to the police station. Judge Lynda stepped in. So, nothing progressed on the case. Still, it's good to know the wine club is rooting for us."

"Wine Club?" Violet asked aloud. "Oh, the town ladies, yeah, at least there's that. And yea, still leaves us with nothing on who did it. And if Crupts is still trying to pin Edmund's murder on you, well, it's just more and more suspicious. However, I'm glad you're not talking to me from a jail cell."

"Regina thinks he wants an easy win without doing the police work."

"Hey, maybe Regina just likes to see you in her handcuffs." Benjamin could hear her smirk.

"Hardly, I supplied the cuffs."

"Ben? Since when do you keep handcuffs, you perv."

"No, they were plastic..."

"I gotta another call. You'll have to make up lame excuses later, thanks for taking Willow, night perv."

"I'm not a—" and the phone went silent.

"Perv." He said to the darkness.

He was happy that Willow would be there when he arrived home. He'd cooked a few sweet potatoes for all the furry beasts earlier that day and forgot them in the oven. On arriving he could see a faint glow coming from the studio. Violet must have left a light on, he thought. Going around back, he lightly skipped up the stairs to his apartment.

Willow ran to him as the door opened. She hopped on her hind legs, pawing at him in urgency. Her distress worried him. Benjamin knew she was usually OK with being left alone when need be. This however, was more pressing than the need to be let out. He opened the door and followed as she raced down the stairs. A crash of metal and glass came from within the studio.

Benjamin ran to the entrance and discovered the back door broken open. In his best stealth mode, he entered, crouching. Willow ran past him, barking. So much for stealth, he thought. Benjamin flicked the lights on, leaping into action.

A masked man pointed a gun at him. Ben stopped his approach. The gunman's voice was muffled under the black mask. "I want the deed or you both die." Willow growled, advancing. Shakily, the intruder's aim snapped between Benjamin and Willow. Several papers were already clutched to his chest. Benjamin gripped a coffee can of paintbrushes and threw them at the intruder's head.

The prowler fired his gun into the oncoming brushes. Benjamin had already ducked out of sight. The bullet tore through the painting of Edmund. Willow bit into the intruder's leg. He screamed, aiming to shoot the angry dog, however, the pain caused him to fumble the gun. Benjamin grabbed the nearest heavy object.

The fifty-pound clay model of Violet, slammed into the gunman's chest. The intruder was knocked to the floor. Reaching for his weapon, Willow bit down on his hand. He screamed while grasping for the gun with his other hand. Benjamin lifted the clay torso and slammed it down on the gunman's head. It knocked him out.

Benjamin picked up the gun and pointed the weapon at the prowler. He was certain it must be Edmund's killer. He looked to the bullet hole in Edmund's portrait, right above the ear. The painting could be fixed, yet Edmund's still gone. Ben, the heartbroken man, the sad man, the angry man, wondered if one bullet could fix all that.

He rolled the clay off the gunman's head and pulled up his mask. He felt some sort of recognition, but the gunman's nose was bloody and possibly broken. It made him squeamish. Disgusted, he pulled the mask back down. Placing where he'd seen that face just wasn't coming to him. Still, there was something familiar. He put the gun to the man's head.

Willow stood on her hind legs and pawed at Benjamin. He didn't respond at first, barely aware the dog was still there. She persisted. She had to. A dangerous and single-minded self-righteousness had taken over Ben. She let out a soft bark. It caught his attention. He looked at her.

"This is the horrible man that took Edmund, your dad."

She continued to paw at him. He didn't want to understand what she was trying to tell him, yet her pleading eyes prevailed.

"Don't be him, I need you to stay my Man-Dog." Try as he might, Benjamin could not mistake her intentions. He couldn't take a life with someone as pure as her present. He un-cocked the gun and hid it behind the big jars of acrylic paint.

Rolling the intruder over, Benjamin used the very tie he was cuffed with earlier to secure the prisoner. Dragging him outside, he peered about in the dark, though he couldn't see the intruder's car. Having no other choice, he dropped the body and went for the keys to Willow and Edmund's driver education car. He left the gunman under Willows growling guard. Retrieving the keys, he uncovered the car and opened the trunk.

On returning, a dozen cats had joined Willow. They circled and hissed at the body, awaiting Gus's order to attack. Benjamin dragged the unconscious creep to the car. Roughly flopping him into the trunk, Ben slammed the lid shut. He felt his heart pounding in his chest.

"You need to calm down." He told himself aloud. Turning, he saw the impressive hit squad Gus had assembled. The thug Tabby's organizational skills unnerved him. Pocketing the car keys, he went inside to prepare Willow and the felines a thank you snack.

He opened and poured the wine. The Zinfandel, combined with the animal's feeding routine, calmed him back to his senses. He emerged a few minutes later with a platter of raw burgers and cooked sweet potatoes he'd warmed for the meowing militia.

When the bowls were empty, the purring avengers disappeared into the dark. Benjamin hugged Willow.

"Please don't be that courageous again."

He stumbled up the stairs. Willow followed, unsure he would make it to the top. Still on alert, she patrolled the room just to be sure.

"It looks like we're fated to go to the police station one way or the other." As he finished his wine, Willow hopped on the bed. He pet her trying to calm her agitation. Slowly her breathing relaxed as she lay only looking at him, her man-dog.

He'd captured Edmund's killer, of that he was certain. Willow sighed and relaxed closer to a slumber. Not wanting to disturb his brave friend, he quietly lay down to follow the sound of her breath, just for a few moments, before he drove to the...

28
Drive Doggy

Violet awoke to a text from Olga.

Patience, please, I am honoring Edmund's wishes.

Running scenario after scenario in her head, she could not fathom an honest reason why Olga absconded with Edmunds investments, and the mystery painting from inside the studio wall. With her scheming parents as role models, she found herself only thinking the worst. Violet wanted to believe her, mostly because of her happy youthful memories. But people change. So far, this was not for the better. She dressed in a gray mood and headed out to help Ben set up for the painting memorial.

Pulling up to the studio, Violet saw a startling sight. All the cats from the stone boat had collected on the car Edmund drove Willow around in, or rather, Willow drove Edmund around in. She parked and approached the oddity, noticing the majority of cats were sitting on the trunk. Stranger still, was that the felines all ignored her. Being breakfast time, she wondered what could possibly be more important. She then heard a thump from the trunk, and another.

As if in a crazy game of twister, the cats spun and jumped, landing on the spot of each thump. Hisses, snarls and growls followed as they swatted the car. Violet was distressed. What if some poor animal had gotten caught inside by accident? She reached to push the open button but was warned off by the snarling beasts. Frightened, she looked to Gus, who sat on the roof of the car with a predator's gaze. For her own safety, instead of opening it, she simply knocked.

"Get me the hell out of here." A voice screamed. Violet jumped back. The cats hissed and snarled, paw swatting the trunk as if pounding drums before battle. Gus crouched for a fight should the trunk open.

Violet had no idea who it was. On the other hand, at least she knew it wasn't Benjamin. Maybe, hopefully, he'll have answers to this. She ran up the stairs to his apartment.

Benjamin slept peacefully on the chilly autumn morning. Deep in a dream, he chatted with Violet. "There are seven student pianos for your class. Four on the floor and three on the ceiling."

"I'll definitely need more space," Dream Violet said, "We must move your bed to my house."

He looked at her and nodded. "I'd forgotten to take my shoes off or get into pajamas before sleep last night. This evening, I'll be sure to do so."

"Ben, your ability to set such lofty goals never fail to impress me."

He glanced at her, making fun of him. "I guess I walked into that one."

She pointed out the door. "Ben, is something wrong with Willow's car? It's knocking."

"Oh, it's just the intruder with a gun."

Benjamin bounded out of bed and out of his dream. The rude awakening brought back the previous evening. There was a knock from outside. Willow hopped off the bed and ran to the door. She looked back at him expectantly. The banging continued.

"Ben." Violet called out, "Who's in Willow's car?"

He opened the door for Violet. Barely saying hello, the taste of the previous night's stress and wine breath had him scampering to brush his teeth.

"The car's trunk." Benjamin said, mumbling through toothpaste, "Is holding Edmund's killer. He's tied up."

"How do you know that?" she asked.

While washing his face and changing his shirt, he told her the story of the noise, the break in, the gunshots, the clay torso and Willows bravery.

"We have to get to the police station now." He ran down the stairs, spun around and ran back up again to grab his jacket before running down the stairs again. "Aren't you coming?" He called out.

"Ben, who is it? Did you recognize him?"

"He's familiar, but it was dark, and he wore a mask. He has no phone, no wallet, no id. I can't place him. And also, I might have broken his nose."

"I want to see." She ran down the stairs and out to the car.

"Violet, why don't we go to the police station first, I don't even know if he's gotten out of the ties."

She looked about and found a thick fallen tree branch. Holding it steady, she looked to Benjamin. "OK. Ready."

Benjamin sighed, "Fine, but seriously, this guy's dangerous. Just be ready." Ben gently moved the furry army off the trunk as Willow stood at the ready. Gus eyed the trunk with incredible focus.

When Ben turned the key, the gunman kicked the

trunk open from within.

"You are dead!" the gunman screamed.

He kicked Benjamin's chest, knocking him to the ground. Wildly wrangling himself out of the trunk with his wrists still tied behind him.

Violet saw half his face and covered in dried blood at that. He'd squirmed his way half out of the mask.

"Both of you are gonna die." He spit out at Violet.

Gus leapt into the air as Willow lunged. She bit into his calf as Gus landed on his head, claws fully extended. The tabby did the twist as the gunman's screams rang out. Gus, then bounded onto the roof of the car as Violet's tree branch collided with his chest. He recoiled back into the trunk. Willow had a patch of his pants fabric still in her teeth. Benjamin was on his feet again and slammed the trunk shut.

"Nice swing," He said catching his breath. "So, did you recognize him?"

"Umm, sorry Ben, I can't tell. The half mask makes it too hard. Let's go with your idea. Next stop, police station. I'll follow you in case he kicks the trunk open."

Ben called. "Come on Willow, you're the arresting K9 on the case." Gus leapt to Violet's shoulder, then to a tree branch and back to the stone boat. Willow hopped into her driver's seat as Ben started the engine. "Sorry girl, we're not going to the pet store today." She didn't understand the statement.

Putting the cars in gear, they rolled to the front of the studio. The voice yelled from the trunk. "You will never see the light of day again." Violet thought the statement kinda funny considering where the threats were coming from. She stopped short before hitting

Ben who jammed on his brakes. Please stay, he said to Willow as he opened his door. Waving to Violet a 'two minute' sign, he ran inside the studio.

He emerged with a colorful shopping bag. Violet stuck her head out the window. "Ben, when did this all happen?"

"Oh, last night-ish." He said fidgeting with the shopping bag and putting something in his pocket.

"Why are you only going to the police station now?"

"Last night Willow and I were agitated, we sat on the bed to calm down."

"And that took all night?" Violet asked.

"No, not really."

"So why are we only going now?"

"Oh, ya see, The wine did such a good job that the next thing I knew, it was daylight."

"Are you serious?"

"Or maybe it was a stress response, and the wine."

"Mmhmm, your action hero figure needs a bit of tweaking." She pointed to the bag. "Are we going food shopping afterward?"

"No, this is his gun."

"Gotcha," she said. "Sorry for all the questions, I'm just trying to catch up."

"No worries," he got back in the car.

Willow did most of the driving into town as Benjamin couldn't find the switch to take control of the steering wheel. Violet followed them through the village. It was a surreal experience to follow a dog driver. The stop light in front of 'A Rise Above Bakery' seemed to take extra long. She hoped the scent of the treats didn't take Willows attention off the road.

The loud screaming and cursing coming from the trunk was putting folks off enjoying their muffins and lattes. Willow barked and growled her own version of, "Don't make me pull this car over." It worked.

As the light changed, Benjamin found the lever taking control of the car's steering. Willow was a bit confused not being able to turn into the pet stores parking lot.

"Park in front." Violet yelled out her window as they approached the police station. "I'm pulling around to the side."

After parking, he opened the trunk. This time, he sidestepped the kicking feet. The gunman's mask had slid back down and backwards. Even blinded, he fought every step as Benjamin and Violet dragged him towards the station door. Willows barking and growling made him think twice about lashing out.

"Willow," Violet said, "Door!"

The furry protector hesitated. She didn't want to leave the action though ran ahead when she realized they were all going in together.

29
Bagels and Baroque Friday

It was Bagels and Baroque Friday at the precinct. Music filled the building across the station loud-speakers. Regina spoke with expertise. "Walnut cream cheese on a walnut raisin bagel is syncopation, pure and simple."

"I cannot agree with you on this." Oscar poised his argument. "It is redundant. Not unlike a stifling bureaucracy. In fact, your Brandenburg Concertos come to mind."

"I beg to differ, my dutiful man. How could you, in good conscience, call that wonderful work bureaucratic? Do you keep the same harsh temperament for Vivaldi?"

"Never. Vivaldi, without question, would be an egg everything bagel with vegetable cream cheese."

"How gauche you can be," Regina huffed. "And to think, you swore to uphold the law."

"Save your confused judgment," Oscar continued, "It was the subtext of the Brandenburg Concertos that I call bureaucratic. So, enjoy your walnut cream cheese on a walnut raisin bagel. Sadly, the colors of life escape you."

"Ah contraire," she rebuffed, "The Brandenburg is not bureaucratic, it is exacting community."

"And the difference is?" Oscar pointed dramatically.

Willow charged into the station, barking with excitement and redirecting the conversation.

"What is it, girl?" Regina asked. "Did Timmy fall in a well?" They both laughed till Violet and Benjamin burst through the door, dragging the masked man fighting to break away.

Together, Violet and Benjamin dropped the bound body on the floor before the front desk.

"We have a delivery of one armed, masked intruder." Violet said. "He's a bit on the ornery side."

"What in the world?" Regina and Oscar yelled in unison and ran to the bound man.

Willow barked and growled at him, leaving no question how she felt. The intruder scrambled away from the growls.

"What is going on here?" Oscar yelled.

"This is the creep that killed Edmund" Benjamin replied as he gripped the plastic ties behind the man and pulled off his mask. "Chief Crupts?" The officers chorused. "Oh Nooooo" was all they could mutter looking horrified at each other.

"Ben, Violet." Oscar gasped. "You've captured and beaten Chief Crupts?"

Violet went pale. She felt the floor disappearing beneath her. All confidence and righteousness fell away. Tunnel vision came upon her and the only sound she could hear was the clash singing 'I fought the law and the law won.'

"OK, you two." Regina did her best to be calm. "Exactly how did you come to this conclusion?"

"Get me the hell lose you two, I'm gonna kill this guy." Crupts bellowed.

"You already tried." Benjamin yelled back. He handed the shopping bag with the gun to Regina. He shot at me and Willow.

Crupts lurched and attempted to kick Willow away.

She dodged the kick, dashed in closer and bit his ankle.

The chief screamed.

"You deserve it!" Benjamin yelled.

"Down girl, and down boy" Oscar yelled at them both, though a part of him felt bad to yell at the pretty dog.

Violet pulled Willow away from the ruckus.

Regina went to the stationery closet to get the scissors while Oscar stood between Crupts and the righteous doggy.

Willow stood back, crouched at the ready.

Violet held Willow's collar; uncertain if she could contain her if she lunged again. She felt sick. As right as Ben might be, in a courtroom, it would be the police chief's word against his.

Regina moved Ben away. "Ben, Violet, please, you don't want to dig any deeper than you have."

"Why the hell are you so calm, she hissed to Benjamin, do you have any idea of the trouble we—"

"Oh right," Benjamin said, calling to the officers, "You all need to see this." He took a flash card from his pocket. "I put a security camera in the day after he killed Edmund." He handed it to Regina. "I also started the web upload when we left the studio. It should be public by now."

"Cut me loose." Crupts yelled at Regina. "That's a direct order."

Regina thought hard for several seconds. Next month she'd have ten years on the force. To be fired or not be fired. It was risky, but something wasn't right. She slipped the memory card into the large TV screen. Oscar navigated the remote to Benjamin's video file, and hit play. Meanwhile, Regina struggled with the choice to cut her commanding officer free.

"I just don't know, these scissors ain't cuttin' it Chief."

"Shut that damn TV off and help me." Crupts yelled at Oscar, "She's useless."

The video lit up the screen. For a few seconds, the lights were on as the armed masked man surveyed the room. He switched off the lights. Nothing on the video showed the identity of the intruder.

Oscar sighed with worry, looking to the disheveled duo. "Violet, Benjamin, if this is all you've got, you might think of canceling any plans for a few years."

The sound of crashing easels, glass jars, metal cans, and cursing came from the black video. Oscar and Regina failed at stifling a laugh. A flashlight switched on; the beam of light lit the figure's face. He pulled up his mask to reorient himself. It was unmistakably Chief Crupts on the video.

"You take a splendid picture there, boss, or should I say former boss."

Crupts lunged to break free, so Regina dropped her weight on his bound wrists, bringing him to his knees. She quickly added traditional cuffs to his wrists. Useless, huh? Let's see how I can manage that whole, 'You're under arrest, thingy.' Willow growled to remind him, should he consider violence.

On the screen, Crupts was moving towards Edmund's office as Benjamin and Willow entered the video and turned on the lights.

Regina and Oscar listened to the threats, watched the gunfire, the dog heroics, the clay torso, and the dog bite which they both agreed must have hurt badly.

"Chief, my chief," Regina said. "You're going in the cage."

"You are all going down." He yelled back at them. The two officers hastily escorted him to the one cell in the small station house.

Throwing her arms around Benjamin, Violet squeezed with her strength. She then released him and punched him in the arm. "Why didn't you tell me you had it all on video?"

"When did you get so strong?" He wheezed.

"I have to apologize to Willow." Oscar said as he pushed Crupts into the holding cell. "You really do deserve another bite." Locking the cell, they returned to the front desk.

Regina approached them, "OK, you two, umm, you three. Let's go through this one step at a time. Oh, where are my manners, please have a bagel, oh erm."

Everyone turned to see Willow eating a bagel that may or may not have slipped to the floor during the commotion. She had decided, the egg everything with vegetable cream cheese, was the best combination.

"So," Oscar beamed proudly. "The furry mistress of taste buds has settled the argument."

"Fine, you win this one." Regina feigned a sorrowful defeat. "Just wait till next week," she challenged.

They all watched Willow's tail wag to the tempo of 'Spring,' from Vivaldi's four seasons.

30
Comparing Notes

Back at the studio, Violet and Ben raced to arrange the coffee tea and snacks for the auction. Violet mixed a bottle of white wine with a gallon of lemonade. Was it OK to skip the coffee half of the day and head right for the wine? After all, it is an art event; she mused.

Benjamin dashed back into the studio to clean up the fight scene from the night before. Violet's clay torso was now a twisted abstract sculpture, however, it was still eye-catching.

A short time later, and with the mess cleaned up, he joined the painters and prospective buyers. Missing the day-to-day normalcy of the studio, he appreciated the cheerful chatter of the visitors over the diverse group of paintings. He was proud to be a member of this community of artists. He felt part of something important, worth saving. The interaction helped to shake off the dreadful experience of almost shooting someone the night before - almost.

The artists clustered into groups, excited yet nervous as visitors arrived. "Oohh's and aahh's," sounded out among the meandering art lovers. The auction buzzed along nicely. Visitors wrote their bids on index cards tacked to the easels.

Some paintings had needed to be situated again. After the scuffle with Crupts, a few easel placements were disheveled. Violet was thankful the drama and threat was over. Her only responsibility was to keep the felines from descending on the snack table.

The portraits in fur gang chatted in a circle. They had all conspired and snuck their beloved pets into the landscape paintings. Bella and Regina arrived late. Regina had quite the stack of paperwork, having arrested her commanding officer. Bella, immediately overbid on Regina's painting. She wanted to ensure it would decorate their living room.

Willow was on duty surveying the grounds. She didn't even approach the snack table. While no one was a complete stranger to her, after the previous night's drama, the volume of visitors kept her concerned and on the job.

Nearly all the paintings were bid on, or happily haggled over. Betty had posted hers on-line and created a bidding war amongst lovers of parakeets. Thrilled to annoy Benjamin, her donation soared above all others. She avoided him all the same. A call for Violet came a few hours into the auction. The internal affairs director was asking for an interview.

"Can you give me a heads up what to expect?" Violet asked Regina.

"It'll mostly be your timeline of events." Regina said. "I'll be back at the station within the hour. Nothing to worry about, you'll be fine."

"Thanks so much." Violet said. "I was visualizing a tiny dark room with a dangling light-bulb."

"Oh, it's not like that anymore, we've added an espresso machine."

That afternoon, internal affairs director, Harold Patton, read over the reports of Oscar and Regina. A distinct scent of bagels emanated from the pages. From his makeshift desk in the station house, he scanned the room for any remaining treats. He hated working weekends. Though on hearing about the crazed police chief shooting up an art studio, he felt a quick lock down on the situation was prudent.

"Are you Harold?" Violet asked as she entered with Willow, licking her lips from the snacks Regina snuck to her as they passed each other.

He waved, "Harold Patton, internal affairs, thanks for coming."

"My pleasure, I want this mess behind me as soon as possible."

"As do we all. I've seen the video your husband recorded. Quite heroic. Taking down a gunman with modeling clay. We might start issuing art supplies to all our officers."

"Oh, he's not my husband. And yes, that was heroic, or crazy. More crazy I think, yes. Definitely more crazy. So Crupts wanted the deed. Why would the police chief have any interest or business with the deed to the stone boat property?"

"We are looking for those very answers ourselves." Harold said.

Harold asked her about the will, Jeremiah's car crash, the studio break in, the murder, and her family. He was attempting to put a puzzle together, and as much as Violet could help, there were pieces that just did not fit.

"Will you answer me something Harold?"

"I'll try."

"How did Crupts, whose incompetence has been well documented and who's criminal behavior is on record, not only avoid being fired, but got himself promoted to chief of our town's police force?"

"That is an excellent question, Violet, and aside from his gun fire and attempted theft in the art studio, it's the question of the hour."

"I've been doing my own investigation," Violet said. "Here's a copy of my notes."

"Oh, well, this is unusual." He glanced but didn't bother to open the folder. "Yes, thank you, I'll take a look at it later."

'Was I just dismissed.' She thought. 'Should I have given my notes to one of the officers first? Who does this bureaucrat think he is? I've been living this case.'

The condescension battle had begun. Except that he didn't ask her anything else. Still, she wanted the fight. After seeing how professional the police performed during Jeremiah's crash, she upped her game, researching the players of anyone who might be after her uncle's studio. She was proud of her research.

Regina was on the computer while Oscar was adjusting the room's security cameras. Harold called out to the room, "Could I ask you all to come over for a few minutes? And might Margot and Abram be available as well?"

The officers brought chairs and gathered around his desk. "Now," he began, "I'd hate to see wild rumors spread about worthless information. So, I'm hoping to spread wild rumors about the actual information we have."

"Is this story time? Margot asked Abram."

"It looks that way," He grinned.

"I wish we'd saved a bagel and coffee for it." Regina said.

Willow looked to her, agreeing.

"May I continue?" Harold asked.

"Oh, please do," Oscar grinned. "she gets peckish in the mid-afternoon."

"Thank you." Harold put a hand on his notebook, gathering his thoughts. "Here it is, Crupts was not promoted to chief, as much as someone inserted him into the position. Now if you were to ask me, I'd say it's impossible. However, here it is."

"Well we knew that," Violet said, "his salary was a top tier of a chief's salary, even though it was his first post as a police chief. Whoever set his salary is where you need to look."

Margot pulled a twenty-dollar bill out of her pocket and handed it to Oscar. Abram pulled a twenty-dollar bill out of his pocket and handed it to Regina.

"Violet, how do you know this?" Harold asked, perturbed.

"Its public record. The state publishes salary ranges, the county publishes the employee and range number. It's a simple cross reference. It's on page two of my notes."

Harold went on. "they suspended Crupts from his precinct in the city. A criminal investigation was underway, but they dropped the case to a reprimand. I'll be looking into the supervising levels on who accepted this determination."

"Oh, it's no mystery." Violet said. "I can save you the trouble. Crupts and a cohort were booting cars and threatening the car owners over lengthy impound-ments. It was extortion, costing the city over a hun-dred thousand dollars a year in fine revenues. The lawsuits cost ten times that, when the scam was dis-covered. It made the news, but the story died quickly. So yes, if you find his supervisors, maybe more light can be shed on that one."

Regina pulled a twenty-dollar bill out of her pocket and handed it to Oscar. Abram pulled a twenty-dollar bill out of his wallet and handed it to Margot.

Harold sighed in defeat. Opening Violet's folder, he methodically scanned each page.

"Three and four is the car impounding scam." Vio-let said. "If you're interested."

"What do the music notes and measures mean?" Harold asked.

"Oh nothing, I was just doodling. Internet searches can be so tedious at times."

"You have the chief's exam in here?" Harold flipped the page.

"Yes, though only the first one. I wasn't able to find the second results."

"My goodness," Harold said. "I hope I get to add something to this inquiry."

Violet smirked.

Harold took a breath. "So as you know, they gave Crupts the chief's exam, which he failed miserably. A week later he took a second exam, against all policy I might add, which he aced."

Regina held her hand up as Abram, Margot, and Oscar gave her a twenty-dollar bill.

"Can we get Jeremiah back?" Oscar asked.

"We'll get to that soon." Harold said. "Still, he is in a coma."

"He's still a lot better than Crupts, don't you think?"

"Do you know about his Uncle,"? Violet asked Harold.

"I do, yes. Letters of recommendations came from: His uncle who is a state legislator, known for down-playing the opioid crisis. And, oddly enough, from his aunt, a nun and mother superior in a church right here in MooiKill itself."

Violet's jaw dropped.

The officers all looked at each other, stunned.

"It was to be the easiest twenty ever." Margot gasped.

"I just did not see that coming." Violet added.

Regina grinned, "Hindsight baby's, hindsight." Lifting her palm up to receive a twenty-dollar bill from each officer.

Harold took a breath, "And a last point," He directed to Violet. "Which I'll bet even you don't know."

"You're on." She said with her best poker face.

Harold's brow knotted up. "Jeremiah's retirement was slated for next year. He was pushed out two years early. An investigation will be underway. Nevertheless, according to a lack of actual policy on this matter, Jeremiah is technically still your chief."

Cheers broke out amongst the officers.

"You do know, he's still in a coma."

Violet reached into her black jeans and handed Harold a twenty-dollar bill.

"A win." He grinned, turning to put the twenty in the food bank jar.

"Uurg," cried Regina, "Why did you do that? Now I feel like I have to do it, or I'll be a jerk."

"What did you plan to do with the money?" Abram asked.

"A nice case of wine for my new wine rack. I'd even share it with the hungry children."

The room went judgmentally quiet as everyone waited for Regina to decide.

Oscar gasped, "The social pressure alone would have crushed me by now. How does she do it?"

"I don't know," Abram said, "She's nerves of steel."

"The suspense is killing me." Margot added.

Regina groaned as she dragged her feet to the food bank box, stuffing her winnings inside.

"And she scores!" The room called out laughing.

"Farewell dear Baco Noir," Regina lamented. "I hardly knew ye."

31
Take Him Away

Two mountain-sized men in uniform entered the station house. However, size was hardly their most striking feature. Lucius wore a short-cropped afro, sporting an intricate multilevel buzz cut with Celtic knot-work designs. He was smitten with the sister of Aidan, his partner transport officer. Aidan, a fiery red-head, did God knows what to his hair, so that it puffed and blazed upwards like flames. Officer Margot, was smitten with Lucius.

"Hey gang," Lucius said, having observed the last of the money passing about. "I thought police officers weren't supposed to gamble on the job?"

"Oh, it's OK," Oscar replied, "He's from internal affairs."

"And I'm winning," Harold added.

Aidan showed his clipboard. "As much as we'd love to join in, we're here for a detainee. A James Crupts?"

Aidan held the clipboard of paperwork. "It seems we have a dilemma. So, who wants to play chief today?"

"I do, I do," Margot yelled.

"OK, we need a signature here and here and we can rid you of all that irks you."

Margot walked the paperwork to Lucius.

"So," she smiled up at the serious-looking man. "It's so nice to see you again, Lucius. What a lovely name."

"Um, thank you." He said nervously. He didn't know if Margot was hitting on him or just making conversation.

"I hear," She continued, "Some prisoners get difficult when transporting from here to the county jail."

"Oh, that's very rare. And we frown on poor behavior."

"Yes, I understand. Yet if Crupts was to display such behavior, it would be OK if, you know, frown on him. A lot."

"Um, well you see Maam, are you asking me—."

His partner Aidan elbowed him quickly.

"Do not answer."

"No?"

"No!"

"It's a beautiful day Margot, don't you think?" Lucius gave her a smile while changing the topic. "Not a cloud in the sky."

"It is at that Lucius." She pressed the clipboard to his chest as she signed away the former chief. "It is at that."

Margot escorted the two men to the holding cell. Moments later they walked Crupts out to a room of applause. His lawyer trailed behind, surprised by the enthusiasm of his exit.

Aidan fixed Crupts with a no nonsense stair, "We'll be putting these ankle bracelets on. Please sit here."

"Get your hands off me," Crupts snapped and twisted himself out of the guard's grasp.

Willow growled and moved between Violet and Crupts.

The furry protector had always gotten the better of him. This was his last chance to inflict any sort of revenge. His career was over. Here or in any police force, and he was desperate for a last kick to MooiKill.

Willow's innate perception of her enemies' body language came from wolves. Fine-tuned over hundreds of thousands of years, she knew the man's movement patterns and saw his means of attack before Crupts even raised his leg. However, he thrust his leg up at the precise moment Lucius and Aidan yanked his shoulders backwards. It changed the angle Willow was expecting. All the canine could do was watch his legs pass by over her head. For just a moment, his body seemed poised in the air, perfectly horizontal and five feet off the floor.

Aidan and Lucius released him, knowing how they themselves could be injured, trying to stop the fall. Violet swooped Willow in her arms and dashed to the side of the action.

Crupts landed with a loud thud, followed by an ear-piercing scream. Everyone in the room cringed. It confused Willow. Why was he screaming as she hadn't gotten to bite him yet?

"You broke my hip." He yelled. "You broke my hip."

"Oh goodness, now what are we going to do with him?" Margot asked the group.

"Oh darn, "Aidan murmured." We keep a stretcher in the back of the van. I'll be right back."

Crupts screamed at his lawyer. "You saw it. You saw it."

In a moment Aidan returned with the stretcher. "Move to the side." Aidan pushed the lawyer backwards with his huge palm.

"You have to release me." Crupts yelled to the room.

215

"Get me released." he spit at his lawyer, "I need a hospital."

"I can't interfere in the middle of a police procedure." His lawyer responded.

"You're fired. You are so fired." The ex-chief bellowed out.

Crupts continued to whimper and cry as they positioned him on the stretcher.

"Want to tell him what to expect Aidan?" Lucius said with a grin.

"Well, Mr. Crupts," Aidan began in his best game show voice. "You'll be traveling first class today to as a guest of the MooiKill justice system. First stop will be the lovely emergency room of our scenic county hospital. In prestigious style, your injuries will be evaluated and treated, all while never escaping the secure comfort and style of accessorized handcuffs."

"It sounds like a dream vacation." Oscar pitched in.

"And it doesn't stop there." Aidan continued. "Because with all the class of a five-star hotel, you'll be enjoying the comforts of our county lock up facility that's so glamorous, only like-minded VIP's like yourself are allowed accommodations."

The gang gave a last round of applause to the former chief's exit.

Crupt's Lawyer held the doors open for the transporting officers. "We'll speak in the hospital," He called after them.

"Fired!" And a whimper is what he heard in return.

"Violet," Regina pulled her aside. "It might be a good time for you to take Willow home. We need to minimize the whole biting thing for Willow." Violet nodded in agreement.

"Harold, please contact me if you hear anything new." Violet asked. "I'll be on the trail as well."

"Certainly, Violet, please do as well. And good hunting with your trusty sidekick." He waved her folder, smiling. While he didn't precisely apologize for his initial dismissive behavior, he now openly showed appreciation for her contributions.

"Come on baby," She called to Willow, "Our work is done here."

"You two make quite the tag team." The lawyer said, holding the door open as Violet and Willow exited.

Smirking at his joke, she paused, and remembered she was talking to Crupt's lawyer. "Oh, where are my manners, get away from me, you slime ball parasite."

"I understand your reaction, but it's, former slime ball parasite. My client, your favorite police chief, just fired me for not finagling a dismissal of charges. Oh, and he fired me several more times a minute ago. It seems a video of him shooting at someone is taken seriously around here."

She relaxed, knowing he was as disliked by Crupts as she was.

"Oh, it's an excellent policy," She spun in a circle trying to locate her car.

"That creep killed my uncle, and almost killed my best friend, and Willow, my newest friend."

She leaned down to pet Willow, who was still excited. "Instant karma, right girl?"

"Well, remind me not to mess with you, Karma." He said to Willow.

She looked at him with suspicion. It was not her

name, and she was not amused. He smelled like plastic that was trying to smell like the sea shore.

'Damn,' Violet thought, 'that's a nice suit. And he has such a nice haircut. And it's just a little gray on the sides. And now he's caught me looking him over.'

He did notice, and met her gaze. "I'm going to take my life in my hands and ask, are you free for dinner?"

"Do you always hit on the opposing sides of legal actions?"

"No, well hardly ever, but I'm not representing him anymore. And honestly, he wants a magic wand to make his moronic criminal schemes disappear."

"And you don't have such a magic wand?"

"Not the size he needs, no."

Regina popped her head out from the station door, "Violet dear, could you please ask Ben to take down the video of Crupt's break in, it's getting too many likes."

"Will do," she said, grinning. Taking out her phone, she rang Ben's number and walked to her car.

"Violet" Lance spoke.

"Oh sorry, what is it?"

"Would you like to go to dinner with me?"

"Oh, I don't know about that."

"It'll be uneventful and relaxing, and nothing like the day you just experienced."

A myriad of questions flooded her mind. Why was he asking me on a date after knowing me for two minutes? He was Crupts lawyer and Gretchen is Crupt's aunt. Is Lance somehow connected to the two of them? And who's footing the bill for that nice suit? She regarded him thoughtfully, Damn, should I take a chance? At least find out what his intentions are?

"I could certainly use that. I'll need to take Willow home. Why don't we meet in the village circle in an hour?"

"It's a date," he said. "See ya there."

She reached her car and heard a strange tinny voice calling her.

"Oh crap, Ben." She lifted the phone to her ear.

"Is there a reason you're calling me?"

"Yes, she said." Pausing. "I swear there was a reason."

"And it's cause you wanted me to hear some jerk ask you out?"

"Oh, you heard that," she cringed. "Sorry."

"Yeah, I heard. Talk later."

"Regina." She remembered.

"What about Regina?" He asked, not masking his annoyance at her.

"She asked that you take down the video of Crupts in the studio."

"Did they let Crupts go?"

"No, he's going to the county jail for holding, though, first to the hospital cause he tried to kick Willow and ended up with a broken hip."

"Every day brings more reasons to love her." Ben said.

"Well, there's more to the story, I'll drop her off in five minutes."

"Right, cause you got a date."

Violet grimaced with discomfort.

"Sorry, that was an accident."

He hung up the phone.

She told herself she shouldn't feel guilty about it.

And she hadn't done it intentionally. And they aren't dating, so he has no reason to feel bad or offended. And she was only wanting to know the lawyer's angle. Damn, so why the feelings of being a jerk?

32
Date Night

"So how is it you know Crupts?" Violet asked. His name felt sour even to speak it. She adjusted herself in the passenger seat of Lance's sports car. The interior looked more like a science fiction spaceship.

"He'd approached me wanting another opinion on a murder case. He said the small-town goobers weren't moving quick enough. It was a strange request as my opinion can be expensive."

"And your assessment of his request?" Violet asked.

The lawyer grinned, "Is this a date or an inquiry?"

"Yes, you're right, that was not polite." She replied.

"Oh, I was joking, it's natural to be curious."

"On second thought," she smiled back. "Since he was, at the time, working for the town of MooiKill when he hired you, and I am a taxpayer, your opinion is public record."

"I think you may have picked the wrong profession." Lance laughed. He was enjoying the turns on the parkway that hugged the river. "Are you comfortable?" He asked.

In her own car, the heat dial shot out full blast Sahara, or nothing at all. This dashboard offered an independent weather system for each seat. She looked for the monsoon setting.

"Gone silent on me?" he asked.

"Oh no, Your dashboard intrigued me."

"Wow, that's the first time I'd heard that line." He smiled at her. "OK, I guess you really want to know."

"I'm juggling so many unknowns at the moment, I would appreciate it." She answered.

He reached across, patted her hand and returned his to the steering wheel. She gave a squeeze on the hand sanitizer she kept in her bag. Violet found herself wanting to like him. There was an effortless way about him. A natural confidence and lack of drama. She gave him her best smile as she stealthily disinfected her hand, 'just in case.'

"So, this guy, Benny."

"Huh? Oh, Benjamin." She corrected him.

"Well." He smirked. "Crupts wanted Benjamin in the hot seat. Was there some history between the two? He pegged him as a drugged-up loser."

Violet nodded, "No, they were complete strangers. Still, that's not the first time some idiot made that judgement about him. He is his own person, and definitely unique in his life choices. And his behaviour. And his thought process. And unlike Crupts, he would never destroy another person's life for career brownie points. That was a despicable thing he tried to do."

"I agree," He said. "Fortunately for Benjamin, he only attempted to do it, and was honestly terrible at it. Today was his final fail."

"That's reassuring to know. Thank you Lance, for clearing his name."

"No problem. Your uncle, even in death, has a lot of connections in town, and by extension 'Benjamin'. Much more than Crupts could have imagined."

She winced, hearing him bring up Edmund. She turned her focus to watching the landscape blur by.

"Are you two some kind of item by chance?"

"Oh no," She said, looking into his eyes, "We have a history, but no, I mean, that ship has sailed." She felt a little shame referring to her relationship with Ben as a sailed ship. He was a solid friend, and her rock when situations went bad.

Entering the restaurant, Violet noticed the vibrant music. She could tell it was her friend Jasmine before they even walked into the dining hall. Jasmine was a great fan of forties music and musicals. Violet swung by the piano with a smile, though was met with an imploring face in need.

"Violet, please take over for five minutes, I'm having an emergency."

"Sure, what cha' playing?"

"Oh, just follow it through from here," pointing to a measure in the sheet music.

Violet slid her toe over the sustain pedal as Jasmine slid hers off. She proceeded with the tune while not missing a beat, the room, none the wiser. Jasmine stood up, surprising Violet, looking like she was expecting to give birth ten minutes ago. "Congratulations," she said to her friend before Jasmine scurried off to the ladies' room.

"This is a sweet tune. It's called 'My dreams are getting better all the time'" She modeled the notes as close as possible to Jasmine's style. "Do you mind? It's only one song."

"My mother used to sing that song to me." He said, leaning on the side of the piano. Violet's brow crinkled at his words. She had to admit, he was very good looking. The kind of face that could easily lie and always be believed.

The waitress brought him a drink without even ordering. He's a regular here, she surmised. A very well to do regular. These little pieces of information irked her.

'Couldn't I just have a friendly date?' She asked herself as he smiled that pretty smile of his.

"You must think I'm just a money chaser." He said. "But I would have loved to be a musician, well, if I could play as well as you, of course. It must be very fulfilling."

"Thank you Lance, though talent does not keep the wolves away. And there are a lot of wolves."

"Well, I only understand your situation as Crupts explained, so consider me knowing nothing." He grinned. "But if that art business was to be yours, and you were to live above it. You'd be modestly set." She looked at him. It scared her a bit how she wanted to trust him.

After a few minutes, Jasmine returned from the ladies' room with thanks. Violet smoothly switched positions from pianist to dancing with Lance.

"You're right. The studio is a modest business. I could be very happy there."

"And I'm sure you will be. But long term, I certainly wouldn't undervalue the real estate. You know, someday when retirement is on your mind. You could easily get two mil for it."

"Oh, that's ridiculous." She said. "It's a quarter acre and shaped like a pie. It couldn't possibly be worth that much." She looked out the floor-to-ceiling windows of the restaurant. The setting sun cast a golden light over the evening dancers. "Could it really sell for that much?"

"A lot of people with a lot of money want to live on the water."

"True, and thank you, it's something to think about, at some later point in time."

They did an impromptu twirl that was perfect. He was regrettably an excellent dancer to boot. 'Darn it.' She thought, 'Why are such questionable men always good at such things.'

"Two million dollars? Really?" She reluctantly questioned him.

"Not that I'm personally buying it, but yeah, two million could make a lot of life's challenges go away, Violet."

"So, just thinking out loud, how would it work?" She pondered.

"Oh, it's rather easy. In fact, let's say I was working as your personal broker..."

"Fast mover there, buddy," she laughed. "OK, let's say that."

"Well, there are processes involved, but the transaction honestly comes down to a handful of forms and signatures."

"Honestly, now?" She teased. "Just like that? It's really that easy?"

"It absolutely is. Well, minus my fee."

"And what is your fee for this? I don't remember you telling me. Than again, this is make believe."

"Oh, It's standard."

"So no numbers, yet you're telling me it's standard."

She smirked. "That much, huh?"

"Well, in settlement cases, it's one third. But for some reason, maybe hearing you play my mother's favorite song. I'd do it for twelve percent."

On their next twirl, she flipped her hair for dramatic effect.

"It's very tempting. On the other hand, wait, what am I talking about. Half the Stone Boat Art Studio belongs to Benjamin. I can't sell it without his permission."

"I've seen the will, Violet. You are right, half the business belongs to Benjamin, but not the property. You can move the business to town and attract twice the customers you currently do."

It would be tight making a living there, she thought, Edmund didn't even take a salary.

"OK Lance, let's make this happen. I'm feeling spontaneous tonight. And can we order some wine to celebrate?"

He waved the waitress over and requested a bottle.

Pulling out his phone, he focused. "I'm printing the paperwork from my car."

"Oh my god, amazing what one can do these days."

"Violet, I'll just be a moment." He rose, kissed her cheek and moved towards the door. "Hurry back now," her eyes sparkled at him.

Her phone vibrated, a message from Regina. *"Did you actually go out with that guy?"*

"Do you have spies everywhere?" She wrote back with a scared face, emoji.

"As a matter of fact I do."

"Than if you must know, yes, you've caught me, I'm out with Lance, having a wonderful time. I'll call later, still,

you'll get no confessions from me."

Lance returned. "Oh my," she took in his orderly stack of forms. "Should we order dinner first?"

"If you like." He replied cheerfully.

Violet ordered the vegetable lasagna and Lance the salmon.

"Eight signatures and we are done. The transfer of funds would happen during banking hours tomorrow, with a check waiting for you at the bank."

Violet flipped through the papers, signing the certificates, promissory deed, and so on. She tapped the stack neatly and slid them back into the large envelope.

"Ready for delivery my good sir. Assuming your car does that too?"

"It does everything," he said. "I'll go make you a copy and fax these off before dinner even arrives. One of us has a lot to celebrate tonight." With exuberance, he returned to his car.

Violet filled her glass. The golden glow coming off the distant mountains was beautiful. Time seemed to slow down as she watched the breathtaking landscape. She was neither disturbed or surprised as Lance's car slowly creeped past the window. And how amused she was that Jasmine's piano sounded like an old film soundtrack. The confident scoundrel was making his getaway. She savored her lasagna and wine; it was a rare treat.

"Will your date be returning soon? Asked the waitress."

"Oh, I don't believe so, he is quite the busy fellow."

"That's a shame. Shall I wrap his dinner to go?"

"Would you please? And by chance a cork for the wine?"

Finishing her dinner, she said goodbye to Jasmine and asked the hostess to call a cab.

"Yes, of course," She said, "I'll put it on Mr. Crupt's account?"

"Huh what?" She asked.

"Lance Crupts, shall I put it on his account?" asked the hostess again.

"Oh, well, yes, of course." she answered, stunned. He'd one surprise left for her, after all. She assumed Lance was a criminal lawyer. Now, it was obvious he was the family real estate lawyer. Though back to the core matter. He was nothing more than an underling relative of Gretchen. Another dot connected, and again, wanting the stone boat property.

She watched the stunning outdoor fountain splashing water. Two marble cherubs cascading water from one bowl to another to the lower basin. The delicate sound held her attention while waiting for her cab. For a few brief moments this evening, Violet lived the fantasy life of the wealthy. Like a visit to a theme park. "It was OK," she said out loud to the statues in the fountain. "Though all this glitz clutters my attention." The cherubs had no opinion.

Her car arrived shortly. Once she'd given directions to her driver, and called Regina.

"How was your dream date?" Regina asked.

"Not the nightmare I expected. Still, he gave himself away almost immediately."

"How so?"

"When I thanked him for clearing Ben's name, he

took credit for it as if he'd done anything."

"Did he now? Well, I've been looking into him myself." Regina said. "Guess who his cousin is?"

"None other than your very own ex-chief Crupts." Violet laughed back.

"Right you are, I bet you've been studying. OK, for extra credit, in what area of law is he about to lose his license?"

"tic toc tic toc, I pick real estate fraud for three to five years in jail!"

"Right again," Regina yelled. "So, what did he want from you?"

"He wooed me till I signed over the stone boat property to him. I'm getting two million dollars tomorrow. Honestly, I've seen more convincing scam's on the internet. Oh, wait, I seem to be passing him. He's pulled over on the road, but I don't see any flat tires"

Violet's taxi slowed to a crawl. She could see where Lance's car spun out. The skid marks illustrating the reckless swerve into a ditch by the roadside.

"One should never fax and drive." She said to Regina.

"Good thing to remember, still, Vi, you're not making much sense. Did you sign the papers?"

Passing his car, she couldn't help but look. He was punching the empty passenger seat while screaming into the phone, probably at the person he'd faxed the paperwork to. She relaxed back into her seat for the ride home.

"I didn't not sign them, it's that the new owners of the stone boat property have made the purchase from one, Serious Lee."

"Regina burst into laughter." Oh, my goodness, would I have loved to see his face.

"He did have good taste in clothes though, and a fancy car. In the station, he let everyone presume he was a criminal lawyer for Crupts defense."

"That's right, I guess it was just a family reunion. Seems they're still weaseling away for ownership of the stone boat. And to make matters worse, he lied about the song his mother sang to him. It would make her like a hundred years old."

"Huh? OK now I have no idea what you're talking about."

"You're right, priorities. Still, ya learn a thing or two playing music in a nursing home."

Regina interrupted, "One sec work call."

Violet debated giving Benjamin, Lance's dinner. He'd never touched it. It was a dilemma of integrity. Is giving her ex the dinner her date never ate, generous or insulting? Ben enjoyed such quandaries. In this case, she was certain, he would not. Taking a pen from her bag, she wrote Willow & Gus on the container. If he took a bite or two, it was on him. Her concern for his feelings could be exhausting.

Regina came back on-line. "Gotta go, girl. Crupts escaped. He faked the broken hip injury. It was all a performance. Oh, and call Ben, can he stay at your place tonight? There's a chance Crupts is armed."

The line went dead. While not quite a step ahead, being engaged in the investigation agreed with her. She enjoyed the ride home.

33
A Curious Ailment

Waking early, Violet drove to the art studio to check on and feed the cats. The crisp autumn air helped push away her evening with Lance and his attempt to steal away the property. To be honest, she thought, the stone boat belonged to the cats. They were fiercely territorial and knew you had to care for something in order for it to belong to you. Otherwise, it was just a thing, taking up space in your life. Still, she thought while gripping the old door. In the meantime, there was no better reality check than the demands of a baker's dozen of hungry kitties.

She walked the large metal tray of food bowls out to the Boat. She'd memorized the feeding regiment Edmund wrote for Benjamin. She missed her lost uncle, regretting what could have been. Was his care of animals a stand in for the family he lost?

After placing Willow's bowl temporarily on top of the boat, she maintained her balance while opening the door latch with her foot. As per the instructions, they were having raw chicken that was frozen to kill the microbes, then thawed. The chicken was mixed with sweet potato and a little broccoli. She placed a small amount of dry food under the bottom lip of each bowl. An inquisitive treat, when finished with breakfast.

The cats were vocal in their hunger and dove into their food without the usual glares of 'who are you and what right do you have to cross our threshold.' She nudged a few speedy eaters back into their own bowls when they tried taking advantage of the more ponderous appetites.

Gathering up their bowl's after being licked clean, she backed out of the boat to feed Willow. There was a noise, the sound of feet shuffling behind her.

A man stood holding a large rock. The sun at his back blotted out his features.

"I'm not alone." She yelled.

The figure lifted the rock. She slammed the serving tray into him.

The man lost his footing as he stumbled backwards.

"Get the hell away from me you—."

"Rose, Rose, it's me, Father Frank."

"Father Frank? Dammit. You nearly scared the life out of me."

"Oh, I'm sorry Rose." He said lowering the rock. "I wanted to give you this." He offered the rock in his hands.

"And my name's Violet."

"Ahh yes, I knew you were a Flower, and apparently, a flower with a temper." He added, smiling.

"Yeah well, It's good to see you as well, so what's with the rock? I thought you were attacking me for a moment."

"Oh dear me, I do apologize. I heard about poor Edmund and thought of you." He looked at the rock in his hands, then looked confused about something. "How this must have looked, this stone, it fell out of the boat." He pointed to the stern and port's edge. "The branch there must have fallen and hit the corner over here."

She took the food bowl off the roof as Willow danced around awaiting her breakfast, Violet put it on the ground. "Some watchdog you are."

"Willow and I are old friends. Well, OK, it's only been about three years, yet I honestly can't remember Edmund without her. They went everywhere together."

Violet lifted the rock and tried to push it back in place. She pulled it out again and picked up a small stick, scraping out the moss growing inside. Pushing the stone in again, and at just the right angle, it fit like a puzzle piece.

"You seem to have a knack for this boat. Too bad about everything. Family can be tough. Though time heals most wounds, I guess. Animals help." He pet Willow's side as she finished with her breakfast.

While Olga was off saving the world, Frank preferred to work locally making the world a better place at home. She remembered the priest as an energetic dynamo running everything from drug rehab clinics to activist rallies to bake sales. The poor soul standing before her was sad, confused, and irritable. Uncomfortable in his own skin, he looked back to his church and rectory.

"It's all so much to keep up," the priest groaned. "There's so much in disrepair. I'm not the man I used to be."

"Are you certain you want to sell it?"

"Goodness, no. I'd never allow the church to be

sold. We have to change with the times, that's for sure, but to throw in the towel? Never."

"Frank, you're bleeding."

"It seems I am, how could that have happened?"

"Oh no, the serving tray. I didn't know it was you, and I pushed back as hard as I could. Don't go anywhere, I'll get a bandage."

"Please, I don't want to be a bother." She was already entering the studio, rummaging for the first aid kit.

She emerged seeing him holding his hand out, watching the blood drip off his thumb. She padded his hand down with a towel and washed the wound. Squeezing a bit of ointment over it so it wouldn't become infected, she wrapped the bandage.

"Have you seen your doctor lately?" Violet asked.

"Oh, I'm sure I have," Frank answered, "If Gretchen says I did, than it must be. My darn memory has been so challenged lately. I know she can be a bit harsh, mind you. Still, I'd honestly be lost without her."

"Yes," Violet said, with a nagging thought of something she couldn't pinpoint. Something about his behavior didn't feel right.

"It would seem, she's done wonders."

Violet slipped the bloody hand towel into a separate baggy.

Father Frank got down on one knee to pet Willow. "You are such a special dog. You know, one thing I wouldn't mind at all, is another bless your pet's day, it's on the feast of Saint Francis."

"I can only imagine how much fun that must be." She said smiling at the two engaged in a furry belly rub.

"For me, it's better than Christmas. For the Mother

Superior however, it's a day in hell."

"Oh?" Violet asked, "is the sister not fond of animals?"

"I don't know one way or the other. She's just so gosh darn allergic to them, it's impossible to find out."

Violet looked to Willow's tail wagging back and forth and grinned at the thought of it being a weapon against the nasty woman.

"Father, do you by chance know what medications you're on?"

The older man's gaze wandered, looking for the names or even the colors of the pills.

"Too many. Gretchen sorts them out for me." He reached into his pocket. "This one here, I have to take with each meal, an extra dose if I'm feeling achy." He put the canister on the boat's roof and gave the formerly loose stone a pat with his non-injured hand. I never tire of telling the story of this boat, yet Gretchen is so tired of hearing it.

"Like I said, she can be a bit stern, although she takes care of so many things. Well, I best be getting back. I never used to need naps in the midmorning. I'm just so tired of being tired."

The priests' malaise dawned on Violet. She had seen it before, several times in fact. Packing up the first aid kit, she pocketed the hand towel. "Are you in touch with Olga by chance?" She felt guilty asking him while feeling unwell.

"Oh yes, we talk once in a while. Gretchen feels her calls exhaust me, thought in truth, I think it might be Gretchen who's tired of her. Either way, it will be wonderful having her close again."

"Yes, Frank, that would be wonderful. I'm so glad

you're in touch. It's nice to see you again. Maybe you could talk to your doctor sooner than later, you know?"

He waved, making his way across the lawn back to the rectory. After gathering the food bowls on the tray, she noticed Frank had left his pills on the stone boat. Balancing the tray, she put them in her sweater pocket to return to him. She made a mental note to wash the bowls later, then a bigger mental note to let Benjamin do it. She locked the studio and raced herself to town.

On the drive, Violet reminisced about her short stint as a phlebotomist ten years prior. Having completed the coursework, she'd taken a job, drawing blood for the small lab in town. On a sweltering July day, she absentmindedly wore a short sleeve top to work. It showed off the dancing skeleton tattoo she'd named Lucy, after the famous early human ancestor. When she flexed her muscles, Lucy really danced. It put a few priggish patients off. They made the assumption she'd be drinking their blood on her ten-minute break.

Once word got around that the lab hired a vampire wannabe, business dropped off. Gary, the owner, used language so colorful, even Violet was impressed, and more so when he said he'd fight any prejudice and that her job was safe. However, in conversation with Sally, his wife, she'd learned their twin girls were entering college in three months. Business continued to fall. She resigned with the excuse of a music gig three towns over. In his heart, Gary knew there wasn't any gig. September grew closer. And he couldn't afford to fight her. They remained friends, and the couple came to her 'actual' musical performances for a while, even though they preferred classical.

"So, you want what, tested for who?" Gary asked, "looking at the hand towel in the plastic bag."

"Well, would common addictive pain meds be too vague?"

"Oh, sadly no, it narrows things down a lot, I'm afraid. And the who?"

"I'd be in a holy mess if I shared that information."

Gary winced at her choice of words.

"I know it's an odd request," she said. "The thing is, it's about a possible intervention before more damage is done."

"Been there myself." He squinted at the blood-stained cloth, "It's not a proper sample, I can already tell you it's contaminated."

"All I need is a red light or green light."

"I can give you that Violet, but between us, this never happened."

"What never happened?" she smirked.

"Exactly."

On the drive back to the studio, Violet's thoughts went to the priest. He was the last patient whose blood she drew. He was kind and forgiving about her needing three tries to get the needle in just right. Frank was a patient of Dr. Stewart, who used Gary's lab almost exclusively. If her instincts were right, many laws were about to be broken to save that man. Today, she'd a reason to smile.

34
Good Morning Jeremiah

Judge Lynda slipped a ribbon into the book she was reading to Jeremiah. "Maybe we can finish this later. I'd like to know what happens to the horse."

"I would too." His voice was raspy from three days unconscious.

She jumped, surprised, and leaned over to see his brown eyes struggling to focus. "It's good to see you awake, Jeremiah." She pushed the nurses' button.

His eyes scanned the room. "Car accident? I was run off the road, wasn't I."

"You were, friend. Three days ago. Abram, Margot, and Benjamin have been all over it. We've kept a group chat active."

"That's nice." He murmured, closing his eyes again.

"How? Um, why is my painting teacher involved?" Jeremiah asked.

"Oh, he is quite the creative craftsman, I'm hoping to see the results of his work later this morning."

"Looking out for me, huh? And to think you were once my nemesis. You're doing a terrible job of it, you know."

"I'm temporarily off my game, that's all. Truth is, you've been an unworthy opponent as of late, yet still, the best I've got. Oh, and I have something for you."

"What's that nemesis?" He smiled and yawned.

"Your banter is already boring me."

She grinned ear to ear. "Ready for it? You are no longer retired."

"Wait, what? How in the hell?"

"I know, I remember, you told them a dozen times, it was two years away. Internal affairs, plus your crew, and Violet are all over that one."

"Why would they be all over that? It's administration. And why Violet?"

"Violet opened a can of worms, and it just keeps on slithering. A string of corrupt admin actions including a state legislator in Albany, who is Crupt's Uncle, and now a nearly disbarred lawyer who is Crupt's cousin, and his aunt, the Mother Superior of our very own Holy Spirit Church. As you were being retired against policy, Crupts was promoted and inserted into your position. Harold, from internal affairs, exposed your retirement. Violet exposed Crupt's misdeeds."

"I'm missing my coma already. Still, no to Violet. I told her to stay out of it."

"Well, ownership of the Stone Boat property is being challenged by Gretchen, who, as I said, is Crupt's aunt."

"His aunt? Jeez. Lynda, please, do all you can to stop Violet. Lock her up if you have too, it's just too dangerous."

"Why? She found the information and the links to Crupt's family. Are you afraid of a little competition?"

"I'm afraid of her getting killed. Whoever murdered Edmund is scary, crazy, and strong. Has there been any progress in the murder?"

"The current person of interest is Crupts. He escaped during transport and honestly, with all the other charges, I'm sure he's making as much distance as he can."

"He's a nasty piece of work." Jeremiah said. "Do we know for sure he was there the night Edmund was murdered?"

"I hope to learn soon." Lynda squeezed his hand and stood as the nurse came in. She looked excited, and retreated in search of a doctor.

"Thanks for visiting and all the reading you've done."

"Could you really hear me read to you?" She asked.

"And your dirty jokes." He laughed weakly.

"Oh my, that must have been your wife. You know how Joanne can be."

He grinned, "Joanne's never told an off-color joke in her life."

"Well, there's a first for everything." Lynda said.

"Not buying it." He smirked. "So, what else do I need to know about?"

"You need to know you have to heal. That's all. I'll call Joanne right away." She left as the doctor entered the room.

35
Discovery

Violet and Willow entered the courtroom in full strut. Violet held a folder of findings in one hand, Willow's leash in the other. Willow scanned the room, wishing she could give it the full sniff down. The leash, Willow assumed, meant, 'I need you with me just now'. Violet didn't understand that to Willow, Violet was putting out scents of nerves, anger and fear. Of course, she was staying with her. For the others in the room, her nose twitched unpleasantly. Way too many people wore sickly sweet scents. It was difficult to get a genuine idea of individuals, yet there were bad people here, like rotten old food that should be left alone.

Gretchen and her three lawyers sat behind Lance, who made a point not to recognize Violet.

"Good Morning." Violet sang to the room, hoping to irk her recent date, his client, and their minions.

Lance flinched and would not meet her gaze.

"Good morning, you two." Margot said breezily, as Violet and Willow moved to her row. Margot was pensive and kept checking her phone, belying a forced cheer.

"You OK there?" Violet asked.

"I'm fine, it's that darn Abram, he'll be late for his own funeral." Ten o'clock means Ten o'clock, wouldn't cha' think?"

"We're here today for a Discovery." The voice of Judge Lynda immediately took ownership of the courtroom. "What we learn today may or may not lead to a trial or lawsuit by one or both parties. In addition—"

Violet's phone lit up. She tried to multitask her attention with Judge Lynda. Being intimidated by the legal process, she let her focus slide to something more comprehensible.

Her phone displayed the message,

"Dancing on the moon - OPI."

It was a message from Gary. OPI, was the abbreviation for opiates. The phrase was the joke his office used to mean: 'This blood sample contains more drugs than blood.' She cut and pasted the note with an explanation of its meaning and a question to Regina and Benjamin.

"How do we get Father Frank to the hospital for testing and treatment?"

Benjamin answered first.

"I'm on my way. I just saw him wandering around by the boat. Stall the discovery, fenders are on the way, I'll be there in minutes!"

Fenders? Violet thought. She didn't understand about the fenders, nevertheless, he was on it.

"Will meet you at the hospital." Regina added.

"Also," Violet texted, *"Does he know he signed a power of attorney over to Gretchen?"*

"Will ask, depending on his status." Regina replied.

Putting her phone in her pocket, she heard a rattle. Darn, she had forgotten all about Frank's pill bottle, the very pills he was now searching around the stone boat for. If she'd given one to Gary, the testing might not have been needed, or at least processed quicker.

Looking closer, she noticed that, 'Not For Resale' was stamped across the bottle. Looking closer, it also lacked Frank's name or pharmacy or doctor, just the manufacturer, Oplyne Pharmaceuticals. This was no prescription medication, just samples given out by the salespeople of the manufacturer to doctors. Father Frank had been sick for three months. Had he been on these for three months, and without a prescription? What or who was Gretchen's connection to these highly monitored drugs?

Violet! Lynda called out. Where's your head?

She looked around the room to see everyone seated, looking at her, and waiting to proceed. Lance wore a smarmy smirk.

"Your honor," Lance began. "If we have everyone's attention, we wish to submit a motion for a bad faith claim against Violet Eklund. Before any question of who owns the property, my client made a generous offer to purchase the property."

"Stop." Lynda said, "Exactly who is your client? You've listed the church of the Holy Spirit. Is there another party involved?"

"Just the Mother Superior and the church your honor."

"Hmm, OK, proceed."

Lance continued. "She agreed to the sale of the Stone Boat property, yet intentionally and improperly signed the legally binding contracts. We feel she has offended the letter and spirit of the legal process."

"Do you now." Lynda fidgeted with her chair. She'd not gotten it back exactly how she liked it before Crupts played with it.

Lance placed the motion on her desk.

"So, Lance, you convinced Violet to sell her family property to you over dinner. Is that right?"

"It was a business meeting that took place over dinner, yes."

"Did that diner by chance include alcoholic beverages?"

"It may have your honor."

"It may have?"

"I believe Violet drank a glass of wine."

"And did you drink anything at this meeting?"

"No, your honor, I was driving."

"Ah, responsible fellow. Did you pay for Violet's glass of wine?"

"I did your honor, and her dinner."

"Very generous," She said. "And it was a glass, not a bottle, yes?"

"It was a glass, but I may have purchased the bottle."

"I can see that," Judge Lynda said, holding up the receipt to Lance and Violet's dinner.

"How did you—" he gasped.

"It seems Lance. The waitress brought the receipt back to the table after you scooted out. You must have been in a terrible hurry to forget your date at the restaurant."

"Our business matters were complete, your honor. Or so I thought, had Violet acted with any sense of integrity."

"You know, Lance, that's the very point I'm getting

at. Although first, let me say, I'm in a wine club myself. And this is a very nice wine, I've enjoyed it once or twice. It's very expensive. Even on my salary, this would only be for very special occasions."

"Your honor, I do not believe the cost of the wine is the issue he—."

"So, it got me thinking, why would you order the entire bottle, if your date needs to stay clear-headed enough to read the property sale and contract? And you're not drinking, as it would be irresponsible to drink and drive."

"Your honor, I was negotiating the sale of a property, there's nothing wrong with treating my client well or even trying to impress my client."

"If she were your client, and not a buyer, shouldn't you be looking out for her interests? It looks to me that Violet drank the entire bottle."

"I don't know if she did or didn't your honor. I fail to—"

"You certainly did fail." she interrupted. "How can you let your client sign a property sale contract, after drinking an entire bottle of wine?"

"I may have indulged in a small glass your honor, it would not have put me over the limit."

"Ah yes, a small glass, yes, I mean how could you resist. Still, even a small glass leaves your client quite tipsy on the remainder, don't you think?"

"Look," Lance barked, losing his cool. "Her ability to hold her booze is on her. Not me. And further—"

"And that brings us back to integrity, Lance."

Abram quietly entered the courtroom so as to not disturb the conversation.

"You see," The judge played with her glasses. "Integrity goes hand in hand with transparency. So, Lance, that creating a situation where great damage could be done, although not directly by your own hands, is as lowly an act as causing the damage yourself.

The unique sound of handcuffs slapped on Lances wrist. Lance attempts to twist away, but Abram yanked his body in a circle and slapped cuffs on the other wrist.

"What's going on here? Get these damn things off me now. I've done nothing illegal!"

The doors of the courtroom swung open as Benjamin entered, carrying something large and cumbersome. He was followed by Oscar, who quickly dragged a table from the side of the courtroom directly in front of the Judge's bench. Violet was stunned at the speed of their arrival, and hoped that Father Frank wasn't tossed out the window to Regina, as they drove by the hospital.

Oscar looked to Judge Lynda, then Abram, pointed to Benjamin, and gave a thumbs up.

"Lance," Abram said. "You're under arrest for blackmail against Mr. Miller and vehicular assault against a police officer, our very own Chief Jeremiah."

"I did nothing of the sort," He yelled.

"No," Abram explained. "However, as the judge just explained, you own the building in which Mr. Miller runs his engine repair shop. Mr. Miller is six months behind in his rent. Yet you knew that. You also knew his history in demolition derby racing. You blackmailed his eviction for running Jeremiah off the road."

"I made no such deal. That drunken bum lies about

everything." Lance yelled.

Everyone watched as the two men arranged the display.

"That's so interesting," Oscar said, "We thought someone might be lying too. Which is why Benjamin made a plaster mold of Jeremiah's car dents,"

Benjamin lifted the mold of Jeremiah's fender and door panel and showed it about the room.

"He also made a mold of the attacking vehicle's fender and door panel, which we have here. Wouldn't you know a perfect match?"

The two men fit the molds together like jigsaw pieces.

Lance's face went pale.

"Mr. Miller is giving a full statement." The Judge said. "I suggest you do the same. And while I make no assumptions of your guilt. It's unlikely you'll be sipping that lovely wine at the Château Horizon anytime soon."

"Wait, why is some local art teacher allowed to do forensics that will hurt my case?"

"Officer," Judge Lynda asked. "Would you explain why the police department requested the local art studio to make its molds?"

"Oh, well, Benjamin taught the beginners sculpting class my wife took. I figured he's cast hundreds of times more than we have, and besides, why not use the local talent?"

"I'll allow it." She turned to Lance. "Mr. Lance Crupts, I want you to listen carefully. By now you must know our illustrious former police chief, your cousin, is under suspicion of murder, attempted murder, and burglary. If you have any knowledge of his actions or whereabouts, it might secure you a hole less deep than the one you've dug for yourself."

Lance weighed the value of his silence and took a breath. "He didn't kill the old man, Edmund, was it? He didn't kill him."

"And how might you know this?" Lynda asked.

"He was with me the night of the murder. I was with him till three or four in the morning I guess."

"Where were you and what were you doing?"

"Oh, well, we were in a social club just enjoying ourselves, you know."

"And the name of this social club?" She asked.

"The Gentlemen's Oasis."

"Are you referring to a strip club, Lance?"

Violet watched him squirm inside his expensive suit.

"No, I mean, I guess some might call it that."

"OK, Lance deals off, if I have to go fishing for information you can—"

"OK, ok, yes, it's a strip club and James drank a bit too much. In fact, he drank way too much. Anyway, he got handsy with a dancer, and she wanted nothing to do with him. So, when he grabbed her ankle."

"He grabbed the dancer's ankle?" The judge clarified.

"Well, he was just having a little fun. The dancer grabbed the pole really hard to pull away, and he was drunk and thought it was a game so he pulled, and she didn't like it, so with her free leg she kicked him in the head and a tooth came flying out of his mouth right into my drink. He let go after that. And after that, the bouncer threw us out of the club. I took him and my drink with his tooth in it to the emergency room. They gave him something for the pain, then said he'd have to see his dentist in the morning."

"And where is your cousin right now?"

"I swear your honor, I have no idea."

Judge Linda paused deciding whether Lance had anything more to offer. She motioned to Abram, who escorted him out of the courtroom, reading him his rights.

Benjamin went to Violets isle and whispered. "Frank found a pill in his pocket and is sleeping in the car. So, we came here first to get the evidence in. I'm off to meet Regina at the hospital now. I'll be back asap!

The previous night in the restaurant was still fresh on Violet's mind. She was surprised by how this picture of self-confidence and entitled greed had been reduced to a bumbling scammer desperate for survival, or at the very least, minimal jail time. Still, she thought, I'm not out of the woods yet. Gretchen's proven herself a ruthless ring leader. Could she have arranged Edmunds murder? And by who? She certainly had the opportunity to observe his comings and goings.

36
And Then Some

"Violet." Called the Judge "Do you have anything more for the court?"

"Why is this proof needed now? Nether Edmund nor any of my ancestors have ever needed to prove this before."

"Because," the Judge said, "This is the first time it's being challenged. I'm aware of the legends as much as anyone here. Still, a legend, even if a delightful story, is not the same as a title of ownership."

"It's far from a delightful story." Violet approached the bench with the pages she did have written by Bishop Elias Eichler, and his gratitude for Erland Petri and Ada Dotter.

Carefully opening the folder, the Judge silently read the pages. "This is fascinating Violet, it truly is. Still, there is no mention of land ownership."

"I have the tax records and survey records, both going back nearly two hundred years. I have many articles about the building and boat going back to the first newspaper, all stating the owner as one of my ancestors. The deed, however, has disappeared from the town records."

"I'm sorry to hear that Violet, I am."

Her back against the wall, Violet reached into her pocket. For all the movies where the hero defeats the villain in that last decisive moment, this did not feel like a victory. To destroy another person takes a personal toll. Even if a vile creature like Gretchen. She stepped out of the aisle, approached the bench and put the pill bottle in front of Judge Lynda.

"What's this?" asked the Judge.

This is the real reason I'm being asked to prove my family owns the Stone Boat property. "Father Frank doesn't have dementia. He's been over medicated by Gretchen. And she's taken his power of attorney in an attempt to sell—."

"Violet." Lynda snapped. "Do you have anything pertaining to your family's ownership of the Stone Boat property?"

"I have the fact that my uncle painted the portrait of the Oplyne Pharmaceuticals CEO, and that he made it clear he wanted the Stone Boat property for himse—."

"Violet!" The Judge interrupted her. "For the last time, do you have any actual proof of ownership?"

"It's over two hundred years of family history." Violet stated. "I have proof of every generation who's lived there. This has to count for something."

Lynda sighed in exasperation.

"Do you have a deed, a land title, a sale agreement?"

"No, I do not." she mumbled. "Father Frank—"

"Go sit down." The Judge snapped.

"What?" Violet protested, "But she—"

"Sit down." The Judge hissed at her.

Miffed, shocked and humiliated, Violet took the pills and went back to her seat. She looked to Margot for some support, though she was buried in her phone. The curt dismissal from the judge sent her hopes plummeting.

She looked across the aisle. The three lawyers besides Gretchen were busy comparing notes and texting. Sensing her dismay, Willow stood on two feet and pressed herself into Violet, offering what comfort she could.

"Your honor, Gretchen spoke laboriously while adjusting her wheelchair to face the judge. I first must apologize for the brazen behavior of my nephews. They are well-intentioned, yet their exuberance was thrust on my personage with no knowledge on my behalf. Some mistakes have been made, however, their hearts serve a greater good. They are both fine young men and certainly no murderers."

"How in the world could she say Crupts was a good man?" Violet grumbled to no one. Judge Lynda gave her a warning glare.

A cough came from Gretchen, pulling the attention back to herself. "Violet's misguided accusations, I can only assume come from the grief and guilt she must feel, having ignored and shunned her uncle all these years."

Violet was seething in rage and now forced to hold her tongue. She could feel her blood pumping like a drum.

"Your honor." Gretchen continued. "I have reviewed and copied the earliest of town records in existence. They began recording in the eighteen fifties, stating that the stone boat property, which at the time was a cabinetry shop, and was located on the property between the cemetery and the church." She paused and sighed, as if the explanation pained her. "In my exhaustive search, there's no mention of land ownership or deed. From all records, we have only proof that we permitted these businesses to operate in the building. The matter of taxes always being collected, is merely an administrative error by the town. And the stone walls built, were to keep the church's livestock contained, not to separate or define properties."

Violet listened to the heartless ghoul perform her story as if it was a children's tale. Furious, it seemed she was the only one who knew the nun was lying.

Long-lost feeling of family, legacy and belonging, crumbled all over again. These manipulative scoundrels crawled through the legal channels, stealing her newfound history. All the while, the Judge listened attentively to their lies. How could she have been so wrong about Lynda?

"If Violet could not find tangible evidence," Gretchen concluded, "that the plot they insist on calling the Stone Boat property, belongs to her family, we ask, as you did days ago, your honor, that she relinquish her claim."

"I asked nothing of the sort," the Judge replied.

Violet's phone buzzed. She ignored it. It buzzed again. 'This hurts too much.' Her phone buzzed again. Standing to leave, it buzzed again. 'Fine,' she thought. Glancing at her screen, she saw a photo message of a beautiful large open field surrounded by forest. A sign in the foreground read. Edmund & Olga's Animal Sanctuary. The next photo was a selfie of Olga, her big hair blowing in the wind, her beautiful wide smile shining with the rich green field behind her. The third image was of a cement truck pouring a foundation cement into large rectangles. A large assembly of building supplies lay in wait to the side.

"Im sorry for my secrecy." said the text message from Olga. "With everything going on, I felt it best to honor Edmund's wishes quietly before lesser intentions tried to intercede."

"Violet," the judge stated. "Before you go, you need to understand—,"

Gretchen and her minions seem to have won. She couldn't tolerate another minute of these land grabbing parasites and the two faced bureaucrat allowing it to happen. The words from judge Lynda sounded in the courtroom, though Violet barely heard them.

"Without you having proof, I'll have to find in favor for Gretchen and the church."

"A few more steps, Violet mumbled, A few more steps and I am out of here."

Judge Lynda grimaced seeing Violet heading for the door in such dismay. "In that case," she raised her gavel. "I'm bringing this discovery to a clos—."

The doors burst open and bopped Violet's nose, pushing her back into the courtroom.

"Would the original deed be enough?" Olga yelled to the room as she stepped through the doors carrying a large rectangle wrapped in fabric. Bella Petters followed close behind and was bursting with smiles and excitement. Bella was head librarian, the town's unofficial historian, and wife to Regina. Violet followed the excitement rubbing her nose as Benjamin entered with Regina.

Olga looked to the Judge. "What I took from the art studio walls, I believed, belonged to me." She looked to Violet. "I discovered it wasn't entirely the case."

"Please clarify." the judge asked. Her gavel poised, wavering as whether to drop or not. "Are you saying you're the person who broke into the studio, cut open the wall and stole what exactly?"

"Oh, not stole, and technically, I did not break in either. I am not ashamed of what you're about to see and hear, though it is rather personal. It was a work of art Edmund and I shared. For its intimate nature, I would rather have stayed private, although this situation has forced me to reveal it."

She pulled away the fabric revealing a breathtaking painting of Olga, nude, reclined, and unabashed in her direct gaze to the viewer.

Gretchen glared at her lifelong rival. "What unholy lack of reason moves you to bring such a lewd spectacle into this courtroom? What lurid madness has taken your senses?"

The surprise of the painting shook Violet out of her hopeless mindset. In that instant she saw his life. Quiet, rich, and in love. The hand that made such a painting, and the eyes looking back to the painter, were unmistakably, deeply connected. The pit of anger and despair she'd dug herself into dissolved.

"Olga, it's so beautiful." She said.

"Thank you, Violet. I hated keeping it covered away, Edmund insisted for my security."

"Olga?" The judge asked with curiosity. "It's a beautiful painting, however, you said you had the deed."

Violet glared at the judge for bringing the subject of the deed up again.

"Yes," Olga said. "I passed the painting in front of

258

a bright window and saw two rectangle shapes. After peeling the backing off a little, I called Bella. She has experience with old paintings, so who better to ask."

"Bella. Please?" Asked the judge.

Bella threw a soft cloth over the table and unzipped a small pouch of what looked like surgical instruments. Carefully lifting the painting over, she peeled away the backing paper with a scalpel. Once removed, there was an ancient browned sheet of paper on the left, and a newer document on the right. Bella looked to Judge Lynda.

"Behold our town's history." Her grin was pure joy.

"This document is a letter written and signed by Bishop Elias Eichler in seventeen ninety-nine, and the deed to the Stone Boat property."

"And the other document?" Lynda asked.

Bella looked to Olga, smiling.

"That, your honor," Olga stated, "Is the wedding certificate for Edmund and Myself."

"You and Edmund were married?"

"Forty wonderful years, yes."

The Judge's mouth hung open, as did many others in the room. Most were smiling, an obvious few were not.

"Oh my," The judge stammered. "That answers so many questions about Edmund. I can't imagine this will go over well with your superiors."

"Your honor, I have no superiors, as does anyone else. Still, if you mean, I'm in for a fight or two, it's well worth it to head off this gruesome travesty." She looked to Gretchen with disgust. Gretchen returned in kind.

"Olga?" The Judge asked, "Are you making any claim on Edmund's estate yourself?"

"No, your honor, my claim was on the Man. And I don't mind telling you, it feels damn good to say that out loud. I know full well Edmund's wishes for Violet and Benjamin, as I was present for the signing of his will."

Violet, Willow, and Ben walked to the painting. Discovering the life Edmund and Olga shared, she needed to see it up close. Feeling the eyes of both Gretchen and the Judge on her, she took several photos of all three documents just in case.

"Bella?" the Judge asked, "Is it possible to remove the documents from the painting?"

"No. Edmund was a talented painter, though not so knowledgeable when it came to humidity. When he hid the painting in the wall, I assumed to protect Olga, it pressed the painting side to the sheetrock, and while that saved the front of the canvas, the documents tucked in the back faced the outer stone wall. Which is where the humidity entered. It's been wet and dry so many times, the deed, has fused with the canvas. At this point, any attempt to separate them would destroy both the document and the painting. We might, with expert help, separate the wedding certificate."

"Fascinating," the judge said.

"Isn't it. I am just so excited." Bella said. "It clarifies the origin of the Stone Boat property. I'd always thought the stories hearsay or anecdotal, although this is the real thing."

"Bella, are you able to read the entire deed?" The

judge asked.

She lifted the canvas as if performing a ritual. "Your honor, I thought you would never ask."

Olga blushed. The painting faced the room for Bella's reading.

Bella cleared her throat and began.

37
Dearest Descendre

On behalf of our humble congregation, we wish to express our eternal gratitude. Your service to our community in dire need, I am emphatically certain, would not have survived. Ada, the purposing of our church and your own home, to be hospital and hospice when the yellow plague struck, surpassed all skill in care and arrangement.

I have witnessed firsthand the testament of your union, whilst Erland's minuscule complaints over his homemade gin to clean the ward and instruments of the sickened. You have proven to me the reasons for the boiling of sheets.

You have lessened in multitude our lost brethren and Sistren. souls pray ascended. Gratefully, and for reasons unknown to all except our lord, you, Ada and Erland, were spared. Perhaps to take care of the blessed lot of us.

For these reasons and others too countless to speak in worthy detail, I construct this deed in honor and gratitude.

Set forth this day of October 20, 1799

Be it established and proclaimed that:

Erland Petri and Ada Dotter

Are here recorded as the true and legal owners of the property located at the triangle plot separating the Church of Thy Holy Spirit, and Thy Holy Spirit cemetery. Church road, MooiKill, New York:

In prayer: Bishop Elias Eichler

Witness this day by: Madaline Riegler

Bella's eyes were rimmed with tears. Lowering the painting to the table, she looked to Violet. "Well, it seems Bishop Eichler has spoken on your behalf."

Violet's arms were tightly wrapped around Olga. Ben's arms around the both of them, with Willow. Tears for who was lost, and tears for who was found.

Judge Lynda looked to the fuming mother superior. "Will you be continuing your claim on the property, Gretchen?"

She gave no answer, her steely eyed glare focused forward and nowhere else. She stood, shedding her persona of a sympathetic elderly servant of the lord. Turning her wheelchair and waving her legal minions for assistance, she walked to the exit as a court aid delivered the Judge a message.

"Oh Gretchen," Lynda called out. This pertains to you. It appears you no longer have power of attorney for Father Frank. The police will be in touch with you for further questions." Gretchen responded, by standing up, to hastily depart from the courtroom.

Gretchen's three lawyers rose to exit the courtroom, one folded the wheelchair. They were stopped by Abram. "What might be the hurry for you folks? I was thinking we could have a chat about your employer."

Oscar burst through the door.

"Violet, Benjamin, The art studio's on fire!"

38
The Purring of Fate

Being a psychic and a kitty is a curious thing. All the tomorrow's look like all the yesterdays, yet from the other direction. Both heading towards the present, informing Eve. She always blinked twice as a nod to both.

She read the leaves falling into the river like tea leaves in a cup. It confirmed her agitation as she hopped about the boat. Normally she was happy to watch the world float by. Today, she needed to turn the wheels of possibility. There was too much at stake.

Watching the tragic villain bumble about the studio did not disturb her at all. The fire set would soon be out. She sensed the fire trucks coming down the hill from a bit away. They would arrive soon. As far as she was concerned, it had been taken care of. A delicious scent in the distance connected the dots of her plan.

Gus knew enough to stay away from the fire. However, he wasn't sure of everyone. He sat vigil on the roof of the Stone Boat, at the ready to dissuade any curiosities from the other cats. When the flames were out, Eve ran to him and bopped him on the nose. Taking the challenge, Gus took chase after the sleek black cat. Ordinarily the picture of stillness, Eve bound up the hill to the church rectory.

Gus gained speed, expecting to soon tackle and

tousle about with the disrespecting cat. So Eve pivot-
ed and leapt through an open window. Dashing fireplace to chair to table, she spun to a stop beside an
egg and cheese pie. Gus, within swatting distance of
her tail, followed suit. On seeing the pie, the prince of
the Stone Boat granted forgiveness.

Eve took a quick taste, and possibly a second. Still,
the black cat's to-do list was not complete. She left
Gus to fully enjoy his early dinner, he was seemingly
oblivious to the figure opening the door.

Gus, who rarely tasted such rich food, felt this meal
a proper debauchery for a prince. Still the sentiment
was not shared by the figure picking up a knife. The
human's body language spoke volumes, even to the
face enmeshed in cheese pie. The arm raised. His
nose twitched. A scent remembered.

39
A Little Charred

Violet raced as fast as her car would take her. The engine sounded like a treadle sewing machine laboring through leather. Reaching into the back seat, Ben took hold of Willow's leash. He knew if she felt the studio threatened, she would charge inside, even if on fire. As it was, she was pensive. The humans were pumping out stress. She barked her frustration out the window. On their arrival, the fire truck was just wrapping things up, soon to pull away. Violet spotted and waved to Virgil Embers as she parked. Virgil was the fire chief of MooiKill. Benjamin ran back to the Stone Boat to check on the cats.

"How bad is it?" Violet asked.

"I can't believe how lucky we were." Virgil replied as he photographed the outside of the building. "Only the front of the studio was ablaze. We caught it while heading back to the firehouse from training. We honestly saw the fire before anyone called it in. So not bad at all."

"Can I go in Virgil?"

"Yes, there's no structural damage. Just step carefully."

She cringed, passing the old door scattered about on the grass. Picking the door handle out of the shards of wood, she wondered if it was repairable. More than a century old, it at least deserved an attempt.

Broken glass and wood cracked under foot as Violet entered the building.

"The arsonist ran out back and got away on a boat. We only saw him from behind. If his prints are on record, the gas can will lead the police to him."

"Please tell me you didn't see any cats in the studio."

"Not a one. I've heard about Edmund's catboat. As far as I know, they're all safe. The fire was in its early stages. The front wall, floor, and seat here were only beginning to catch, the curtains went up quickly, that's what scorched the ceiling."

"Where do I even start to clean it up?" she asked.

"I'd suggest replacing all the sheet rock. No matter how much you paint, the smell always comes back. A fire's not a memory anyone wants to revisit."

"Yes Virgil, thank you, can't disagree with you there. I'm so grateful you all showed up like you did."

"Glad we're here as well, Violet. OK, I've got a report to write and communicate with the police. Call if you have questions, we'll send you a copy."

The beautiful front bay window was gone. Shards of glass littered the sill. We could replace it, she thought. Everything looked so foreign being scattered about as it was.

Benjamin entered from the back. "The cats are accounted for, except Gus and Eve. They've gotten into chasing each other lately, so possible they scooted off together. I fed the others and gave them a small sedative. It will be easier to relocate them to the Paw Palace Hotel for a few days, at least till we get this cleaned up."

"That's a good idea. Would you keep Willow with

you, there's so much broken glass, it's not safe." She looked to Benjamin and let loose a sob. "It's just a building. Why do I feel this so personally?"

"It's not just a building." He hugged her. "It's the second act of violence within a week. And thank goodness no one was hurt this time."

"I didn't think of that," She squeezed him tight. "Whoever did this was obviously in cahoots with Lance and the former chief. Not to mention the pharmaceutical company wanting the property. Still, who did kill my uncle? Virgil said the arsonist escaped in a boat. Was that the murderer?"

Ben took her hand. "Let's catch up with Regina later and see what she knows and where this is at. Do you want to go to the Paw Palace with me? Get your head out of this for a bit?"

"No thanks. I need to do something. I'll start cleaning up here." Giving her a long hug, he left with the sleeping cats.

The phone rang. Her anger rose. It was Judge Lynda.

"What do you want?" Her animosity bloomed, remembering how she'd been treated in the courtroom

"Violet, I need you to listen to me. Oplyne Pharmaceuticals has been dumping opiates into this region's population for the past twenty years. We were aware of their land grab attempt for the Church, yet we couldn't have them knowing we knew."

"Why didn't you fill me in on it? I'm glad that Jeremiah's out of danger, Still, obviously neither of you think I'm trustworthy."

"It has nothing to do with trust," Lynda said. "When

you slammed that vile of pills on my bench, I saw several investigations put at risk. And Jeremiah's concern was for your safety. As evidence revealed, it could not have been Crupt. Edmund's killer is still at large."

Violet stood her ground. "I could have helped."

"I decided you've enough on your plate."

"I do not agree." Violet growled coldly.

"I'm aware of that, I wanted you to know my reasons. Goodbye Violet."

She hung up the phone and was still very angry.

Like a passing shadow, Eve caught her attention, silently landing on the windowsill from outside. She delicately pawed at the broken glass. The sun bounced around the sharp, shiny things. She was fascinated. Violet couldn't shoo her away lest the kitty be cut by fast movements. She nonchalantly wandered in circles till she was close. As softly as possible, she lifted the jet-black cat with yellow-green eyes into her arms.

"It's all going to be OK, right Eve?"

"Maaaaybe." An inner voice replied.

On hearing this strange silky voice in her head, she nearly dropped the cat. But the feline was intent on staying in her arms and hunkered down. Claws gripped the weave of Violet's sweater. That voice, was it hers? Not hers? She looked to Eve, bright eyed, in full purr, and loving every second of this exchange.

"The very moment it's mine," She said to the cat. "Someone tries to burn it down. Let alone the family history mess."

"This place is your place, the stories belong to your family." Said the voice again.

A shiver ran up her spine. "Oh, great. My breakdown, in the form of a cat." She wanted to throw the mysterious kitty far and fast, yet it froze her. Eve's paw reached up and patted her cheek. Unblinking eyes peered into her. The next pat was a single claw. The pain pricked open a fear, personal, deeper. The fear of claiming what was truly hers. Violet crouched over as a cold sweat covered her body.

"It belongs to you." The words purred again. "Silly human squabbling cannot decide otherwise."

This time she expected the voice. It was less jolting, though still crazy strange. Claiming what was hers, was the genuine fear. And fear of her own anger for all she'd lost. Living hand to mouth with her parents led to living on near nothing as an adult. For years she fooled herself with an empty solace of having nothing to lose.

The purr soothed her mind. The purr gave clarity as she wandered about the mess of the room. Righting a table, moving the chairs out of the way. This was hers now. And hers to defend. Mentally planning a revitalizing of the studio space, the cat kneaded her sweater arm excitedly.

"Please don't pull any threads." She asked the little mystic.

"I will try." responded the voice.

"Ah ha, it is you!"

The cat then closed her eyes, settled quietly, and admitted nothing.

She opened the back door and the lithe creature slipped out of her arms. In a few bounds, she crossed the fence to the cemetery. Looking back to Violet for the quickest of moments, Eve disappeared within a broken statue of an angel.

From the other direction, Violet watched a dusty golden cat sprinting across the church lawn. It was Gus. Running up a tree trunk, he leapt branch to branch till landing on the roof of the stone boat. He was filthy, and with blood splattered across his paws, cheeks and ears. She wet a towel and ran him. Examining him for injuries she discovered there were none.

"Whose blood is this Gus?"

He nuzzled the woman who held some of his beloved subject in her. He needed to tell her who the terrible smell was. Moving closer he head butted her nose, murmured again about the terrible smell, then nuzzled her cheek. She smelled nice, and a little like Eve. She was not at all like the other one whose skin and blood were still stuck in his claws. Gus reached over and licked up the drop of blood he'd left on Violet's cheek.

"Thank you, so glad you stayed, pretty boy. If you only knew."

Gus watched the woman walk away, frustrated that she didn't speak cat, and wished, if she only knew.

Flipping open Edmund's toolbox, Violet took the biggest hammer she could find. The thought crossed her mind to wait for Benjamin's help, however, the hammer felt too good in her hands. She wanted this for herself.

Gus watched her through the window from on top of the boat. He decided the raging woman smashing walls inside would make a good ally, and an excellent new subject.

40
Tearing up the past

Exhausted, having smashed the day's turmoil away, Violet swung at the last piece of sheetrock still attached to the wall. It broke away too easily. The hammer swung too fast. Her tired arm couldn't stop the hardened steel from slamming into her knee. When the cursing stopped, she limped back to the nearest round painter's table.

On the front lawn of the studio lay a pile of smoke-damaged sheetrock, on top of a large tarp. It was a mess for another day. Inside the exposed wall revealed a collection of antique knick-knacks going back two hundred years or more. Accompanying the knick-knacks was a lot of old booze left over from prohibition.

Her knee hurt like hell. Still, she'd finished what she started, and that was a grand feeling. She sent a text to Ben.

"Please grab two ice packs, and what time will you be back?"

He answered,

"The kitty palace was full, I'll need three stops to place all the cats. Be back in thirty minutes with the ice."

Next, she texted Regina, inviting her and Bella to come peruse the findings behind the wall. Bella would see the historical relevance to items that Violet only saw as dusty trinkets.

She gathered the assortment of old misshapen bottles strewn around the room onto a round table. The tabletop rotated like a lazy Susan. The antique glass refracted light everywhere, bringing magic to the dusty room in transition. They must have belonged to her grandparents during their bootlegging days. Another surprise was discovering a second painting hidden in the walls. It was not of Olga, although unquestionably by Edmund's hand.

The painting was a youthful woman standing, her face open, vibrant and unsure. The energy of her stance and gaze danced off the canvas. She wore a beautiful pastel blue peasant dress. Her left hand rested on her hip. Her right hand posed on the gatepost of the stone wall, separating the studio and the church grounds. The mystery was, why was this painting hidden?

"Who are you?" Violet asked the woman in the canvas.

"You should have let it burn." Came the graveled voice behind her.

Violet spun around, expecting some mystical cat talking at her. Instead, she saw Gretchen in the doorway. Her knee throbbed from the quick turn. The nun was covered in ash. Bloody scratches criss-crossed her face and hands. Grey eyes burned wildly.

The preliminary drawing for Olga's painting lay on the table beside her. Gretchen clawed it into her hands. "This is how I knew." She waved it over her head before tossing the delicate artwork to the floor.

"You sent that yellow rat to attack me! Furthermore,—"

"Well, if it isn't the holy ringleader of criminals." Violet cut her off.

"My nephews are no criminals. And I will have every one of those rats put down. They are a menace."

"You're the menace Gretchen, you brought this all about."

"Ah," Gretchen sneered as she approached, "The lost child playing detective? It's curious why everyone's complimenting your perception. You can't even see what's in your own hands." She swung her walking stick, hitting the painting. Violet backed away.

"Don't you dare hurt this painting?"

"My painting urchin! Can't you tell?" Gretchen hissed, "The lord gave her eyes, yet she cannot see."

Violet looked closer. The shape of Gretchen's face and eyes were there. Long gone was the purposeful innocence in her expression. Over decades, soft brows sharpened into a predator's gaze. Yet the shape of her face was unquestionable.

"Oh, I see you now," Violet said, as the painting's subject moved closer. "Like a reverse painting of Dorian Gray, the good version of you is trapped inside the canvas. Is that why you want it destroyed?"

The seething nun gripped her cane. Like the wheelchair in court, Violet could see she didn't need its assistance. The ornately modeled handle was decorated with a brass gargoyle.

"Tell me, Sister, do you have a bible quote for arsonists?"

The nun stepped even closer, "How dare you accuse my family?"

Violet's anger rose "Oh?, How dare I? How dare you

drug your own pastor? You poisoned that sweet man into a junkie to steal the church and sell it to the corporate parasites he's fought to save the community from. How dare you, Sister? You hypocritical monster."

Gretchen's nasty demeanor failed to intimidate Violet. Pushed to a defensive place, the nun felt every bit the cornered animal. She slammed her cane down on the table, smashing a coffee mug. The mug said, 'Music is the Souls Coffee' It was Violet's favorite. Her secret love of kitsch callously violated. Inwardly, she boiled over, 'Of all the ancient whiskey bottles she could have smashed, she thought, why did this nasty creep have to break my mug?' Psycho nun or not, Violet was all in.

"You and your worthless piece of garbage nephews will be in jail."

"I've done nothing but the Lords wor—,"

"Oh, really? Is the Lord's work poisoning, real estate fraud, aiding a murderer. Nun or not, you're going to jail."

"You know nothing about this. I've told you ignorant child, my nephews murdered no one." Gretchen snarled, moving closer. "This property rightfully is holy ground and every generation of yours has defiled, soiled and sinned against the Lord."

"Oh, you're giving us way too much credit, sister." Violet spit back at her, knowing the disrespect would rile her.

Gretchen swung again at the painting. "That horrible reminder of his sins needs to be ashes. He was a vile demon seducing me away from God. And he debased Olga, even marrying that weak-willed harlot."

"My uncle Edmund was a vile demon?" As angry as she was, Violet couldn't help but laugh over the idea. "He was many things to many people. However, a vile demon is a bit of a stretc—."

Shame slammed into Violet before she could finish the words. Like Gretchen, her parents demonized Edmund. Refusing to face their own addiction, they berated Violet for her tears in how they were wrong about him. She knew Edmund would never put them out in the street and knew he and Olga loved her.

Her parents were relentless in how he'd stolen their chances of being millionaires. In the end, agreeing with their delusions and denial, was the only way to remain part of her family. The child mourned her uncle's loss, and to appease her parents, mourned his trust. Over time, the wound scarred over, losing awareness that it wasn't really her own choice, only survival.

"The drawing of that harlot was lewd! Just like the painting" Gretchen bellowed, snapping Violet from her thoughts.

"I found it hidden away. She was proud of her blasphemy, inviting his lust." Emboldened with her accusations and her gargoyle, Gretchen moved closer.

"The drawing of the nude! That's what you're going on about. You must have stolen it from Olga!"

Up close, Violet saw Gus's handiwork. His nails had carved deep into her face. "What did you do to bring that pretty kitten's wrath on you?"

Gretchen pulled back defensively and swung her cane. With no choice, she held up the painting to protect herself. It saved her, though not the beautiful blue peasant dress.

"I will clean this sin he seduced unto me." Violet grimaced as the nun swung again.

She quickly ducked but tripped and stumbled backwards. Stabbing pain shot from her injured knee. Gripping the table's ledge, she hobbled to the other side. The tabletop spun, refractions from the antique glass flashed everywhere. The nun swung again. Slashing at the painting, she tore the background river off the canvas.

"He bought her that dress to lure her in."

"Lure who in?" Violet cried, 'oh crap,' she realized. 'She's gone third person crazy.'

"All the while knowing how to seduce the girl." Gretchen spoke on.

Violet felt a shiver up her spine listening to the manic woman.

"He told the novitiate where to place her hand on her hip. You can't deny his lustful intent. He wanted his own hands on her."

She swung again, tearing off her younger self's other hand and the fence post she rested it on. The fence post, something about—.

The gargoyle barely missed the tip of her nose and startled her back into the moment, as more canvas tore away. Paying attention to the lunatic's story was getting dangerous. Her throbbing knee made it clear she couldn't make a run for the door, let alone her car.

"The demon and novitiate raised that fence together. He taught her well, it was his temptation. She worked hard to please him. He corrupted her with pride and accomplishment. He made her want a life with him. He made her want to abandon her promise to her family. Abandon her promise to God. She was nothing but tormented craving."

The nun's eyes were crazed. Violet couldn't help but pity her self-tortured life. The next swing took out the young Gretchen's throat. She gasped at her own sense of feeling muted.

Violet yelled back. "How could you let some jackass man define you? They know nothing. And yeah, it's hard when we're young and everything is so romantic. But it's a fantasy. Don't let yourself be fooled by some idiotic fantasi—."

The gargoyle smashed the jug of whiskey, ending her attempt at reason. Violet spun as the shards of glass flung into her hair. The shock rattled her back again to the present danger. 'Ok Violet,' she said to herself, 'do not commensurate with the crazy person trying to kill you. Ok, good talk. The fence posts. Damn, why is that so important?'

The next whoosh of the gargoyle took out the younger Gretchen's delicate matching shoes. 'Damn it Edmund,' she thought. 'The girl had an insane crush on you, and you went and bought her shoes? Were you asking to be murdered?' Quickly running out of painting, Violet limped clumsily to keep Gretchen on the opposite side of the table. It was all she could do to not be brained by the brass gargoyle.

Her unblinking glare sought an opening to attack further as she continued. "The day came to witness her vows. The day he betrayed her. Surrounded by unrepentant sinners. Her family, flawed believers to the core, sacrificing her to the service of the Lord in their blasphemous barter. They believed it would secure a seat in the kingdom of heaven. It was their folly."

Parrying the next swing with the remnants of the younger Gretchen, Violet saw the last swatch of canvas twirled into the air as the young face full of promise floated to the floor in a puddle of broken glass.

"Yet he did not rescue her. He refused the girl, uttering cowardly claims of misunderstood intentions and neighborly friendship. He handed her back a heart shattered, seeped in lust, wanting, and broken promises. Her failures lay in mockery before the Lord."

"Dammit, Gretchen, you had a crush." Violet screamed. "And yeah, awful families happen. It can be terrible, I know. Still, you don't stew yourself into a psychopath because he wouldn't be your boyfriend."

Enraged over the younger woman's words, Gretchen lunged closer, swinging the cane. With a sharp twist of the frame, Violet hooked the gargoyle's chin and yanked the cane out from Gretchen's grasp. As the frame disassembled mid-air, she caught the makeshift weapon before Gretchen could grab it back.

Violet blinked, shocked as a realization slammed into her. The drawing Gretchen stole was at the murder scene!

"Fence post!" Violet blurted out. She remembered Edmund taught Ben how to use the old fence post digger. That's how Ben stabbed the clay, that's how she stabbed the clay, that's how Gretchen stabbed—.

"You killed my Uncle Edmund!" She screamed at

Gretchen, who was still lost in her murderous trance.

Violet swung high and hard, smashing the bottle in front of the crazed nun. Stunned and aware she no longer held the upper hand, the nun lurched out of her manic state.

"Story time's over, murderer." Violet swung the cane as Gretchen ran for the back door. The gargoyle landed on the nun's shoulder; Gretchen spit out a string of profanities that could have made the gargoyle blush.

Hobbling after her, Violet needed to use the very cane nearly planted in her skull moments before. Yet she needed it for any chance of catching the hell-bent nun who'd done her worst to destroy her heritage.

She limped out the back door, gripping the gargoyle. Closing the distance to this queen of mean, she questioned why Gretchen ran towards the water. The question quickly answered as Crupts stepped out from behind the stone boat. Violet met the barrel of his gun, staring down at her. Far more angry than scared, she stared back.

41
Showdown

"He had the gall to marry that harlot!" Gretchen cried to Crupts, "Debasing her vows before God, posing shamefully, he chose that wanton temptress over, over...,"

"Yeah Gretchen, say it." Violet yelled, "My uncle chose a kind, loving woman rather than a crazy psycho."

Crupts rolled his eyes. "Auntie, you have the rest of your life to rant about your old boyfriend, we have to get out of here."

"You told your family he was your boyfriend?" Violet spat in disgust. In the distance, she could hear two cars arrive. The sound of doors slamming echoed back to the boat. Crupts eyes flicked, he heard as well. Unlike Gretchen, still screeching over her girlhood travesty.

"Shoot the urchin and be rid of this stain." Gretchen barked at him.

"Auntie, get in the boat, I'll be right down."

Violet thought about rushing Crupts. His shaky gun betrayed his moronic bravado. But he couldn't hide his fear of the messed-up plot.

Gretchen walked to the edge and stopped. She wanted to see. She wanted to see him shoot her. Because dead or not, she wanted to hurt Edmund even more.

The gun jerked her way as he sneered. "I couldn't care less about you, or your relatives. It's nothing personal. Well, it kind of is. I honestly hate all of you." He smirked, yet his face was deathly pale and covered in sweat.

'If ever there was a family who needed therapy.' Violet thought. Yet it was clear he planned to shoot her. A blur passed by her peripheral vision. 'Please be who I think it is.' She prayed.

"So you're the genius," Violet blurted out. "You're the smart one?" Her nonsensical rant bloated his pride, but she needed to distract him.

"James." Gretchen yelled from behind him.

He didn't respond to his aunt.

"You figured everything out yourself, didn't you?" Violet said. "They didn't appreciate you, and you had everything under control. And we both know you've murdered no one."

"Well, there's no time like the present is there." His shaking hand stiffened.

"James!" The nun yelled again.

From the tree's, a figure charged through shadow. Her eyes set on the foul smell who threatened her human. Take out the bigger one first, then the other awful smell. The one who took her man. Willow did not growl, she did not bark. Her paws barely touched the ground as she flew towards the dangerous man, her teeth impaled on his behind.

The ear-piercing screech from the disgraced chief scared a mile of birds into flight. His body twisted, falling to his knees. Gretchen ran forward trying to grab the gun away, yet stopped when she saw her other nemesis.

From over Crupts head came a hissing growl, soft golden fur swooshed across his nose as sharp claws tore into his face. He screamed in pain and raised his gun to smash the little beast. But the feline was faster and ripped away from his head. His claws extended, landing on his next target. The murderer of his most favorite subject. In the church, she got away the first time. But the murderer was on his turf now.

Crupts pointed his gun at the cat, his senses too mangled to see. He was also pointing it at his aunt's face. Meanwhile, Gus's claws and teeth dug into the fire and brimstone nun, as Gretchen screamed, flailing her arms. The realization that her nephew's gun was pointed at her head, made the torment all the worse. Mercifully for Gretchen, yet not so much for Crupts, Willows teeth clamped on his wrist, giving him new reasons to scream.

He dropped the gun. Violet lunged to grab it, but Crupts was closer and kicked it down the slope. Before he could follow, Violet reared back and punched him in the nose with all she could muster. With another yelp, Crupts tumbled backward towards the water, a hand covering his already broken nose.

Not wanting to interrupt Gus, Violet swung the cane, smashing Gretchen's shin with the brass gargoyle. The nun lurched away, tripped and fell towards her nephew. The descendants of a wolf and tiger doubled down on their fight to avenge their loved one. Following them down the embankment, the fight was far from over.

Yet in an agony inspired jolt, Crupts threw Willow

off him. She landed in the idling boat just as Gretchen fell onto the deck. Gus was tossed into the air. Ten pounds of hiss and claw landed on the throttle, pushing the engine to full speed. Willow dashed in, biting the nun's leg. Gretchen screeched, falling backwards out of the boat. The thrust of the engine jarred Willow against the seat. A large overstuffed suitcase fell into the water.

"My things!" Gretchen yelled.

"The boat." Crupts added.

The boat, loosely tied to a tree branch, spun in circles on the shore's edge. Propeller blades cut into the riverbed, pummeling Crupts and Gretchen with mud and algae. The force of the engine pulled loose the rope, and the boat flew from shore, spinning in larger and larger circles.

Gus gripped hard on this spinning oddity in water. His front paws held the throttle for dear life as his back paws gripped the dashboard. Water is meant to be occasionally sipped. Having it completely surround him was just wrong. He hissed at the situation. His early kitten trauma of floating down the river, returned.

Willow assessed their situation. This car on water was out of control. Everything was spinning and unfamiliar, except the seat and steering wheel. It was sort of like the one in her car. The one she and her man had shared. She hopped on the seat and put her paws to the steering wheel, as she did many times before. For a moment she felt her slow-moving man with her. They were still a 'We'.

He always patted her head before they started. She

reached over and patted Gus's head. Now, the steering wheel would work just fine. Gus answered with a hiss that transformed into a worried long cry. He was not happy with the situation. He wanted to continue turning those rotten smells into scratching posts.

Willow turned the wheel and the boat made less of a circle. She turned it a little more. Soon they were moving in almost a straight line. However, they were heading towards the opposite shore. She remembered turning, although on roads, she always used the shape of the road as a guild. Water was so different from the road with curbs and lines. She imagined Edmund pointing this way and that. Eventually, she saw his fingers pointed towards the pet store. It was her favorite turn. She tried that turn and the boat turned with her.

From across the river, she could now see the stone boat peeking between the trees. 'Home' was in front of her. Edmund, had always driven slower when nearing home, however, the sounds Gus made were a clear plea for dry land. Willow adjusted the steering wheel, just like when trying to not hit garbage cans. The keen-eyed dog focused on the open space next to the stone boat. Gus looked up to see they were heading home, and not a second too soon.

Meanwhile, on the shore's edge, Gretchen and Crupts emerged dripping in thick mud and algae. They began their humiliating crawl up the slope, grasping fistfuls of grass to keep from falling back. On one such grasp, Gretchen's hand landed on the gun. The corners of her mouth curled as her bitter purpose was renewed.

Regina and Bella arrived to see the knick-knacks from the open wall. Violet limped towards them. "Thank heavens you're here, Regina, do you have your gun?"

"What in heaven's name is going on, Violet? You look like a wreck."

"It was Gretchen," Violet implored. "She is Edmunds killer."

Regina immediately dialed for back up as Olga and Benjamin arrived with the ice. Ben ran to Violet, shocked at the state she was in.

A gun shot into the air surprised them all.

Bedraggled, yet armed with a gun and a manic grin, Gretchen snarled, "Freeze. Keep your hands where I can see them. All of you." Pointing the gun at Violet, her face went sour. "You've ruined everything you pitiful heathen."

"Aunty," Crupts said. "Gimme me the gun. You don't have experience—."

"Shut-Up you bumbling moron. You've failed me. Your self-glorifying cousin, your loathsome uncle. You've all failed me. I gave you the chance to help. To thank me for all I've sacrificed. Ungrateful family, ungrateful sinners.

She snarled at her nephew, "Fetch my suitcase you idiot, can you at least do that?"

He scurried down to the shoreline.

"With you all disposed of, I'm sure they will blame my nephew." Her smile grew with expectant madness. As the gun moved slowly towards Violet. "Starting with you."

Crupts still smarting from the acidic words of his

aunt, groaned. The suitcase was floating thirty feet from the edge. Covered in wounds and exhausted, he tripped and fell down the slope. Damning his rotten luck, his eyes lifted in time to see the oncoming boat, smash open the suitcase. The vessel continued at full speed directly towards him. Crupts tried to scramble away, but his shoes were stuck in the thick mud. It briefly registered that the boat was being driven by a dog and cat.

The realization he would never get out of the way in time, hit him hard. With all his remaining strength, the disgraced chief yanked one foot out of the mud, while raising his arms over his face.

A wave of mud splattered the shore as the boat hit the embankment. On hitting the rock, the engine broke free of the stern. Still, the speed alone enabled the boat to fly up the embankment before coming airborne.

The ear shattering crash shocked Gretchen. Her hand jerked just enough to miss Violet as she fired the gun. Violet, filled with adrenaline, pushed Benjamin and the rest of her friends out of the path of the airborne boat. They fell safely in the leaves as Violet found a soft landing on top of them. Bedraggled and hurting, she still smiled at having a gang to land on. As if in slow motion, she watched the boat floating through the air. Willow, at the helm, still steering, while Gus leapt off the throttle grabbing hold of a passing tree branch.

The boat crash landed over Gretchen, slamming her yards away into the stone wall. The hull was torn open with the grinding of wood, and stone, then finally, falling to its side.

For a moment, all was silent. Violet's arched her head, looking, praying, that her canine rescuer was not hurt. Willow scrambled out from under the helm, hopped off the side of the boat, and pranced happily to be reunited with Violet and Ben.

Wearily, one by one, the gang approached the boat. From the tree branch, Gus jumped and landed on Benjamin's shoulder, digging in for extra security.

Surveying the situation, Regina called into the station. "Hey babe," Her voice still shaken from the shock of the event. "I'm gonna need a bit of backup at the Stone Boat Studio, no, scratch that, a lot of back up. Yeah, and an ambulance, no two ambulances, and a flatbed tow-truck, and a pulley rig."

Benjamin walked towards the slope. Gus hopped from his shoulder to the stone boat. The golden tabby curling up in his basket, hissed at the entire day, then settled in for as quiet a night as possible. Ben heard his former nemesis groaning, before he could make out Crupts shape, flattened into the mud.

"How bad is creepy Crupts?" Regina called out.

"For a pancake, he looks just fine."

Violet walked to the nun, still sprawled next to the stone wall she'd slammed into. Surprisingly, she was conscious. The old nuns hands patted the area around her, searching for the weapon she'd lost. Violet jabbed the staff of her new cane into Gretchen's hand. Reaching down, she picked up the gun hidden by a few leaves. "You will not be needing this anymore."

Willow came to Violet's side and delivered a few angry barks at Gretchen. The murderous nun yelped at the cane pressed into her hand and pulled away the moment Violet released her.

"She's awake." Violet said as Regina approached. "And she murdered my uncle Edmund." With a bit of reluctance, she handed the gun to Regina who was sitting Gretchen upward and cuffing her. Ben, having climbed up the slope, came to Violet's side.

"You know," he said, "that cane. It weirdly suits you."

"It's just temporary, till my knee feels better."

"Still, it kinda fits your whole," He drew circles in the air around her. "You-ness."

"Oh, so now I'm the eccentric cane lady, huh? Should I start speaking in a fake European accent, walk around holding one of the cats? Is that it? After everything I've gone through today, is that what you're saying, Ben? That I'm bonkers."

"Yea, I guess it is." He smiled and put his arm around her as they listened to the approaching sounds of police cars and ambulances. She had wanted to rile him up, if only to feel normal again, but his arm around her, was just a bit better.

42
Hello Again

Eve sat on the edge of the Stone Boat intently watching leaves fall to the water. Of particular interest was how they floated or spun their way downward, and how the water welcomed them with a soft landing. She read them like tea leaves, communicating what was to be. The warm September evening was perfect for watching nature take its course. Gus was curled in his throne basket, at peace with his rule.

Olga, followed by Willow, climbed up the ramp Edmund built years earlier and joined the two felines on the bow.

"It's not a private party, I hope." She whispered, finding herself a seat. Willow touched nose to nose with Gus and exchanged a recap on the day's excitement. Eve gave Willow a slow blink, and a nod of welcome, as they both lay within petting range of Olga, should the urge arise.

It was a cloudless night. The mist rising off the shore was unusual. All the animals took notice. In its own time, the shape of a person formed between Olga and Willow. With a wagging tail, Willow could see Edmund within the mist and nudged in next to him. With eyes full of love, she nuzzled into the apparition. Gus could also see Edmund. And he could not deny it was Eve, invoking the soul who banded them all together.

Olga gazed out on the water, searching for peace from the recent turmoil. Edmund's ghost looked to her adoringly. Eve hopped up on Olga's right shoulder and blinked prettily at her.

"Oh my," Olga said, "You're even more beautiful up close."

Eve blinked at her again. Olga smiled at the cat, unaware that the gesture was an instruction. Having no other option, Eve bopped Olga on the temple three times.

Olga felt her eyes twitch. She was a little put off at Eve swatting her. Still, she blinked herself while turning away. As her eyes opened, she found herself looking at Edmund. He was still rather hazy, yet she knew it was him. She looked back to Eve, who held up her paw, ready to bop her again. She turned back to Edmund, this time blinking as instructed. Her husband became clearer.

"Are you really here Sweetheart?" She asked.

"You look like you see a ghost." His rumpled laugh was so familiar to her.

She took his hand. It felt like many tiny sparks warming her skin, yet still, her Edmund. "It crushed me that we never said goodbye."

"Interestingly enough, there's no need to. I think you have Eve here to thank for that. She has some unique skills."

Willow moved closer, putting her head on Edmund's lap.

"Hello pretty girl. You know you're in charge now. Have to keep those kitties safe."

Willow gazed into his face. Her tail wagged like she might achieve lift off.

Olga reached over and embraced him, surprised she could even do it.

"Why am I able to hug you?"

"You'd have to ask Eve. I'm just a pretty face."

"You certainly are dear. Oh, speaking of, my scandalous painting now hangs in your living room."

"Oh?"

"Yes, Violet has moved in."

"With or without Ben?"

"Well, that's still to be seen. They're both inside now. He's helping to clean up the mess from her fight with Gretchen, and Violets icing her knee."

"And another thing!" Violet screamed from inside the studio.

Olga gave an affirmative nod to Violet's volume. "Oh, and yelling at her parents for all their lies about you."

"Darn chowder heads," he looked back to the studio.

"Are you referring to my in-laws, dear?"

"No, to Ben and Violet. When are they going to figure each other out?"

"Maybe I'll make them my next project,"

"I think saving the world might be easier."

"Oh, speaking of projects," Olga said. "I purchased the land for our animal sanctuary. This morning, we poured the foundation."

"How exciting! You designed one mean rescue center. Now you know, it's not meant to gobble up all your time."

"Yes, dear, I've a meeting with the veterinary college next week. Just like you planned."

"Just like *'We'* planned. I so wanted to do this together."

"And you think we're not? You're not getting out of lifting feed that easy." She nudged him. "You had better polish up your levitation skills."

"Look at you, the taskmaster. No wonder the cemetery stays so quiet."

"And I might drag that church over there out of the dark ages."

"You're not off fighting evil again?"

"What's the use of saving the world if I can't come home to my sweetheart? Besides, it'll make a nice retirement project."

"Great, now that I'm dead you're going to stick around?"

"Awww, you know I've been planning this. Than again, maybe a better question is, will you be sticking around?"

Edmund looked to Eve. She purred with a musical resonance. "I don't know. You should ask her, it's my first time in the afterlife."

"Well, if you're taking up a 'here after' residency, let's not spring it on the kids just yet."

"Agreed," Edmund said. "They have the monumental challenge of, you know, holding hands once in a while."

She took his hand in hers, remarking how warm he felt. "Violet's forgiven you. Once all the pieces fell into place, she realized you'd been there for her all the while. Maybe you knew that, with universal knowledge and all."

"Did she really forgive me? Not a pity dead uncle forgive, but for real? I hope so. And as for universal knowledge, no. What I get is a random mishmash of information, plus what I already knew. And that I might be good at finding nick-knacks. Like that you put your left sneaker in the cloth's basket and that's why you can't find it, cause you're overdue on your laundry. No mental omnipotence. Maybe that costs extra."

"I did tell you to pray more, and I'll do my laundry when I feel like it, or just go naked in that giant tome over there."

Gus found his way to Olga's lap. He kneaded his paws into her sweater and purred at the return of his lost subject.

Edmund wrapped his arms around Olga, hugging her close. "If you hear any chains rattling, it's me visiting." They leaned into each other, watching the river flow by.

Eve walked across Olga and Edmund's shoulders, stepping down to share Edmund's lap with Willow. Her long tail flickered. The woolly mammoth was still slightly over the otherworldly kitty. The cat blinked and touched nose to nose with the Willow.

She shared news of the near future. There would be big changes for some, and lazy days of sameness for others. Some happy, and some were simply adventures that needed living. And no one more than Violet. Still, big changes or not, Willow knew, she would be there to protect Violet and the cats. However, the other worldly kitty, kept to herself, the changes in Willow's future. That would have to come out in its own time.

Willow, like Gus, decided the midnight kitty was also part of her pack now. Eve returned to watching the leaves fall onto the water, regretting she could not share everything. Willow sighed in contentment, nuzzling closer to her man, and drifted to sleep.

The End

Dear Reader

I hope you have enjoyed Perils Portrait.

Please join the Stone Boat Newsletter to receive free digital art prints of MooiKill, the Stone Boat and its residents. They can be printed and framed, or used as your computer's background image. (Instructions will always be provided.)

There will also be the occasional short story, as well as videos and demonstrations on your favorite arts and crafts.

And lastly, posted updates on the next 'Stone Boat Cozy Mystery' release. To join go to:

https://timothyswriting.com

If you are feeling generous, I would greatly appreciate a review of the book, or even a simple rating, which can be found at:

https://www.amazon.com/dp/B08LMNMM97

Made in the USA
Las Vegas, NV
03 March 2022